50¢

C0-AZV-704

CORRIDOR OF DEATH

Slivers of concrete and marble ricocheted in Stryker's face as a half dozen bullets slammed into the wall near his head.

"Get down!" he yelled at Thomas as he dropped to one knee and returned the fire, never really seeing what he was shooting at. After three discharges, he forced his finger off the trigger. His ears were ringing with the harsh noise of cartridges exploding underground.

Thomas was still running. Twice, he slipped in the blood coating the smooth floor, but he got right back up and kept rushing to his sergeant's aid.

Suddenly, there was silence.

Stryker and Thomas didn't want to lose the killer. They stepped out into the corridor—and a bullet shot from a doorway shattered Thomas's thigh. The young MP went down.

Stryker jumped forward and sprayed the doorway with lead, then darted to the side and came back for Thomas. Without holstering his .45, he dragged his partner back several feet.

Stryker looked at his bleeding friend and made a promise. "I'm gonna go out there and waste him, Thomas. Count on it!"

THE SAIGON COMMANDOS SERIES
by Jonathan Cain

#2: CODE ZERO: SHOTS FIRED   (1329, $2.50)
When a phantom chopper pounces on Sergeant Mark Stryker and
his men of the 716th, bloody havoc follows. And the sight of the
carnage nearly breaks Stryker's control. He will make the enemy
pay; they will face his SAIGON COMMANDOS!

#4: CHERRY-BOY BODY BAG   (1407, $2.50)
Blood flows in the streets of Saigon when Sergeant Mark Stryker's
MPs become targets for a deadly sniper. Surrounded by rookies,
Stryker must somehow stop a Cong sympathizer from blowing up a
commercial airliner—without being blown away by the crazed
sniper!

#5: BOONIE-RAT BODY BURNING   (1441, $2.50)
Someone's torching GIs in a hellhole known as Fire Alley and Sergeant Stryker and his MPs are in on the manhunt. To top it all off,
Stryker's got to keep the lid on the hustlers, deserters, and Cong
sympathizers who make his beat the toughest in the world!

#6: DI DI MAU OR DIE   (1493, $2.50)
The slaughter of a U.S. payroll convoy means it's up to Sergeant
Stryker and his men to take on the Vietnamese mercenaries the only
way they know how: with no mercy and with M-16s on full automatic!

#7: SAC MAU, VICTOR CHARLIE   (1574, $2.50)
Stryker's war cops, ordered to provide security for a movie being
shot on location in Saigon, are suddenly out in the open and easy
targets. From that moment on it's Lights! Camera! Bloodshed!

*Available wherever paperbacks are sold, or order direct from the
Publisher. Send cover price plus 50¢ per copy for mailing and
handling to Zebra Books, Dept. 1629, 475 Park Avenue South,
New York, N.Y. 10016. DO NOT SEND CASH.*

SAIGON COMMANDOS
YOU DIE, DU MA!
#8

JONATHAN CAIN

ZEBRA BOOKS
KENSINGTON PUBLISHING CORP.

ZEBRA BOOKS

are published by

Kensington Publishing Corp.
475 Park Avenue South
New York, NY 10016

Copyright © 1985 by Jonathan Cain

All rights reserved. No part of this book may be repro-
duced in any form or by any means without the prior
written consent of the Publisher, excepting brief quotes
used in reviews.

First printing: July 1985

Printed in the United States of America

Dedicated to the memory of Vietnam veteran Jeffrey C. Davis. A Washington, D.C. police officer for over fifteen years, Jeff chose the pre-dawn hours of September 16, 1984 to claim that right all warriors worldwide hold dear to them: the power to decide the time, place and manner of their death. Jeff's tortured soul drove him to suicide. We will never know if this tragedy was a result of his Vietnam experiences — he left no suicide note. He died at the foot of a tree which lies in the heart of the Vietnam Memorial at the nation's capital. Officer Davis served with the 101st Airborne Division in Vietnam during 1968.

ACKNOWLEDGMENTS

The author wishes to extend his special thanks to The Brotherhood of Military Police (Rt. 2 Box 284G, Carbon Hill Alabama 35549 USA), which has assisted him with research during the writing of *Saigon Commandos* by reuniting him with military policemen who served in the Republic of Vietnam during his Tour 365 of Southeast Asia.

J.C.

"Show me a hero and I will write you a tragedy."
—F. Scott Fitzgerald

Though the author served as a military police sergeant with the U.S. Army in Vietnam, Thailand and
Korea, portions of this novel have been altered and
fictionalized to protect the lives of those men and
women left behind, abandoned during the surrender
of Saigon in the spring of 1975.

The phrase "Saigon Commandos" was a derogatory term invented by infantrymen in the field to refer to almost any soldier stationed in the "rear." But some of the military policemen fighting snipers, sappers and other hostile hooligans across the sleazy Saigon underworld affectionately adopted the title, proud to be lawmen, and not jungle grunts, battling crime in the toughest beat in the world.

Jonathan Cain
February 1985
Honolulu

PROLOGUE

The Maximum Security Stockade, Ft. Leavenworth, Kansas

Escape sirens sliced through the pre-dawn stillness. Outside the high outer wall of the stockade, police dogs barked, howled and tugged at their handlers' leashes, sensing the unfolding hunt.

Inside, prison guard Paul Southfield lay on the cold cement floor of cellblock Alpha-seven, blood pouring from an open neck wound. His throat had been sliced from ear to ear. The left side of his face was against the cement as his eyes strained to follow the giant slowly lumbering away, a straight razor in one hand, drops of crimson sliding off its sparkling surface.

Should have known, Southfield decided as he felt the bubbles rising against the gash in his jugular. *Should have sensed a change in the bastard! All that talk lately about going back to Vietnam. All that steam about killing screws and returning to "ice the*

13

pig" who jailed him wasn't just steam after all. *Should have known . . .*

Southfield was drifting in and out of shock now, and his mind was flashing back like a broken film projector to events of only moments ago: When Boardchek first came up behind him . . . wrapped a thick, muscular arm up under his chin until he couldn't breathe . . . lifted him off his feet . . . plunged the straight razor into the tight skin below his ear and ripped his throat out.

Ripped his throat out.

Southfield had seen all the murder movies. Where the bad guys came up behind the unsuspecting victim and neatly, quietly sliced open his neck.

But his wound was not clean. Boardchek had not been able to tear through him with one single slash. He had had to hack. *To hack.* The blade caught onto gristle or chipped against bone, and he had had to hack at Southfield's throat several times, ripping the skin to shreds as blood sprayed out at them both.

Finally the cold steel found his jugular, severed it with a crude, probing jab—and Southfield's life began flowing forth like spilled paint across a child's water-coloring set.

Should have known. He cursed that single moment of carelessness when he turned his back on the monster everyone on Alpha-seven called "Fist." *Should have known I couldn't trust the goddamned maniac. Should have known he was up to something.*

Southfield watched Boardchek plod toward the door at the end of the corridor, ignoring the secondary alarms that were triggered as he kicked it down with one blow. Southfield had no doubts the madman would make it over the concertina-lined fence. And past the attack dogs, who always started their search on the other side of the compound, where most escape attempts usually began. And always failed.

His heart went out to the MP in Saigon who would meet the Fist next.

And then Southfield died, his eyes still open, staring lifelessly at the monster climbing over the sparkling barbed wire.

1.

The Suspects Wore Silk

Saigon

The explosion shook buildings along the entire block. The target structure, a two-story brick affair which had been converted from a whorehouse into a fancy office building, now stood in shambles. Two walls facing the street were gone, and half the roof had collapsed. Smoke still rose from scattered piles of debris. A thick pall of it hung over the Tu Do street side of the structure, where the hot sticky air blanketing the city was blocked and pushed back by the cool breeze swirling up from the Saigon River.

CID investigator Robert Quinn cautiously combed through the rubble, searching for clues that might lead him to the bomber, a motive — or both. Sometimes he could even tell what kind of explosives had been used. A lot of his friends at the Criminal Investigations Division didn't waste much time on these sort of calls. Especially when the victim business was Vietnamese-owned. But an MP patrol jeep had called this one in—had even exchanged shots with a rooftop sniper in the vicinity seconds before the explosion—and CID rolled on all shots-fired calls. Quinn had a reputation for solving the difficult ones nobody but the line cops were concerned about. Just last week he responded to a double homicide which he proved was only another in a recent string of American boyfriend Vietnamese girlfriend murder-suicides. He was eager to impress the brass this time around too. (Though impressing the brass was more a hobby than something he'd waste time over. It was a plastic sort of challenge—just another game with the guys.)

"Have we got dogs on the way?" he asked the MP private standing at parade-rest in the smoldering doorway. Behind the nineteen-year-old, red lights atop two Saigon firetrucks were throwing lazy crimson beams through the drifting smoke. The flashes bounced off a distant plate glass window, making it look like there were twice as many emergency vehicles at the scene.

"Couple APs from Tan Son Nhut are en route, Mr. Quinn," he replied, straightening slightly. "They're bringin' Shogan and Bear down with 'em, though I don't know why. Shogan's a narc mutt, and Bear isn't good for nothin' but tearin' your leg off or pissin' on your unit right after ya wax it." Two Phantom jets descended from the dark skies behind the youth, their glowing after-burners rattling windowpanes as they headed for the airport six miles away.

Quinn grinned, but made no reply as he directed

his flashlight down at a fractured ceiling rafter. The kid in the doorway was full of shit, he decided. Shogan and Bear were ace mutts, but leave it to the jeep jockeys to find something to badmouth them about. Quinn loved watching the Vietnamese police stare wide-eyed in awe and astonishment as the dogs went to work at a crime scene. The two barkers had tracked the robbery suspect last night after a liquor store holdup on Nguyen Hue, and Shogan tried to eat a terrified VC he caught in a tunnel complex some tower rats discovered running beneath MACV— the Military Assistance Command complex in Vietnam. But Bear was his favorite.

During midnight chow, back when he was on the MPI shoot team, Bear was always good for testing the local food purchased at the open-air markets. The dog would eat anything. He *loved* holsters. Quinn's day was made when the APs got the ass at the bar girls loitering inside the meat market and sicked Bear on them. Bear hated Vietnamese, but he especially hated whores.

"So tell me about the sniper." Quinn kicked over a charred and broken table with a Chinese typewriter laying on its side next to it. Five burned and curled-up fingers appeared in the strong, probing beam of his flashlight, but he didn't react immediately.

"Not much to report, sir." The private was tall but underweight. His jungle fatigues seemed to hang from his shoulders. But he was a six-month-plus vet. The uniform was so thin it shined metallic green. Housegirls hand-washing it every morning were the culprits. One boot was scuffed, the other reflected the crescent moon in its spitshine. With his right hand he twisted the end of a mustache he was trying to grow. "I'm with one of the joint Army-Air Force patrols, Mr. Quinn. Me and Moorhouser were cruisin' ol' Tu Do there, and some Adam Henry drops a belt o' tracers on us, sir. Kimbo just happened to be snoozin' and losin' behind the Hog-60, and he popped a belt back, but I think the bastard beat feet on us. Sergeant Stryker's got a reactionary force up on the rooftop now, going through the motions, but I think the sniper's long gone. You know how Charlie is — he don't hang around long after the Signal 300 goes out over the air. All the big-city Cong got monitors these days, ya know?" He watched the investigator pull a bloodstained silk scarf up through a ring of floating smoke, and childhood memories of some magic act gnawed at the edge of his mind's eye like a nervous tic.

Quinn focused on the idling V-100 Assault tank parked across the street. A Captain America mural was painted across the front. On the sides, below the huge white MILITARY POLICE stencils, the words *Sat Cong* glowed in the dark. That was Vietnamese for "Kill Communists." Quinn's smile grew. He loved it.

The MP private stared back at Quinn. The CID investigator inspired him. Quinn was one of the good guys. He backed the men on the street to the hilt. Never mind the throw-down pieces. If you wore the shield and the arm band, it was always a righteous shooting — within reason. Just don't let the fuck-up be flagrant. Never mind all the hypocritical loopholes in the law that placed the criminal's rights before those of the victims. Quinn enforced jungle justice.

He did what was *right*.

Quinn was the MP private's role model. At twenty-nine, he already had twelve years in law enforcement, coming into the MP Corps when he was seventeen, even though the minimum age at that time was nineteen. He was now the equivalent to a civilian detective, had his choice of shifts (being on call five p.m. to five a.m. for emergencies didn't count, of course) and had won enough valor medals to keep the brass off his back. He had been in Saigon five years, arriving in 1962 with an MP detachment assigned to one of the first infantry units sent to the Republic, so he knew the city like the back of his hand. He was not an officer, so there weren't as many games to play, and he wasn't a non-com, so there was none of that "incompetent leading the unwilling to do the impossible for the ungrateful" syndrome. He was a warrant officer — a *mister*. Quinn was feared by some, and respected by most. He was often easygoing, and mellow — but never anyone's fool. *Just let me do my job. Leave me alone and I leave you alone. Just don't rape the UCMJ in my presence.*

Quinn stood an inch under six feet, and had an athlete's body that wasn't rippling with muscles but would get him through a bar fight if cover cars were tied-up in traffic. His hair was as black as his Vietnamese wife's, but much much shorter. Hers fell to her waist. Every three weeks *he* stopped by a barber shop on Nguyen Hue for a crew cut. Tonight it touched the tops of his ears, and he had combed it straight down in front. His eyes were just as black, with a peculiar Asian cast to them though he was an Irish-Italian mix and the name was British. Quinn

21

was clean-shaven, but his eyebrows were so dark and thick people often remembered him as "that guy with the sinister mustache." He had a thin, inch-long scar running horizontally along his left cheek — souvenir of an easy narc toss gone bad — that strangers also remembered.

The only thing the MP private did not like about Quinn was his taste in women. He couldn't understand why so many of the guys were living with the locals. Maybe it was something about their exotic appearance or the stereotype that said they were all eager to serve Western big-bucks masters with blind loyalty. Would they really walk on your back after the nightly massage? Maybe he'd ask the CID agent about it someday, at Mimi's or the Queen Bee, but tonight it was by-the-book business.

Quinn dropped to a squat and pulled on the charred hand protruding from the rubble. Severed at the elbow, the arm slid out and he casually dropped it. "Got a D.B. here, looks like —" he pulled a pen from his pocket and pushed some chunks of board away, revealing a body — "probably Vietnamese."

A woman in a silver *ao dais* appeared behind the uniformed MP and, sensing her presence, the private jumped to the side, hand automatically riding the exposed butt of his holstered pistol. The shiny black pantaloons beneath the form-hugging gown gave her an out of place, futuristic appearance — almost like a beautiful alien who had beamed down to investigate the results after Earth's first thermonuclear exchange.

"Ma'am?" Quinn let a slab of broken cinderblock fall back on the dead man and, eyes staring up at the woman now, slid the pen back into his pocket. "Can I help you?"

She stepped forward, breeching the crime scene, and spoke a few words softly in Vietnamese, then stood there in silence, waiting for the investigator's reply.

"What did she say?" The MP in the doorway edged closer, arms folded across his chest. "You speak Viet, don't you, Mr. Quinn?"

"She knows our friend here." He pulled a wallet from beneath the corpse. "Says he works at the embassy over on Thong Nhut too. Says he's been getting death threats. Says she's his wife." Quinn's eyes shifted back to the woman's, and he read off the name on the national ID card melted into the black plastic wallet. "Tran Chi Minh?" He guessed her age to be about late twenties.

The woman's eyes went wide with surprise. "No!" she gasped in English. "My husband name Che Dan! Pham Che Dan!" Her fingers fanned across trembling lips, and she switched to Vietnamese again. "The company was receiving threats too," she revealed. "Many workers were frightened away. Those, like my husband, who supervised, were forced to work longer hours. But nobody should have been working here so late at night, sir. Nobody except my husband."

Quinn's eyes dropped to inspect her slender figure. *Ao dais* drove him wild. He bought his wife a new one every payday, despite the mild rebukes from the former beauty queen. (She wanted to save money to send their children to Paris for an education somewhere down the line. And this humored Quinn—she was the first Vietnamese woman he had ever met who dared to plan for the future.) "This Tran Chi Minh . . . was he an employee?"

The woman started to speak, then hesitated. She shook her head slightly, confused — or trying to look confused. Quinn thought he saw a hint of deception in her eyes. "Maybe they were working late," Quinn shifted course. "What kind of business is this?"

"Was this," the MP in the doorway joined the conversation.

"Just an accounting office." She stuck to her native language. "But we also handled some importing and exporting accounts. This and that, you know . . ."

Yes, I know, Quinn smiled to himself. *You dabble in the black market, just like every other national on this block.* "Tell me about the threats," he said. "Were they VC-related?" His Vietnamese was slow and pidgin. He loved the local culture, but the language, with its wide range of tonal inflections and accents, was something he had yet to master.

"I believe they were from a . . . competitor in Cholon, though I am not positive. My husband doesn't talk much anymore. What I'm telling you now is what I overhear at the dinner table."

When he's entertaining business associates, Quinn decided silently. *When you're serving them rice cakes and chrysanthemum tea.* The open sky above the missing ceiling erupted into a roar of rotors as a Huey chopper suddenly appeared over the bombing scene. Hovering fifty yards above the smoking debris, its downblast was not that powerful, but the engine noise drowned out all else occurring on the

24

block. Dual spotlights attached to the craft's landing skids lit up, and as the bright silver beams lanced down through the smoky night, Quinn shot them the all's-fine sign with his fingers. A giant of a soldier was standing in the helicopter's open hatch, and he flashed a toothy grin back down at the CID agent in acknowledgment.

"Good ol' Egor." The MP in the doorway identified the Dustoff crewman. "Always hovering somewhere over your shoulder, like a guardian angel."

The MP's best friend. Quinn's thoughts again strayed from the investigation at hand. *Tommy Johnson — what would we do without ya?* Then his mind flashed back to the MP-Down call where Nilmes caught an AK round in the forehead several weeks earlier. Johnson had swooped in on that Ten-100 also, and after crazy Carl was tossed into the slick, a rooftop sniper began using the red cross on the side of the Huey for target practice. Several direct hits were scored as the chopper rose up through the tenements, but it did not crash. Nilmes would spend the next month telling the troopers at choir practice about how he watched Egor balanced precariously on the outside skids as the chopper skimmed the rooftops, speeding for the hospital — the corpsman stuffing rags into the bullet holes from which fuel was pouring!

The bright spotlights extinguished quickly after playing across Quinn's face, and the helicopter banked to the left and disappeared between a leaning tenement and long line of palm trees rising behind a string of flophouses in the nightclub district.

The sound of the rotors began to fade, then

abruptly started growing louder again. The Huey was circling back around. A garbled transmission crackled across the pak-set on the MP's belt.

"What was that all about?" Quinn motioned for the private in the doorway to turn his portable radio up.

"Arc-Angel to the Mike Papa's on the ground at Nguyen Van Thoai and Thanh Kok."

Quinn recognized Egor's calm voice.

"You've got possible hostile movement on the whiskey side of your crime scene. Looks like a Victor November Foxtrot, over."

Quinn's mind quickly translated the military jargon: *Whiskey means west*. The rest was Vietnamese national female. He motioned with his chin for the MP to reply, but the young patrolman was already reaching for his radio.

"Arc-Angel, this is Car 36-Bravo. Description, over?"

"Same-same any-street Saigon, 36-Bravo," came the dry response. "About five feet, slender, long black hair, blue and black *ao dais*. Is now heading northbound along the alley that parallels—"

"Want us to spotlight her?" the crew chief's gruff voice cut in.

Quinn rushed for the doorway. His eyes met first the woman's, then the private's.

"Want me to radio you some back-up?" the MP called after him as Quinn sprinted into the edge of darkness.

"Negative!" His .45 was in his hand now. "And tell Egor that's negative on the spotlight too!"

And he was gone.

Racing down through the maze of alleys, silent as a gust of wind, deadly as a prowling panther.

The chase was one of the few things about the job that attracted him anymore. Since he had been promoted and plucked from the street to fill a Criminal Investigations Division slot — CID was an agency outside the Military Police Corps in which they usually wore no uniforms — he rarely got in on the in-progress calls: robberies, hot burgs, rape screams or street fights. Everything seemed after the fact now, though once in a while he might monitor an MP-Needs-Help call and roll on it. But for the most part, CID work entailed just what the initials said: investigations. Putting the pieces of the shattered puzzle back together after first blood had been drawn, trying to trace evidence after an often violent explosion — not all of which involved bombs.

There *were* times, like these, when an on-scene investigation could escalate into a bona fide foot pursuit. During a chase, he could put his latent survival instincts to the test — pitting the skills taught to him back at The School, honed and polished by years of experience on the back streets of the Orient, against those of the competition — was just about at the top of his list of adrenalin highs, in between robberies-in-progress during a stake out, and four a.m. so-quiet-you-can-hear-the-city-breathe warehouse walk-throughs.

He knew which way she'd run, though something in his gut told him this might not be the woman again at all, but a suspect actually connected with the bombing. Now *that* would throw his gears all out of sync!

Around two corners and a full sprint down a narrow corridor—guided by the moonlight—then around another bend in the alley, and he caught sight of the edge of her *ao dai* as the woman darted into a dark doorway, out of breath. Perhaps she had not expected the pursuit. He had always ignored her in the past.

The woma⁻ had been turning up at many of his field calls the last few weeks. Just standing in the background, watching him, observing his method of interviewing witnesses and clearing the crime scene . . . always looking away when he glanced in her direction.

You couldn't miss her. She was as beautiful as an Early-Out order. Or Extension papers, for guys like Robert Quinn. She had the high cheek bones and narrow facial contours of Hue royalty; the waist-length hair that sparkled like midnight blue—regardless of the hour—and drove American men on their first Tour 365 wild; the dark exotic eyes of a mysterious enchantress, yet with a schoolgirl's innocent twinkle in the depths of those same sloe eyes.

She was definitely younger and prettier than Xuan, but his wife possessed an ageless magic that had captured him the first night they met. He had never tried to escape.

That was five years ago. Nine months before Mang, his son came along. Little Lien, the boy's sister, arrived during the following Tet celebrations, making the New Year twice as exciting. He couldn't imagine life without them, though he could still remember life in his early twenties, when the thought of raising and being responsible for children frightened him much more than war.

His automatic pointed toward the stars now, Quinn took his time closing in on the doorway. He could hear her breathing hard. He imagined he could hear both their hearts racing in competition. In his mind he saw them laying in the grass beside the Song Saigon — she atop him, his eyes taking in the heaving chest, the pursed lips, the tightly closed eyes, the edge of her long hair tickling his loins as she leaned backwards in ecstasy. But the water slapping against the banks was drowning out the labored breathing he heard now.

His mind's eye shifted to another more practical scene: He was in front of her, in the dark doorway, pressing the pistol up against the bottom of her rib cage, feeling through the weapon's metal, the harshness of the coarse fabric against her skin as her entire body tensed with the contact.

In the distance, faint as a whisper of warning, gunship rotors flapped against the night. A Cobra was dropping flares along the northern edge of the city. Green and yellow orbs of hissing light seemed to hang motionless over his shoulder, though they were actually far, far away.

"Good evening," he gave his best Bela Lugosi vampire greeting as the shards of flickering light shot down into the dark doorway, finding her, and the flares reflected in her troubled eyes. But the words were lost on the woman. Smiling, Quinn holstered his .45 in the sheath of leather hanging under his left arm. "Who are you, my dear?"

She did not answer, but allowed her eyes to drop to the ground in reply. Total submission. She was his to do with as he pleased, or so it seemed.

Quinn's smile faded. His hand flew up, cupped her chin, and lifted her face so their eyes would meet again. "Who . . . are . . . you?" he repeated slowly, in a demanding tone. "Or must I . . . *frisk* you for identification?"

The slightest hint of a smile danced across his lips, but she refused to look at him. "My name Lan," she said. "I swear, I not VC."

Quinn glanced down both sides of the alley. It didn't pay to get too comfortable after the midnight curfew—but they were still alone. The bad bad Victor Charlie was not sneaking up on him.

"But why you follow me?" he shifted into pidgin English as she dug through the folds of her gossamer-thin gown for the national ID card.

"I . . . like . . ." She swallowed hard, searching for the words. Then she switched to Vietnamese, and her voice became very low. "You interest me."

"You flatter *me*." He glanced at the unsmiling picture on the large, laminated card without really seeing the face. But then his expression turned serious, and he whirled her around to face the door. She gasped as Quinn slammed her up against the wood, and the knob struck the edge of her rib cage—where his mind had rammed the gun barrel only moments before. His eyes fell along the narrow waist to the curve of her hips. "You have an MP radio?" he asked.

She hesitated before saying, "No, but my girlfriend have MP boyfriend . . . have paks- . . . paks—"

"Pak-set," he helped her out, feeling the smile return to curl the edges of his lips. He fought to remain stone-faced.

"Yes." She smiled too, blushing—though he could not see her color change in the dark. "He have pakset his hooch. He work swinger's shift."

"Swing shift. Fifteen to twenty-three hundred hours." Quinn lost the battle and grinned openly. The recent change to eight-hour shifts wouldn't last long for the line MPs. It never did. Just long enough to get morale up, then another hundred men from the thousand-strong battalion rotated back to The World, and the 716th returned to the six-and-one schedule of half-day and eighteen-hour shifts. Six days on the street, one day off with your tealok. "At least you're not humping rucks through the pungi-laced paddies," Stryker would always reply to the whiners.

"Yes, swing shift. Sometime I play cards her hooch. Cook shrimp . . . eat *pho* soup. We listen *dinky-dau* MPs all night."

"What's her manoi's name?" His left hand kept her shoulder against the door, but the grip softened.

"She say . . . Uke, no?"

"Ah, yes." Quinn released her. "The Uke."

He let her turn around to face him and her eyes fell to inspect his build before she caught herself. But the message was there. Plain and obvious.

"I am married," he knifed her bubble bluntly.

"Yes . . . I know," the words came out sadly.

"Happily married." He almost sounded like he was trying to convince himself more than her.

"I only *watch* you, Quinn the Eskimo. I only watch you from distance. I never interfere. I never make trouble you. You wife never know—never *soc*

31

mau you." Her eyes pleaded for compassion.

"Quinn the Eskimo?" He sounded amused now.

Her smile returned. "Angi — she call you that. Always sing your name. You bic, no?" Her accent turned French with the last sentence, and she resumed humming the popular Manfred Mann tune.

"Ah, Angi. Nick's manoi. Yes, I understand. I *think*. But Quinn the Eskimo?" His expression said, *Now come on, honey!*

"Because you cold. Some Vietnamese girls no can say Quinn. Some no can say Eskimo. *They* call you Iceman, 'cause you so cold. Never talk. Never flirt. Never smile at the counter."

"Oh, really?" He folded his arms across his chest in the mandatory manner.

"The bargirls talk bad about you."

"I can imagine."

"Lisa at the Purple Palace says you are faggot," she replied matter-of-factly.

"The Moanin' Lisa?" Quinn laughed out loud. "Haven't ya heard? She's dead, goin' on three or four weeks now."

Lan's face went blank with shock, then she finally said, "I did not know, because I do not frequent those places."

"I see. Well, I assure you, miss, I am not a homosexual. Just happily married with no desire to practice the common Vietnamese custom of taking two wives. I don't think *mama-san* back stateside would go for that too much."

Lan's feet shifted nervously and she wringed her fingers like a tear-soaked tissue. "You no mad me?" Her English kept the smile on his face. So innocent, so childlike. The same qualities that had attracted him to his wife. And now *she* was so different. Still loving. Still obedient and subservient. But also cold and calculating now when it came to protecting her family from the war-hardened culture, and her husband from all those "fish in the ocean." But this was Saigon, Pearl of the Orient. And the South China Sea held only sharks and piranha.

"No mad you." He returned the ID card. "Perhaps we could even begin a sort of . . . working relationship." His eyes involuntarily dropped to the modest breasts jutting out proudly beneath the closed Oriental-style tunic collar. In his mind he saw himself on top of her, holding her legs apart, pushing her feet down on either side of her head as their bodies ground against each other, threatening to spark a fire in the silent, filled-with-a-thousand-eyes rain forest. "In a purely business-type relationship." He shook the vision from his head without her noticing.

"I know Saigon well." Her eyes lit up with eagerness. "Better than even your wife!" But she bowed slightly, showing respect for the older woman. "She married woman now . . . and mother. She out of touch with street scene. With . . . with . . . under . . . under—"

"Underworld." He cocked an eyebrow, curious how she would phrase her offer.

"Yes, underworld. Please understand me, Mr. Quinn. I am good girl. I am 'new' girl, OK? But I keep eyes open all time. I watch everything, everybody. I know all streets Saigon. I know all alleys with no names. I know all secrets Vietnam!"

"All the secrets?" He allowed just the slightest

33

amount of skepticism into his challenge.

"Most secrets," she changed her line. "Stealing, killing, raping, robbing—I see it all. Black market? I know the tophats. Car *kipe*? I show you where parts *di di*. Spies? Whether Danang or Dalat, it all begins in the capital, Mr. Quinn."

"Impressive." But the CID agent was always cautious. He had been burned bad by snitches before. "You'd be the most beautiful informant in my bag of dirty tricks—I'd have to admit that. But how do I know you're not just all talk and a pretty face?" His smile broadened and he wished Raunchy Raul or the Stryk were present to hear his next question. "How do I know you're not just trying to get into my pants, honey? To blackmail me or something? Gimme an appetizer, sweetheart." He gently ran his fingers along the straight line where her hair fell against her cheek. "Something I can bite into—something I can dissect and verify."

She half-smiled, confident she had the right amount of bait under her blouse for this kind of fish. "The boom-boom you see tonight?"

He did not think immediately of the explosion scene but flashed back to a floor show he and Bryant had attended with the boys from Decoy where two naked women, tangled together on the stage beneath a pulsating strobe light, probed each other's body cavities with empty "33" beer bottles. It had been appropriately disgusting for Mac Dinh Chi street.

"Yes." He shifted gears again, remembering suddenly the charred hand sticking out of the rubble only moments ago, beckoning him forth across that invisible line into the Otherworld. "What about it?"

"Talk flutters through my housing project like a butterfly," she said, easily switching to longer, multi-syllabled words, but Quinn did not seem to notice. His eyes were watching the flares drifting beyond her shoulders. They always mesmerized him when the mist rolled thick beneath the moon. "Or a hum-mingbird," she continued. "We wait all week for this to happen. I can give you names of people who prob'ly do this."

"Oh, really."

She looped her dainty hand through his muscular arm as if now, their business arrangement secure, he was expected to escort her home. "And Tran Chi Minh?"

"Yes, I expect we will find him under one of those piles of bricks in the morning. What about him?"

"He walks and talks and breathes Saigon now just as we do." She laughed. "He is definitely not lying dead beneath bricks. At time of the boom-boom, he *bookoo klicks* away—at his mistress house in Gia Dinh!"

2.

Every Man Has a Woman Somewhere (Who Loves Him)

He could not understand the sea of flashing red lights rushing toward him, head-on, like the giant tidal wave in *The World of Suzie Wong*.

"They're going the wrong way!" CID agent Robert Quinn gritted his teeth as he swerved to the side of the road to let the two dozen vehicles pass. A blue and yellow Renault taxi, its lights off, roared by. Slamming against its rear bumper was a black '67 Plymouth Fury—the battalion's new, souped-up chase car. Four bright crimson beacons twirled frantically on its roof, and dual sirens under the hood sent shrill yelps and a leopardlike wail out at the tenements rising up on both sides of the boulevard.

Americans hung out the passenger windows of both cars, exchanging shots, bright flashes exploding from the barrels of their weapons. Eighteen MP Jeeps followed closely behind the chase car. Some were loaded down with young troopers to the point of throwing sparks from the protesting undercarriage as they bounced through each intersection's dip. Others were two-man gunjeeps.

Quinn heard windshield glass shatter and a hollow-point strike metal as the "convoy" roared past.

"Christ!" he muttered to the warrant officer seated on his right, "I musta missed the pursuit broadcast."

"I think they were on channel four," his partner, Christiansen, replied dryly—outwardly calm though his gut always belly-flopped when someone else was doing the driving on a hot run.

Quinn's head was already throbbing. The small flashing light on the dashboard always did that to him. Xuan had sewn him a dozen half-covers, so the bright red beams only shot out through the windshield and not into his eyes as he swerved in and out of Saigon traffic, but he had misplaced them all over the years.

"Think they got enough back-up?" Christiansen watched the militiamen dive out of the way and flaming oil drums bounce about as the chase slid through a curfew checkpoint up the block, then disappeared down a narrow side alley. Sparks flew as several of the American patrol Jeeps failed to negotiate the sharp curve and the vehicles' sides scraped against brick and cinderblock in their haste to get through the bottleneck.

"It appears that's a rog—" Quinn had originally been responding to a Ten-100—an MP-Needs-Help call—at Mimi's Bar on Tu Do street, and after the chorus of echoing sirens in the concrete canyon behind him faded, the CID agent floored the Pontiac's pedal. Rear tires spinning, the unmarked, heavily dented dark green sedan shot back into the middle of the street. Before it got back to high speed again, two MP jeeps screamed by from behind — on either side — also responding to the Ten-100.

"Well fuck *me*," Quinn said calmly.

"I hate eating the smoke from *them* goddamned beat cops," Christiansen muttered. But Quinn knew he wasn't serious. The younger red-haired agent was still a 95-Bravo hotdog at heart.

"I could kick it into overdrive and blow 'em off the road." He grinned evilly, flipping the European hi-lo siren back on.

"But you won't." His partner wiped sweat from his brow and sighed. "Fuckin' foreign equipment," Christiansen growled in reference to the weak blasts of sound moaning under the hood now. He began working the spotlight handle hanging down by his right knee. Though it was only a few minutes before the midnight martial law curfew, the streets were still clogged with cyclos, taxis and troop lorries. He splashed light into the windshields of oncoming traffic, forcing them to the side of the road, out of the way, and aimed for the rear-view mirrors of vehicles in front of them the drivers of which either ignored or didn't hear the siren. "Don't really matter," Christiansen decided, trying to sound like he was coasting after finally patrolling over the hill. "Let the rooks be the first onscene. Let 'em take the first rounds too."

Quinn's smile grew. Where had he heard those lines before? Ex-Green Beret Mark Stryker's face flashed before his mind's eye.

"Car 22-Echo's on scene." They listened to units

going Ten-23.

"In the back!" an excited voice broke squelch. "In the back! *Step it up!* We got ten fighters, and an arm band on the bottom!"

Quinn cut a corner too close and crashed through a flimsy vendor's wagon, but its owner was nowhere around. What was left of the shattered contraption remained chained to a concrete lamp post while watermelons splashed across their windshield and rolled off the roof of the car.

"Now *that* takes the cake, Bobby-san!" Christiansen's spotlight was coated with pink mush. *"That's* gross!"

"A real man wouldn't complain, son!" Quinn's smile was ear-to-ear now as, elbows raised in delight, he swerved in and out of startled pedestrians. "A *real* man would eat this shit up!"

"Reminds me of my old lady's disposition when she's on the rag." Christiansen wiped chunks of watermelon off his exposed elbow—it had been hanging out the window.

"Reminds *me* of that old adage: What does thou do with—"

Sirens also wailing, a land rover loaded down with heavily armed Vietnamese QCs cut in front of them at an intersection, raced along behind the two MP Jeeps for several blocks, then swerved down a side street, en route to an unrelated call.

"Let me rephrase that." He had not even seemed to notice the Asian MPs. "If you were Raunchy Raul and you found an abundance of tampon strings on your person upon waking, to what use would they—in their present position—best be utilized?"

"Does it have anything to do with dental floss?" Christiansen sounded like he didn't want to know. He sensed Quinn shaking his head in the affirmative, but he refused to look, choosing the sidewalk scenery rushing by instead.

Three prostitutes stood on a street corner, intrigued by the rare American car as they bent over slightly to inspect the men behind the flashing light on the dashboard.

His face bathed in sliding shades of electric red, Quinn stared back, zooming in on the woman in the middle. She wore a low-cut blouse of purple silk. And it was plentifully stuffed with just the right proportions of chest. The smooth swell of flesh beckoned him like a warm blanket in winter—even taunted him as she shifted feet, searching for a more comfortable position and the breasts jiggled about. But what could he do? Quinn was so faithful to his wife he made himself sick. And it didn't help matters much when—jokingly, of course—Xuan reminded him each night before he left for work that she'd liberate his loins with a rusty straight razor if she ever caught him butterflying behind her back. He'd always respond with *"Lai day, ho mo kai,"* and a convincing kiss that appeased her for the next twenty-four hours.

He locked eyes with the prostitute as they passed and found it hard to pull away and concentrate on his driving—and the matter at hand. *A brother cop was calling for help, for Christ's sake!* What was it about these Saigon women? What lay in the depths of those dark, hostile eyes that was so mysterious, so foreboding? So challenging? They were not to be compared

41

with hookers in Miami or Hollywood. Or Paris, for that matter. Back stateside, the only thing floating beyond the false eyelashes were dollar signs and a contemptible smirk. But in these women he saw smoldering hate, mixed with . . . desperation. A look that told you the color of your uniform meant nothing, only your money. They despised all men equally, regardless of their loyalties. So many were orphans of war, forced to survive on the streets any way possible. And that realization, all moral and social arguments aside, touched better men than Quinn to the bottoms of their soul. Some left the country with their values and outlook radically changed, forever haunted by what they saw in Saigon.

Quinn stared hard at the woman, trying to memorize the details of her face. He would like to return after the call, talk with her, buy her a baggie of ice coffee or steaming cubes of sugar cane, convince her all Americans were not bastards. But the midnight curfew was rapidly approaching — she'd be long gone by then, secreted deep in the dark crevices of her leaning tenement world with a five-dollar joe, shivering with disgust beneath his pounding, groaning frame, miserable until the dawn because she had no gods to pray to, no Buddha to believe in. Her only solace was the hard-earned greenback.

"Waco, this is Blue Diamond 6," Christiansen called into the mike calmly as they skidded around the last corner and a sea of flashing red lights suddenly spread out before them. "We'll be Ten-23 at Mimi's, over." In the distance — on the other side of the thirty MP Jeeps clogging the street — sirens bounced off tin and teakwood walls as other units arrived, pulling up from the opposite direction. "I can smell it!" He pulled a lead-laced sap from under the seat as he jumped out of the car. "This one's gonna be a ball-buster!"

"Kick ass and take names," Quinn agreed with a grin, completely forgetting the woman on the street corner several blocks back.

Nightsticks were still cracking when they waded through the army of night-shift jungle fatigues and day-shift khakis to where three prisoners were lying face down, handcuffed behind their backs. They were all unconscious. Two MPs were wrapping a first-aid bandage around the forehead of an injured private. The white letters on his black arm band were splattered with blood. *Bet he buys a laminated one after tonight*, Quinn mused as he and his partner changed direction toward a wall of helmet-topped giants on their left. Out of the corner of his eye, the CID agent noticed all three drunks were black. His ears told him the belligerents shouting challenges at the line of peacemakers were also BLA sympathizers.

Some of the ten privates wearing the green sword and gold battle-axes of the 18th MP Brigade combat patch were also black, but they were silent, and wore stone cold expressions as the obscenities and racial slurs and allegations of treason to their "brothers" were hurled at them. The only sergeant at the scene was checking the wounded MP and seemingly ignoring the rowdy GIs, though he appeared preoccupied and irritated by all the distracting noise.

Quinn assessed the situation in a matter of seconds. Though the MPs had the place under control, no one was taking the initiative to silence the disturbance once and for all and clear the building. Adrenalin was flowing in everyone, and the action was still rolling, the situation still potentially explosive — perhaps the cuffs had just been snapped on moments before he arrived. He understood how and why events were unfolding the way they were. But this was not one to play by the numbers.

Quinn pulled the black plastic folder from his back pocket and flipped it open, then slid half the case into his shirt pocket so the gold CID badge was showing. Then he waded through the sea of young shifting troopers and stopped nose to nose with the tallest, most vocal antagonist. "You got a problem, *chump*?" he asked, smiling the way a uniformed MP would not have been allowed to use body language.

The off-duty soldier with the beer-drenched fatigues and flaring nostrils rose up on the tops of his toes so that he was a couple inches taller than both CID men. *Same old game of mindpsyche*, Christiansen sighed, feeling the tremor coming. "Who ya callin' a chimp, *whitey*?" His eyes told Quinn he was about to pounce — or seriously thinking about it.

"I am ordering you and your fellow *chumps* to disperse, soldier. *Right now!*"

"Ordering *me*?" the soldier bellowed uproariously, like some Jamaican comedian, and the men on either side of him laughed along. "You and whose mofuckin' army, lillypuss?"

The soldier next to the tallest drunkard spoke a rapid-fire warning. "Better watch yo ass, bro — whitey's flashin' a shield. Looks like the Man."

"*Fuck* the Maaaaan!" an anonymous loudmouth

44

in the rear ranks chanted.

"*Fuck* the Maaaaan!" several of his comrades joined in. Someone jangled a ring of keys like a tambourine, until they began sounding like a troupe of donation-hungry religious fanatics invading an airport terminal back in The World.

"Ice the pig, brothers!" another incited the small mob to riot.

Quinn sensed the arrival of the breaking point. Through his peripheral vision he saw rooks on either side swallowing nervously as their eyes darted about, unsure of themselves. And he saw the vets and double vets unmoving—almost grinning, as they anticipated, and invited, the command to "kick ass and take names." Quinn also sensed the change in force fields between himself and the soldier in front of his face. A change that indicated increasing hostility and an imminent explosion. He was about to be hit—no backing down now.

So Quinn struck first.

The edge of his hand shot out with blinding speed and struck the soldier on the bridge of his nose. He teetered back on his heels, and Quinn's other fist slammed into his gut, doubling the corporal over.

The man's belly had been rock-hard, and that worried Quinn slightly. His fist hadn't inflicted disabling damage, just a temporary loss of wind. He would have to go in for the kill quick—without actually delivering serious injuries—before the bigger GI rebounded. Before there was any chance of retaliatory pain.

Quinn doubled over himself now, as if bending to pick up a dropped article, and his boot launched a side kick at the dazed soldier that caught him in the glass jaw, shattering his composure. He flipped over backwards, eyelids fluttering—totally out of it.

"You can't do that!"

"That's fucking police brutality!" The scrotes took up the usual chorus of protests.

A beer bottle flew through the air from the clouds of smoke in the back of the room, missed Quinn's head by inches, and bounced off the helmet of the MP behind him.

A gorilla of a man, wearing a military police uniform, burst into the room after stomping up the stairs with unusual agility and, pausing a microsecond to assess the situation, homed-in on the two investigators, and altered course for the proposed point of impact. An expert at gauging a mob's temperament and the appropriate degree of physical response, he drew his nightstick and threw a body-block at the line of drunks, yelling, *Charge!*" at the top of his lungs.

"It's Smitty!" one of the Saigon Commandos yelled, and the buffer of black helmets surged forward like a disturbed school of piranha reacting to a slab of meat tossed into their lagoon. Any semblance of order dissolved rapidly as the squad of MPs merged with those off-duty troublemakers still standing, and pummeling black mixed with white like the stripes on a raring zebra.

"By God, I *love* the sound of breaking billy-clubs at midnight!" Sergeant Smithers exclaimed as a rook guarding the stairwell for escapees phonied one last Ten-100 and more sirens began their mournful cry in the misty distance.

46

* * *

"Does it hurt, father?"

Quinn smiled as his son gently reached out and ran his tiny hand along the swollen cut on his cheek.

"No, no, of course not, Mang. It just makes my wake-up grin look funny, don't you think?"

The ploy did not work. The child did not smile back.

A colorful bowl of rice appeared on the table in front of him, and he glanced down to see Lien staring up at him with large, sad eyes. She looked on the verge of tears, with her lips sucked in to where the edges barely showed.

"It's alright, honey." He reached down and took his daughter's chin in his hand, and the smile that made his insides glow magically appeared. "Daddy's OK." Her little hands rose and clung to his wrist. She stayed frightened for days when he came home from work sporting the routine street medals: gashes, scrapes, cuts and bruises.

"I will love you forever, Father." She wrapped her arms around his neck and hugged him tightly. *"Forever!"*

"Such a big word: forever." He laughed lightly. "Where did you learn such a thing?"

"I should have cleansed that wound before the children awoke," his wife interrupted softly from across the kitchen table, a stern look in her eyes and no compassion in her voice. She slid a plate piled high with sliced tangerines toward him.

"Oh no, no." Quinn held up a hand defensively, though he seemed to miss the intent of her words as the smile remained intact. "It's nothing, really." He ran a finger along the discolored swelling. "Nothing."

"It is not Halloween, my husband, yet you choose to come home looking like a street monster. You scare the children." Her expression remained icy, and when he examined the narrow almond eyes more closely to see if she was mocking him, he found only disapproval.

They stared at each other several minutes, the children beside them obediently quiet, the ticking of a wall clock the only sound in the room.

Then two vehicles roared down the street outside, sirens screaming. Their radios were turned up full-blast, and as the American military police radio jargon filtered through the open bamboo drapes, a smile crept across her lips.

"You lose!" Quinn reached across the table, taking advantage of her weakness: overpowering memories of their first days together that always flooded back when the MP patrols sped past outside on a Ten-39 hot run. He flicked a finger at the tip of her breast. Little Lien's eyes grew wide as she watched her mother react by pushing her chair away from the table. Mang began clapping loudly in approval as he watched his father charge in the usual manner. The boy's face became an ear-to-ear smile, his eyes sparkling with excitement. Both children's prominent Amerasian features came into play as their parents began the nightly ritual. Neither noticed their mother's nipples spring taut beneath the gossamer-thin fabric of her flowered *ao dais*.

Quinn rushed around the table and dove for her legs as she reached the balcony of their two-bedroom apartment. Xuan screamed, kicked at him playfully, then squealed with delight as he sprung to his feet and carried her off toward the sleeping mats.

"Now you pay for your misdeeds!" Quinn laughed as he found the hidden clasp and began unraveling her gown.

"Payback is a sonofabitch!" she replied in French, their secret love language the children could not understand.

Quinn kicked the door shut behind him but failed to secure the lock like he usually did. By the time she rolled onto the bed, she was totally nude. He crawled under the sheets after her and silenced her laughter with a hungry kiss that pushed her head deep into the plush satin pillows. Her long, black hair fanned out below him, framing amber shoulders like an exotic Japanese tapestry.

Quinn's hand was automatically drawn to full breasts that jutted out, beckoning him as Xuan arched her back so he could wrap his free arm beneath her. His lips slid along her throat until his tongue found the swirl of brown comprising the nipple's tip. She shuddered as his lips took it between them, and then his knee slid between her legs, parting the thighs, and her gasp deepened, becoming a long, drawn-out animal sound as he lowered his body onto hers, entering her.

The room filled with the friction of their bonding, but Quinn's smooth, rhythmic thrusts fell silent as he sensed movement behind him.

Glancing over a shoulder, he saw his son standing in the open doorway, peering at them wide-eyed.

"What are you doing to her?" The question was phrased no different than if he'd been plunging a knife into her heart.

Quinn giggled, blushing. Both he and Xuan were at a loss for words. Mang had his hands on his hips and an angry scowl across his face—like a father who'd just walked in on his teenager's first experiment with sexual intercourse. Beneath his left elbow, Lien squatted, Asian style, soles flat against the smooth teakwood floor, fingers cupped over her mouth.

Quinn cleared his throat uneasily, trying to pull a blanket up over his bare haunches without being noticed. "Didn't your mother ever teach you to knock first?" A stupid smile inched across his face. Xuan elbowed him in the ribs.

Mang ran up to the layered pile of sleeping mats and leaned against them. "No more papaya in the kitchen!" His serious expression disappeared. Outside, thunder boomed in the distance and light sheets of rain could be heard starting their advance across the city.

Little Lien raced around the other side of the bed and crawled under the covers. "I'm scared!" she cried. "Another storm is coming, Mommy!"

"Can we sleep with you tonight?" Mang asked innocently.

The color appeared to have drained from Xuan's face as she stared up at her husband. Her ankles were still wrapped around his thighs, but she was frozen. And now Lien was right against her side, trying to hug her—expecting to be cuddled back.

"Of course, of course." Quinn came up with an idea that might spare them both further embarrassment. He was no child psychiatrist, but he read a lot, and there was no way of telling what tiny, insignificant things kids recalled years after their childhood. "But first you must go out into the living room, OK? Today I hid some candy from the PX—butterscotch kisses!—somewhere in there. And you must—"

But he didn't need to say another word. Mang and Lien tumbled from the bed and pulled each other back, trying to be the first out the doorway.

"Very commendable." Xuan looked up at him with starved eyes that had yet to be fullfilled. "Now what about *my* candy?"

Quinn glanced at his watch. "Almost time to drop by the graveyard shift guardmount, baby."

"But . . . " Her smile evaporated.

"No money, no honey."

She tried to slap him, but he caught her wrist just in time. "Nothing personal, Xuan." His tone remained that of a prankster on the verge of being shotgunned. "But duty calls," and he slid down her body like the rainwater sliding down the slick bamboo outside their window. "But I'll leave you with a little something to keep you honest and interested." His tongue rolled across her flat stomach in a circular motion and began working its way down farther.

"Right *there*!" She grabbed his ears and held his face in place, then slowly began moving it about to suit her fancy. "Oh yes, Johnny . . . right therrrrre."

But he was quickly back on his feet and moving across the room to where his pants were draped over a desk chair. "Time to *di di,* honey." He smiled down at her and almost laughed at the combined expression of anger and exhilaration on her face. She hated it when he left her in these states of denied passion, but words never came to her lips until minutes after he went out the door.

Still grinning as he zipped up his trousers and slipped on his tongs, Quinn pointed down at Xuan as she continued to rub her breasts slowly, her mouth slightly open and lips drawn back. "Hold that thought!" he said.

And then he was gone.

3.

Women Should Be Obscene
And Not Heard

The empty windowpanes of the military police
briefing room at the International Hotel shook and
rattled for several seconds as the two low-flying
Phantoms swooped across the steaming metropolis.
There hadn't been glass in the windows since anyone
could remember. Chicken wire attempted to obscure
the view outside—the smog-choked tamarinds along
busy Tran Hung Dao street, and the *ao dais*-clad
maidens that floated by beneath them—and keep the
grenades out. It depended on whether you focused
on the unsightly metal filters—designed to protect
America's boys from hostile natives—or the living,
breathing, constantly swirling *real* world beyond.

A paper airplane glided across the room as the
dual sonic booms rolled down through the concrete
canyons outside, and Sgt. Mark Stryker slammed it
to the ground with a blinding swipe of his nightstick.

"Damn," he muttered, face emotionless but eyes smiling, "Uncle Ho's growing the mosquitoes bigger and bigger down on the farm these days."

"Here ya go, Sarge." A rookie in the back of the room rolled a can of mace up the center aisle. "All ya need is a dose of good ole Uncle Sammy's bug repellent."

"Good for the hairballs cruisin' the bricks, too," the three-tour vet behind him added dryly.

"As I was saying." Stryker tugged at the bullet hole scar in his left ear lobe and focused on the clipboard atop the podium in front of him. "Looks like we're going back to twelve-hour shifts, with you honies from Charlie Company doubling over till the newbies finish in-processing at Camp Alpha."

A low murmur of protests circulated through the roomful of law enforcers. "First the new rule about mandatory steel pots in sniper alley, now this."

Stryker glanced up, an irritated look replacing the sparkle in his eyes, and scanned the fifty-plus MP helmets glowing back faintly at him. "Save your groanin' for your hoochmat," he muttered.

"But, Sarge." A muscular teenager with close-cropped blond hair stood up, scratching the stubble on his chin. "*Twelve*-hour shifts again?"

"Well, this is the fucking *Nam*, ya know," a lanky NCO leaning against the doorway in the darkened back of the room whispered to the staff sergeant beside him.

"Goofy kids," the E-6 replied, folding his thick forearms across his chest, "Always gripin' 'bout this or that. You'd think we were a big city police department back in The World or something the way they act."

"Goddamned punks." The first man cleared his throat noisily but did not spit on the polished teakwood floor—the old *mama-san* sweeping the corridor behind him would have his hide. He lit up a cigar instead, casting the bent-over Vietnamese woman a disapproving scowl. "What kinda place is this anyway? They let old VC grandmothers loiter around while a 716th guardmount briefing is going on." He kicked the dual swinging doors shut silently with a polished jungle boot.

The sergeant beside him nodded approvingly at his actions, but his thoughts had shifted to the man's earlier complaint. *The damned punks.* Fresh off the block, seventeen-and eighteen-year-old cherry boys, mixed, of course, with some rough and tumble hoods the judges had ordered into the Green Machine. They were all his boys; his scowl remained intact as he nodded to everything the sergeant beside him said, but his eyes were smiling the way Stryker's had. *His* boys. His to hone and polish out on the street. His to baby and protect. To teach. To turn into veteran street cops who could hold their own against a sniper hiding on a rooftop or a Honda Honey intent on lobbing a frag into their lap. He relished each new roster of F.N.G.s, and he knew the other NCOs did too—despite all their own groaning and griping about the latest contingent of eager graduates from The School back at Gordon, so far away. So many, many worlds, an ocean distant.

His mind's eye saw the neat, orderly rows of the forests outside Augusta, Georgia. And the convoy of MP recruits racing up through a hidden trail toward a steep hillside lined with "bomb" craters where the dug-in "enemy" — Green Berets from the Special Forces camp at Benning across the way — awaited them . . .

"Twelve-hour shifts," Thomas was still complaining under his breath, *"again."*

"Sit the fuck down, Ants," a stocky soldier with the nametag BRYANT across his chest grabbed Anthony Thomas's wrist and jerked him back into his metal folding chair.

"Don't wimp out on me, Thomas," Stryker replied. "A twelve-hour beat is good for you. It puts hair on your balls!"

A scattering of laughter and applause filtered through the room. Thomas frowned and stroked an invisible rod between his thighs in response as he looked away.

"See what I mean," the NCO in the doorway pointed out the enlisted man's disrespectful gesture to his partner. "Bunch o' fucking babies."

"The only way *he'd* get hair on his balls is from beating his *meat* for twelve hours, not some Saigon side street," the other sergeant agreed.

"That's telling him, Mark!" A third NCO, with a boxer's mug, threw punches at his shadow behind the men in the last row.

"Smitty!" Stryker called back. "Heard you popped another cap on a douche-bag down on Le Loi last night. Congratulations! Heard MPI declared it a righteous shooting."

"Of course." Smitty drew his .45 automatic and licked the edge of the barrel then reholstered it smoothly before re-snapping the rain flap. Someone in the back of the room whistled his approval. Smitty's jungle boots quit dancing and he leaned against a doorframe with his gunhand resting on the butt of the well-oiled pistol. "The little scrote was tryin' to lift a battery out of the deputy ambassador's sedan while it was parked on the side of the Rex Cinema. Made the mortal mistake of turnin' to face me with a foot-long sharpened screwdriver in his hand."

"Strike one, you're out." Bryant laughed.

"Yah. Now I gotta clean my heater," Smitty complained.

"What's this make?" Stryker held up his fingers dramatically and began counting them but ran out.

"Thirty-two." The barrel-chested staff sergeant folded his arms proudly. "If ya don't count the four sappers I decked with a LAW out at Fort Hustler last week."

"The looooong *arm* of the Law reaches out to strike Mr. Charles again," Bryant whispered across to Thomas.

"Outfuckinstanding," Stryker decided.

Thomas leaned over next to Bryant's ear. "A legend in his own mind," he replied good-naturedly, smiling.

Bryant frowned at his best friend. "Personally, I think the dude's one bad mother, Ants. I'm impressed. Thirty-two zaps. *Thirty-fuckin'-two!*"

"By *his* count." Thomas called back the frown, shifting moods on command.

"I'm sure they're all documented." Bryant shook his head from side to side in awe and admiration. "Christ! Thirty-two confirmed kills."

"If ya don't count the four Victor Charlies out at

Hustler," Thomas imitated Smitty's voice perfectly.

"Got a letter from Sergeant Brickmann out Tokyo-way," Stryker changed the subject. He glanced out over the tops of the helmets, past the wire-covered windows, toward the treeline beyond the blackened tenements crowding Nguyen Gu Trinh. Thomas wondered what he was seeing. What he was *really* seeing. In his mind's eye. Where the echoes of old rain forest firefights and rice paddy gun battles never ever completely faded away.

"How's the Brick doin', Mark?"

Stryker held up a large X-ray that had been folded across the middle so it would fit in a satellite recon-shot mailer envelope. The men in the front row erupted into unexpected laughter.

"Well I'll be a . . . "

"That crazy Brick!"

"A man after my own heart."

"Leave it to Sergeant Brickmann."

The X-ray clearly showed a human skull lowered in front of strategically spread pelvic bones. Someone was getting a blow job, and the dastardly deed was being recorded for posterity.

"Talk about a skull job!" Thomas clapped his hands."

"I'll bet the Brick's whanger glows in the dark now!"

"I always heard them Japanese nurses aim to please!"

"Regardless." Stryker flexed his shoulders and the room fell silent. "The Brick's room number and mailing address are tacked up on the bulletin board right under the alert team rosters, so I wanna hear the mail clerk bitchin' about a dufflebag-full of outgoing get-well cards tomorrow. 'Nough said?"

"Alert team rosters!" several men resumed groaning.

In the hallway outside, a weak, sirenlike noise grew slowly louder and louder, until the doors behind Sergeant Smithers burst open and Calvin Schaeffer strode in, a small red light rotating atop his head. A battery operated siren the size of a TCP whistle was also built into the converted helmet liner, and after circling the room a couple times—as if in pursuit of an invisible perpetrator—Schaeffer dropped a stack of red-tint leaflets on Stryker's podium and zigzagged back out of the room without so much as a word to the men.

"That's one crazy-ass bird." Thomas elbowed Bryant as if they shared a long-guarded secret.

"He gives me the ever-lovin' creeps," Tim replied, glancing back over his shoulder to make sure Schaeffer was really gone and not haunting the shadows.

"They shoulda locked *that one* up in the psyche ward long ago," another soldier declared.

Stryker took the top page off the bundle, attached it to his clipboard, then handed the rest down to Thomas. "Plenty o' hot sheets to go around tonight," he muttered, referring to a foul-up at PMO the previous shift. "Pay special attention to the *canh-sat* BOLOs near the top. They're all real bad dudes, OK? Consider 'em armed and dangerous—so y'all be danger*ass* back!" he shifted into a rare Southern drawl.

"Don't worry," Bryant caught Thomas's concerned look, "The Stryk's from San Marcos or somewhere along the West Coast, buttocks breath. I think that's in California."

"Just east of Oceanside a few klicks," Thomas got specific.

"Whatever."

"Ten-two-four, Sarge," several obedient rooks chimed in in response to Stryker's directive.

"Caught some juice through the grapevine that the civilian firemen are at each other's throats again, so give their station houses at MACV and the annex special patrol when you're not tied up on true crime and real police work, OK?" His last dozen words were laced with friendly sarcasm.

"What's the beef this time, Sarge?"

"You hit the gopher right on the head, Clementi: *beef*. They're arguing about food again."

"Another shift war."

"You guessed it. 'B' shift put together some chow filled with dog food and labeled 'em, 'B SHIFT BURRITOS—DON'T TOUCH!' Well, naturally 'C' shift came to work twenty four hours later and went right to the fridge and gobbled 'em up. The next day 'B' shift showed up again, all smiles, asking where their burritos were. After the boys from Charlie shift pleaded guilty to the theft, Bravo shift told 'em to go look in the dumpster out back."

"Where all the empty dog food cans were." Bryant laughed the loudest. He turned to face his partner and told Thomas, "Hue Chean still can't believe it when I tell her there are actually TV ads for dog food on the boob tube back in The World. She thinks I'm twistin' her tit or something."

"Right. So the next day 'C' shift retaliated by filling

a jar of Gatorade with urine. Well, the jizz hit the fan over that one, and Manka's squad had to roll in to quell the Ten-34 that followed."

"Wonder what it is with those guys," Thomas muttered. He didn't like the firefighters at MACV, they always beat him at arm wrestling.

"Oh, you know how it gets when you spend twenty-four shifts with nothing but males."

"The only pussy anywhere close is the Resusci-Annie, locked up in the training closet," someone else added, "and she's not even good for a blow job."

Stryker tapped his clipboard. "Regarding the problems we been having at the Quick Draw Bar down on Tu Do," he said, "I wanna congratulate you men. Shootings have tapered down to just two last week and only one the week before." A solitary pair of hands began clapping slowly in the back of the room. "Curly's Liquorbox over on Mac Dinh Chi is another matter, however. Five more holdups in the last ten days."

"Curly's oughta be solely a *canh-sat* problem, Sarge." A tall, lanky soldier in the fifth row of chairs stood up. "The dude's Vietnamese, and why should I worry about his brother countrymen rippin' him —"

Stryker held up his hands, and the private first class fell silent. "All I'm saying is you clowns might pay a little more attention to this potential hot spot during your 'leisure' time instead of spending all your Short-7's down at Mimi's, flirtin' with the bargirls."

"Aw, Sarge —"

"And speakin' o' cunts," Stryker continued, "my desk top is overflowing with complaints from the officers' dependents about Madame Kwok's hookers causing traffic jams in the main entrance to the Bali Hai Lounge, where so many of the wives meet their husbands for lunch."

"They're lucky their husbands aren't out in the Pleiku bush where they oughta be!" Thomas whispered over to Bryant loud enough for everyone in the first five rows to hear.

"So those of you spending so much time barchecking the Velvet Turtle—" Stryker cleared his throat accusingly—"might consider shifting your activities over to the Bali Hai on Le Loi for a week or two.

"OK, Patterson over at the Rattan Man told the PM he appreciates all the extra patrol he's been getting. Only one rooftop burglary in the last three weeks, and he smoked that *cao boi* himself!" Applause sounded throughout the room.

"With a double-barreled ten-gauge shotgun," Bryant added with respect and admiration in his tone.

"But he's off to Taiwan or Hong Kong or some laid-back exotic port on business till the fifteenth, so let's not slack up on the spotlight checks, OK?"

"About the Liquorbox over on Mac Dinh Chi, Sarge." Thomas stood up, raising his hand like a schoolboy. Beside him, Bryant shook his head from side to side slowly, blushing.

Stryker seemed to be mentally nodding in resignation also when he said, "What about it, Ants?"

"Well, all last week, *I* did spend my free time stakin' out Curly's, anticipatin' a little gunplay, ya know? But every time Lieutenant Slipka drove by, he gave me a dirty look—like maybe I was just wasting battalion time or something." Thomas let a hurt expression color his face.

"Tony was probably just remembering days long past — " Stryker leaned forward over his podium and lowered his voice — "when he was an EM with time on his hands to loiter in search of a hot time in the city, OK? Now he's a busy man, always running back and forth, crisscrossin' the town, tryin' to keep all our asses off the kettle, so cut the Lou some slack. He came up through the ranks. He's been where all of us are now."

"So I can keep parkin' down the block from Curly's, Sarge?" Thomas persisted. "I got your OK on that?"

"Just so you're not dodgin' your regular radio calls, troop." Stryker drilled accusing orbs down into the MP's eyes, and he looked away.

"Aw, not *me*, Sarge. You know I wouldn't — "

"And the rest of you oughta spend a little more time around Curly's too," Stryker's voice returned to its normal volume as it repeated an earlier tidbit of free advice. "Odds are, you hang around Mac Dinh Chi long enough, your heater'll see some use — and you know how stingy the PM's been lately with live ammo out on the range.

"OK." Stryker glanced down at his clipboard, noticing how the room remained silent after his last joke. The men were divided, he sensed. Half were restless, eager to get out on the street. The rest were exhausted — asleep with their eyes open. Some were working a double shift. Others were off duty, opting to attend the guardmount briefing in lieu of returning to a dark barracks and the nightmares that always returned with the hum of gunships cruising overhead, dropping their flares along the edge of Saigon. "Greenlee got sniped at two nights ago at the U-Brew-It over on Le Loi. I don't know why this wasn't covered in last night's briefing." He shifted papers about slowly, painfully aware there was a lot more to be covered before their little "gathering" could be dismissed. "Anyway, Mr. Charles missed by a long shot, and Greenlee and his partner captured a couple suspects fleeing in a cyclo that ran out of gas two minutes into the chase." Scattered laughter. "But I'm sure we haven't heard the last of problems at your favorite all-night coffee shop. Just let it be known. Both MI and CID have gotten more anonymous tips the dozen MP· helmets that congregate every shift at the U-Brew-It provide almost irresistible targets for Cong trainees, so don't *blow it*. Stray from a usual routine. Avoid sitting with your backs to that large picture window they got there—the one without any glass in it. And keep your eyes and ears open, OK? There's lots less lively parts of town you guys could be taking your Short-7's."

Several helmets turned to face the rear doors as the men sensed a latecomer to the room. "Aw, Mr. Quinn!" Stryker abandoned his clipboard and waved the agent into the heart of the briefing. "You all know Bob from CID." He glanced about the room, seeking out nods of affirmation. "Well, he's got a few words of wisdom for your cherry-red ears, so *listen up!*"

"I'll just take a minute of your time, men." Quinn nodded to several MPs he recognized from the street. "We've had a couple bombings in Sector Six this week. One on Nguyen Van Thoai, the other at Thanh

Mau and Chi Hoa. Confirmed fatals at both. Initially, we thought perhaps the owners were after insurance money, but now it's beginning to look like possible contract killings."

"Why would *we* be assisting in a *canh-sat* matter?" an MP in the back of the room asked. "Weren't these both Vietnamese-owned buildings?"

"Yours is not to ponder why." Stryker waved a nightstick at the man, grinning slightly. "Yours is just to do or die!"

"OK, Sarge," the corporal muttered, upset his question had not been answered. Stryker usually didn't operate that way.

"Actually, Jon Toi from the VNP asked our aid on this one." Quinn relieved the tension, as both Stryker and the corporal knew he would. "He figured it was the least he could do, since you guys exchanged shots with rooftop lookouts just prior to both bombings."

"He was hoping we could keep an eye on a couple other locations," Stryker further elaborated. "Mr. Quinn's investigation has revealed some potential future target zones, and the most likely businesses within them." He slid a map of Saigon onto an easel. The city was divided into fourteen sectors. "These are the two most likely hits for the time period we're in now." Stryker stepped forward and tapped his nightstick at the warehouse district a few blocks behind the Presidential Palace. "You men working these beats might want to spotlight the areas a bit more than usual. See what you can come up with."

"We'll keep you posted on further developments." Quinn was dressed in civilian attire, with a T-shirt beneath his safari suit. His chest and sides were lined with perspiration from the tropical heat even though night had fallen three hours earlier. "I know you guys are already swamped with b.s. busy-work, but who knows — we might come up with a basement bomber or something." He unbuttoned his outer garmet, yawned, and stretched, revealing most of the I USED TO GET DISGUSTED — NOW I'M JUST AMUSED T-shirt underneath. It was just the unexpected "statement" the men needed to boost their spirits.

"Where can I get one of those, Mr. Quinn?" a rook in the front row had an eager sparkle in his eyes.

Quinn, a smile starting to form on his lips, stared down at the man, wondering if he had enough time on the street and in this business to even know what the phrase meant. "Ask Ants there." He pointed at Thomas. "He's a jack of all trades, friend. Sells everything on the side you could want."

"Just got in a whole new batch of FEEL SAFE TONIGHT — SLEEP WITH A COP shirts last week," Thomas stood up and took his flak vest off, ignoring Stryker's sudden frown. "But these are the best I've seen in a while." He pulled his fatigue shirt apart to reveal bright red stencils on an o.d. green T-shirt: I'M NOT PREJUDICED — I HATE EVERY-BODY.

"OK . . . awright . . . " Stryker dismissed the guardmount with the wave of a hand. "You've all got your assignments. Two-man units get the old Jeeps again. Those of you riding alone draw the beasts with the Federal electronics systems — just got a *batch* of 'em in last week." He cast Thomas a cold stare. "For field testing in the big city, overseas environment and all that. And don't forget to write up evaluation memos to Captain Douglas at EOW. I'll be countin' to make sure nobody forgets."

"Aw, Sarge," several men moaned in protest as they oiled down their .45 slides.

"Now beat it!" Stryker waved his nightstick in the air before sliding it back in its keeper with a challenging smile. *"Di Di mau or die!"*

"Can I buy you a bag o' ice coffee?" Quinn asked him later as both vets walked out onto the veranda overlooking the long line of fifty MP units. Red lights began flashing, and a dozen sirens blasted a short yelp as the men checked out their equipment and day-shift patrols began wandering in off the street.

"Appreciate it, Big Q, but gotta get out on the bricks with my men. Otherwise half of 'em will swarm over to Tu Do to conduct 'welfare checks' on the bargirls, and the other half 'll begin tryin' to pull the wool over my eyes regarding something or other."

Agent Quinn cocked an eyebrow at the muscular ex-Green Beret, gauging his seriousness, then both men laughed while, below, the radio in a Jeep crackled against the silence of an unusually quiet night.

"Time check," a weary voice requested a Ten-36.

"Zero-zero-thirty hours," WACO cleared the net with the usual unemotional drone.

"Man, am I fucked up," the private out somewhere deep in the heart of the concrete jungle replied over the air. His exhausted tone told everyone the switch to twelve- and eighteen-hour shifts was beginning to take its toll. Both Stryker's and Quinn's eyes arced up in surprise at the rare use of profanity on the radio net.

"Unit *identify!*" The dispatcher now sounded like a father who caught his children playing with matches.

"I'm not *that* fucked up," the patrolman cruising somewhere across the vast metropolis of three million people laughed softly in reply. His voice sounded like any of four dozen MPs currently patrolling the city. Military radios didn't have the best clarity.

Several clicks across the net followed—a policeman's way of applauding something admirable or of laughing about an error. Or, in this case, announcing their surprise.

"Jesus," Quinn also broke into a grin.

"Looks like it's gonna be one of those nights." Stryker's frown deepened as he scratched his forehead.

"Ten-2, WACO!" a different soldier cut in through the waves of static. "MP needs help at the Quick Draw! Repeat, this is Car Niner-Alpha! Ten-2 at . . ." The transmission faded and more static rushed in to drown out the voice.

A three-toned scrambler trilled across the four military police channels. "ATTENTION ALL UNITS," the dispatcher's voice came across twice as powerful as the patrolman's, "ten-2 at the Quick Draw Bar on Tu Do. Cars 35, 36 and 36-Alpha, the call is yours. Handle Ten-39. Units to back, respond."

"Echo-22, from the Majestic."

"Zulu One from the Tan Son Nhut U.S.O."

"Car 12 from Le Van Duyet and Bac Hai."

Climbing sirens could be heard in the background during each transmission.

"Nine-Alpha's a sergeant, isn't it?" Quinn's smile

68

faded. Most NCOs would rather eat lead than radio for help.

"Yeah," Stryker sounded like he was thinking more about the Jeep than the soldier in it. "Vinnie. And he's got *my* unit!"

"Bummer."

"Yeah." Stryker swung down over the railing and dropped the ten feet to the ground. "It must be bad!" A Jeep with its red roof lights twirling frantically skidded up to him and the ex-Pleiku hand jumped in.

Quinn swallowed hard as he started over the veranda railing, careful to keep his automatic snugly in its shoulder holster. Stryker was motioning for him to hurry up and climb in.

More Jeeps roared by toward the compound gate as the CID agent felt himself being drawn to Stryker's side by a sudden swirl of excitement and danger in the air. Sirens wailing in the distance and rain clouds hanging ominous on the horizon were spinning a web of intrigue that sent his adrenalin racing. Saigon sang! She was calling to him. He could feel the spell. And the curse.

He knew of so many men who had lost their souls to the city and had returned to The World forever changed, forever haunted, but the challenge was a call to adventure he could not resist.

4.

Life's A Bitch. And Then You Die.

Quinn knew old Army ammo was being fired at him the moment the man pulled the trigger. With smoke spiraling out behind it, a slug of lead floated lazily toward him — almost dreamlike. He jumped to the side and drew his own automatic as the round flew past, slammed against brick and dropped to the blacktop.

Stryker's .45 was already out of its holster. The barrel barked twice and the Vietnamese man standing above the unconscious MP flew backwards through the air. The gunman beside him, smoke still floating in front of the pistol in his right hand, stared wide-eyed at Quinn, mouth agape, body frozen.

Quinn's fist flew up, and his own .45 exploded seconds after Stryker's. The bullet caught the remaining Oriental in the left shoulder, twirled him around, and slammed him against a door frame. Screaming wildly, his mouth moved all about, twisted grotesquely with horror. But the rest of his body merely collapsed, refusing to respond to the waning rush of fight-or-flee adrenalin.

Stryker laughed out loud as he started toward the three men on the ground. "What a pussy-assed hit, Quinn. Did you take your best shot, or what?"

"Aw, gimme a break, Mark." The CID agent holstered his automatic and rushed to the aid of the fallen MP. "Somebody musta slipped me a hot load. I was aimin' at his belly."

"Surrrre." Stryker broke into a grin as he advanced slightly behind the investigator, gun arm still extended, pistol sights trained on the Asian who was face down, head twitching. His hand still clutched a .45, and as it suddenly shifted toward the Americans, Stryker seemed to spring up off the ground slightly, catlike, and jerk off three rounds at the same time.

The back of the gunman's head erupted in a spray of blood and crimson-slick bone, and his lower torso spun about across the blacktop, but Quinn did not react to the shooting. Instead, he was down on one knee beside the wounded MP—a tall, slender, fifty-year-old sergeant first class. "I've found a pulse!" His forefinger was pressed firmly against the NCO's throat. "And I don't see any blood, Stryk!"

"Yeah—Vinnie's indestructible." Stryker didn't seem concerned. He had just mumbled a few words over his portable radio that Quinn didn't catch in all the excitement. "He's been around since the Boxer rebellion in China, if ya go by the talk always bein' recycled at the Club over at Pershing Field. Probably caught a slug in the flak vest tonight. I got Egor and his chopper flappin' in for a Dustoff, OK? Pound on his chest or something, while I pat down this other douche-bag."

Quinn's head shook from side to side in resignation as he watched the ex-Green Beret flip the second suspect onto his back in search of weapons. Behind him, a sea of flashing red lights was rolling up like an angry tidal wave, sirens crying in the night as they wound down.

In the hazy distance, somewhere along the edge of Saigon, the sound of flapping rotors became audible as the last bouncing siren echoed off the tenement walls.

"Tell us about it again, Father!" The boy jumped up and down beside the table eagerly as he held onto the big man's wrist with two tiny hands. "Tell us how you smoked the *cau bois*!"

Robert Quinn patted his son on the head, ignoring Vietnamese custom which prohibited such contact, and continued reading his *Saipan Post* without looking up. "Mang!" His wife leaned across the table and slapped both the child's hands away in a swift and startling maneuver. "Show respect — leave your father alone!"

The assault had been mild, but little Mang still retreated to his sister's side, stunned. Hurt and shock colored his Amerasian features, but no tears welled up in his sad, dark eyes.

Always the stronger of the two, Lien's smile faded. Frowning, she charged forward and struck down her mother's arms then wrapped her own around Xuan's

73

wrists, temporarily subduing her. "Now tell us, Daddy!" She smiled up at her father then turned and cast a mock glare at her restrained mother, well aware neither adult was really angry. "All about the bad men you *fini* last night!"

Quinn did not move for several dramatic seconds, as he seemed to consider the appropriate response to such a disrespectful act, then suddenly, he smashed his newspaper down loudly on the tabletop and, voice raised, stated, "It went something like this!" He drew a black "weapon" from inside his bathrobe and leaned forward, flashing his incisors insanely at the little girl. Terrified, she squealed with delight nonetheless. Quinn's arm shot out, and he planted the barrel of the pistol against Lien's forehead. "Pow! Pow! Pow!"

Water sprayed from the squirt gun and splashed all across the little girl's face.

"*Daddy!*" Lien and her brother scampered from the room, each trying to laugh louder than the other.

"Don't encourage them!" Xuan snapped at him, lips pursed in reprimand but eyes soft with love.

"Oh, be quiet." Quinn leaned close, brushed her long, black hair aside and began rubbing the back of her neck. He slipped his other hand between the buttons of her blouse and brushed them against the steep valley between her breasts. His knuckles, rough and scarred from years working the toughest beat in the world, slid across her nipples, and, against her will, they slowly bloomed forth, erect and aroused. The way he was.

"Mang is turning into a—how you say? A *wimp!*" Her tone fought to remain cold as his fingers slid

74

down the small of her back and came to rest against the swell of her buttocks.

"Wimp? Christ, Xuan! The boy is not even five years old! When he turns seven, we'll send him to a martial arts class or something, OK?"

"His sister is always there to look out for him," Xuan argued. "But what about the future? She will not always be there. She is, admittedly, the stronger of the two, but what will Mang do when their peers draw them away from each other? Or worse, when the Arvin drafts him to fight the VC—what then?"

"The Arvin? The *VC*?" Quinn asked incredulously. "Honey, this war's not going to be going on that long."

"It has been 'going on,' as you say, for thousands of years, Robert. Mang will be draft age in one short decade. You can promise me this war will be over by then?"

She tried to lock eyes with him, but Quinn looked away, to the small, framed wall plaque holding his medals. "Well . . ." He stared at the dragon walking through the forest of bamboo below the gold and red RVN Service ribbon. Was the beast actually turning to meet his gaze? His vision clouded as he saw his son struggling through a steaming rice paddy, in pursuit of his brother southerners: the Cong. Beads of perspiration slid down his spine, and Xuan's words brought him back to reality.

"Alright, so we won't talk yet about 1977 my Robert dear. But what about school? The children will say his sister protects him, don't you see? That he hides behind her skirts! Is that what you want?"

"Kids can be cruel," he admitted, drifting back

now to his own childhood momentarily. All the while, his free hand was slowly pulling Xuan's blouse down off one shoulder. "But let's worry about it all tomorrow, OK? I'm running late as it is." He had one breast exposed now—the nipple pulsing slightly over the heartbeat but falling back flat and unaroused because of all the conversation. His lips glided past her ear, barely touching it, then his tongue slid down her throat and his mouth swallowed the smooth purple swirl.

Xuan's head dropped back and she sighed but quickly recovered, pushing him away. "Not here, *Robert*! The children could return any time! You always like it best when there is the risk of being caught—just like that night along the *Song Saigon* when the *canh-sats* caught us with your head up my dress! Why? Why you like to take so much chance, Robert?"

Quinn just grinned and fell over the edge of her chair, onto the ground, dragging her down on top of him. "What about the time we did it on your mother's veranda, while she was just down the hillside, trimming those stupid flowers she keeps?"

"Robert!" She tried to slap him playfully, but he caught her wrist in midair.

"Or the time in the back seat of the crop duster over Vung Tau—the one my buddy from Air America took us up in? Remember that time?" He tickled her ribs, basking in the warmth the sound of her giggles brought him.

"We were talking about the children!" Her tone took on a businesslike quality, but he saw right through it. "And it is as much *your* fault as little

76

Mang's when you allow the war stories to invade my kitchen table!" She waved a dainty fist at him. "But that's what it's all really about, isn't it, my dear husband?"

"Whatever are you talking about?" Quinn held his hands up in mock bewilderment.

"You take even more satisfaction from the risks found on the street, than what we have been through during our quest for the ultimate orgasm."

Her sudden fluency took him by surprise. He shook his head about, feigning intense admiration at her up-to-now hidden linguistic abilities, but knew he had to speak fast to maintain the upper hand. "Yeahhhhh," he sighed. "All this talk about sex and violence gives me a hard-on, *honey*!" he revealed, trying to pull her panties down, but she resisted.

"I told you not to buy that TV set!" she scolded him, waving a finger — again playfully. (Where would she be without her Saigon soaps, when all the girls in the building came over — all the other police wives — bringing their sodas and rice cakes?) "Now they watch *Star Trek*, and *Dragnet* when I'm at market, and last night they see story about — "

"What's wrong with *Star Trek,* for Christsake?" he cut in.

"*And last night* — " she tapped her forefinger against his chest with each word — "they see story about your shooting at Quick Draw Bar! How can I keep secrets from then anymore? Mang already says he wants to be policeman someday — like his father."

"What's wrong with tha — "

"*His wishes will be the death of me, Robert!*"

"You know you love it, *woman*!" He slid her night-

77

gown down over her hips and engulfed the other breast for a few seconds of noisy, exaggerated sucking. "That's why you married me. All the black leather and blue steel." He guided her hand to his erection.

"Yessss," she sighed again, weakening.

"Especially my 'nightstick' there, honey. You horny old broads all like us cops' billy-clubs the most!"

The front screen door could be heard opening, then slamming shut. "There, see!" He spread her legs apart with his knee and pushed against soft flesh until, almost stubbornly, she yielded and he slid in, tingling with the suddenly warm sensation around his flesh.

Xuan let out a soft gasp and sat up, arcing her shoulders back as she drew him in deeper. Grasping his wrists, she guided his hands onto her breasts and squeezed his fingers inward. "I will not have my son cruising the streets of Saigon in an MP Jeep!" She swished her hips about in ecstasy, manipulating his hardness to suit her pleasure.

"Yes, ma'am." Quinn's grin expanded with his penis.

"He shall be a doctor, educated in *Paris*!" The French city came out as a gasp when he thrust up into her powerfully, masterfully taking control while letting her believe she was in charge.

"Yes, ma'am. Of course . . ."

"I will hear no more talk of—"

"Oh oh!" Lien stood in the doorway to the hall corridor, arms folded across her chest. Little Mang knelt beside her, hands over his eyes. "Here we go again . . ."

CID agent Robert Quinn swallowed the last of his

Singapore sling, then winked at the woman seated across the table from him as the bittersweet liquor trickled down his throat. Its stem protruding from his lips, Quinn held the drink's cherry between his teeth instead of swallowing it too. Lan reached over the flaming *pu pu* platter and plucked the fruit from his mouth, then ran it along the edge of her tongue, sensually.

Several dozen feet behind the woman, two dancers swayed while a slow tune blared from huge suspended ceiling speakers. Discarding different articles of clothing every few seconds, by halfway through the song they were both completely nude. Beads of perspiration sparkled on the slopes of upturned breasts. Clouds of cigarette smoke drifted between them and the thirty tables in the Tu Do street nightclub.

The blue pall made it difficult for Quinn to lock eyes with either girl and trade thoughts or send that special midnight challenge. Saigon tea was a delicacy he couldn't afford anymore—ever since he slipped on the slender Viet gold wedding band, each of its delicate diamond-shaped etchings adding strength to the spell Xuan held over him.

He didn't realize he was toying with the ring now as his eyes went from Lan's to the dancer's up on the stage, then back to Lan's. He wasn't cheating on his wife. This was purely a business "lunch," despite the hour.

The sweat trickling beneath his collar started only when he thought of Hue Chean—Bryant's wife. Quinn had been there the night she caught Tim entering a bar without her. The young woman had stabbed him over the incident. And that was before the couple had gotten married. *But Xuan . . . Naw, she wouldn't . . .*

"So tell me." Quinn glanced around the bar. "What 'secret information' have you brought to offer for sale on this, our first clandestine rendezvous?" The smile on his lips rippled with a French accent as he sarcastically spoke the last two words.

"I still work on boom boom case." She also glanced about, imitating him — nose in the air as if the voluntary extracurricular activity thrust their status above the other patrons in the bar. "But here are names of some drug dealers who work only GI market. Angi say MPs watch these men *bookoo*, but never get evi — evi — "

"Evidence on them." Quinn's eyes drifted back to the dancers. Far from professional, they were awkwardly out of time as they spun around with a sudden change in tempo, but their tight haunches — smooth and dark — more than made up for any weak points in the choreography of their act.

"Yes. Evidence. Well, beside each name is time and place of their next resupply meet." She slid the envelope across the table for his inspection.

"Very good." Quinn's eyes shifted back to her mouth. It was hard to ignore the way she was still licking the moist cherry. "And how much '*p*' do you require for this information, Miss Lan?" *P* was short for *piaster*, Vietnam's national currency.

She did not answer immediately, but continued sucking on the end of the cherry instead. Quinn decided he had never wanted to be a cherry more in his life than right then. He slipped the tiny packet into his shirt pocket without glancing at the names. He'd hand the information over to MPI, or maybe the DEA. Narcotics bored him. Too much risk for too little satisfaction.

The flow of drugs across the Golden Triangle was a tide no task force would ever be able to crush.

Drug deals were dangerous business. Most anything CID got involved in was unhealthy, but dope was the pits. The Army didn't pay him enough to go after pushers or knife-fight with their customers. That was the sweet tea about seniority. Now that he had put in his time on the bricks, he could practically pick and choose his assignments. And he had already spent two years in Vice—back when he was young, enthusiastic and energetic. And foolish. Back when he loved the street and the night more than his woman. Back when eighteen hours in a patrol Jeep flashed by like a mortar barrage and you were ready for more, often fighting over the voluntary Alert Team rosters. Back when you hung up your web belt, went to bed with your woman, but didn't sleep. You just lay there—listening to the jets landing at Tan Son Nhut and the flares sizzling against the night mist. The thunder in the distance, not really thunder at all but outgoing Arvin artillery. And now and then a lone VC rocket spiraled down into the heart of Lady Saigon, launched from the edge of the laughing jungle. Back when you didn't sleep, but you lay against your woman's breast, cuddled in her arms, listening to her unsteady, hesitant breathing, her racing heartbeat. Listening to the city's energy hiss outside, listening to the clock, knowing it would all end with the dawn . . . dreading the thought of its ending, resisting sleep despite the fatigue, wishing to float in the moment forever, bask in the *heaven* of her heat against you—a feeling that never came to you back in The World, outside the war zone, so far from Saigon.

"I don't know." Lan's words did not break the spell,

81

but only served to reinforce it. Perhaps all the incense and cigarette smoke and odor of alcohol in the club were taking hold of him, deadening his senses, but he loved what he was feeling, what he was experiencing . . . what was pulsing through his veins. He hoped it would never end—that the city would never die, that the war would go on forever. Foolish, he decided. Selfish. Mang's and Lien's faces flashed before his mind's eye. Then a sudden thought shot through him, jerking him back to "reality." What would he do if it every *did* come crashing to an end? *What would he do? Where would he go? Where would they go?* A scarred-up old investigator and his un-American wife and their half-breed kids. The big city? Even the Asians in Chinatown would be suspicious, would never quite accept them. Even the speakers of Mandarin glared at the Cantonese with downcast eyes. So where did that leave his family? Would a Little Saigon ever spring up somewhere in the mainland—the way the ROK families built Little Korea or the Japanese in L.A. formed Little Tokyo? And what of him? Life in a military garrison—where he could meet with all the other warriors and their outcast women—would be too much to handle. It would drive him *dinky-dau*. And it would kill Xuan.

No, only in Saigon were they safe. Vietnam had become home. "I don't know," Lan repeated. "How much do you think information like this worth?" She held her fingers apart. "Six dong . . . *seven* dong?" She was clearly talking inches, and not coins. *Vietnam,* he smiled to himself, allowing his eyes to fall to her breasts, *Land of the sleeping dragon-ladies, where a man could take two wives to suit his fancy. Where the women would kill each other fighting over their man, but where society accepted it all silently.*

Her eyes lit up slightly as she noticed something behind Quinn, and the CID agent turned to spot the tops of four MP helmets bobbing through the crowd at the doorway as a squad from Bravo Company entered for a bar check.

Quinn didn't answer, but a smile rolled across his lips too. As the military policemen grew nearer he recognized his drinking buddy, Bryant.

"Not working Decoy this week?" Quinn asked, as the four soldiers passed by his table. Experienced vets always headed for the stage so they could eyeball the dancers' routine up close.

"Aw, they got me doublin' over to cover some of them skates out at Fort Hustler again." Bryant took the seat between Quinn and the woman, while his three partners ignored the off-duty American and continued toward the strippers. "And what brings you into a seedy dive like this, Bob?" Bryant glanced about with mock suspicion. "I don't see Xuan anywhere around." His eyes dropped to Lan's breasts, as if deciding her measurements. "I suppose you're going to try and tell me this is her sister, up from Mytho for a week or something." His eyes danced with skepticism as he did his best to imitate Groucho Marx.

Quinn poked his stomach with a stiff forefinger. "Well, I can tell *you* certainly haven't been away from Mama's cooking lately, Mr. Potbelly." His smile remained intact. It seemed they were always watching out for each other when it came to temptations of the halter-top persuasion.

"Pleased to meet you." Bryant brushed Quinn aside and bowed across the table, took Lan's hand, then

83

kissed her knuckles with an arousing, sucking noise. Startled by the sound, she jerked her arm back, glancing around to see if anyone at the surrounding tables had heard. "You'll have to forgive my bloodbrother's rude table manners. My name is Timothy Bryant, self-admitted Saigon Commando—"

"A title he's not proud of," Quinn cut in.

"But nevertheless resigned to accepting." He watched Lan frown as she refused to look up at him again. "Oh well," Bryant muttered under his breath, taking a seat again, "that's life in the big city."

"We, as I stated earlier, were discussing business," Quinn assumed a tone of mock seriousness. "*Official* business."

"Sure," Bryant's reply was soaked with sarcasm.

"You have your nerve." The verbal fisticuffs were totally lost on Lan as she began losing her temper.

Bryant patted his crotch. "Honey," he said, "my only nerve you need concern yourself with is the one hanging down between my legs." He locked onto her with a what-do-you-think-about-*that*? glare. Lan's face began flushing as she mentally translated the flurry of words from English into Vietnamese. "I seen the way you been looking at Bob here," Bryant continued. "*All* the way from the other side of the room!" He decided to go for the jugular—it was the best way to have fun with the local girls. "You're after nothing but a *stiff dick,* honey!" He grabbed Quinn's wrist and pulled him out of his seat, away from the attractive Vietnamese woman.

"What you do?" Lan stood up too as the men briefly wrestled without moving their feet. A bargirl at the next table spilled her Saigon tea as she choked at the sight of the glowing MP helmet bouncing across the floor upside-down.

"I'm taking you home to Mama." Bryant totally ignored the woman as he waved his partners back over to their table and worked on twisting Quinn's arm around behind his back.

"Seriously, Tim! This was totally innocent. A genuine business lunch. We were discussing—"

But Bryant's comrades had rejoined him, and the four uniformed MPs proceeded to unceremoniously drag CID agent Quinn from the bowels of the Floating Dragon. "You'll thank me for this in the morning, Bobby-baby!" Bryant insisted. "Once I get you home and tucked in next to *mama-san* Xuan!" It was all just the usual outrageous horseplay to Bryant, but in the back of his mind stabs of painful memory reminded him of that afternoon Hue Chean plunged cold steel into his lower back during a jealous tantrum—fits of anger he had since broken her of.

"Xuan'll *damn* sure sit on his face after we tell her about tonight!" Anthony Thomas slapped Quinn up the back side of the head playfully. "The lifer'll deny it all but it'll be fun watchin' him sweat over—"

"You're just lucky we arrived on scene in time to save your worthless ass," Sgt. Gary Richards cut in. "Better to burst your cock-struttin' bubble in this brusque manner than let you wake up in the morning drippin' with a mean dose of that godawful incurable black syph!"

"Yeah, bro!" Thomas yelled as they exited the nightclub through a tangle of curious patrons crowding the rear doors.

"Right on!" Bryant got Quinn in a headlock as two

bargirls expertly maneuvered up through the customers and tried to snag one the troopers in jungle green.

"Wait till Xuan hears about this!" a busboy holding the doors open for the Americans joined in on the fun. He recognized most of the men from the 716th but knew none of them.

Quinn finally gave up when they got him outside and a rare cool breeze swirled in to coax him back to reality. "Fuck it," he decided, allowing Bryant to lead him over to the nearest MP Jeep. "I'll just set up another meeting with the cunt tomorrow night, you turds," he muttered under his breath. "Or the next. Or the fucking next—don' mean nothin'. I just fucking extended for another year, OK? I got all the time in the world! I got . . ."

A young shoeshine boy darted out from between two parked cars and stopped in front of the MP Jeep to watch the Army policemen drag their fellow American out of the drinking establishment. Quinn's feet also skidded to a halt as their eyes met.

There was something about the boy's face. Something that reminded him of his son. And there was a desperation there that both haunted and frightened him. *This* could be his child. This orphan of war, who lived in the streets, hustling by day and sleeping under parked troop lorries or on park benches in Le Loi Square by night, could be Mang!

A sobering rush flowed through his veins as Xuan's and little Lien's faces also flashed in front of him, and he completely forgot about the woman abandoned inside the bar. The danger in the air no longer excited him. The ominous foreboding that pressed down on the city, smothering it with electric heat until the martial law curfew was firmly clamped down within the maze of roadblocks and ring of flares, no longer impressed him.

It was time to go home to his family. Saigon would be there in the morning. He would still awake with the invigorating fragrance of *pho* soup drifting up from the vendor stalls in one nostril and Xuan's long silky hair in the other. The tropical heat would still be clinging to the shield of shade around the courtyard walls—like some invisible force field thrown out by a montagnarde wizard, or the ghost of some long dead monastery holy man.

But for now it was time to go home to Xuan. He checked his wristwatch. Almost midnight.

Yes, time to return to his family—the den. The warm, safe lair of the clan. Time to go home.

5.

Emotion Commotion

The streets all look different after dark.

Quinn thought back to when he first heard that line. Had it been while cruising the countless white barracks back at The School, where they taught you how to be an MP? Or that first graveyard shift in The Nam, where he sat in the back of a Jeep while two vets — both single-digit midgets — raced down Le Van Duyet toward Plantation Road, joking about VC snipers, missing street signs, and how the fastest way to cut across Cong-held territory from Point A to Point B was just to "duck and go like hell!" Gamble with the gods. Laugh in Lady Death's face, taunting her, making the challenge dance in your eyes so she knows you're not calling the ultimate bluff.

There was truth to the statement. During the daytime, the sidewalks were crawling with vendor stands, freelance artists with their easels, black velvet canvases, and bright metallic oils. And shoppers browsing. Everywhere, shoppers ignoring the terrorist threat, braving the curfew checkpoints to make that final bargain, score that last purchase at the black market.

But now the curbs were deserted, and shadows from the military and police roadblocks climbed the tenement walls as boy-soldiers started up their oil drum fires, turning each block into a kennel of restless devil dogs that strained silently at their invisible leashes but never ever attacked.

Tonight the shadows were uncomfortably long. He didn't like the way they looked—the way the devil dogs no longer appeared to be devil dogs but danced about more like tormented ghosts, trying to escape their tombs.

"And I want you to tiptoe your ass up to your flat without waking the old lady or kids," Bryant was going on and on as Thomas doused the headlights, cut the engines, and let the Jeep coast down the side street to Quinn's housing project. Richards sat in the back seat beside the CID agent. But Quinn was not smiling as his eyes searched the third floor balcony of the building off Nguyen Cong Tru. The Chinese lantern in the window was off—Xuan always left it on for him so he wouldn't stumble over anything on his way to the small PX refrigerator. Now the apartment was completely dark.

"You guys wanna stand by a second?" Quinn requested, sniffing at the air without being obvious. "Something doesn't seem right here."

"He just figures Xuan's gonna kick his butt for bein' out on the street so long without checkin' in." Thomas laughed, but Bryant and Richards were not smiling. As they gazed up at Quinn's balcony, they remembered back to another time, another case, another investigation. An MP had returned home from work to find all hell had ripped up through the floorboards with a blinding vengeance.

Quinn glanced into the guard kiosk beside the compound entrance, but it was deserted. "Is that unusual?" Richards also noticed the sentry's absence.

"Very." The young CID agent drew the .45 from his shoulder holster and started toward the dark, shadow-cloaked stairwell. It had never looked so menacing to him before. "For a rent-a-cop, the guy's pretty dedicated. Ex-Arvin, they tell me."

"One leg, Bob?"

"Same-same. We pay him good bucks to keep alert and sound the alarm should sappers or *cao bois* sneak up on our 'perimeter.' "

"Yeah, I've seen him lots. Never can catch him snoozin'."

"You snooze, you lose," Thomas threw in his words of wisdom.

"The dude's always on his feet," Richards continued.

"*Foot,*" Thomas corrected him seriously. Richards winked at Quinn. *Blame the late hour and the lack of action.*

"You cruise by here that often?" Quinn seemed surprised as the four men started up the stairs. Their rook remained with the vehicle. It was the kind of neighborhood where one out of four MPs on a call *always* stayed with the two patrol Jeeps — to discourage thieves from stealing the tires. Or the entire chassis!

"Sure." Thomas was proud to reveal a tidbit about the Brotherhood of the Badge. "We keep numbers on all the men — even you boys in CID."

Bryant snickered to himself.

"Can't be too careful in Saigontown," Thomas continued, "or Charlie'll come down hard on ya! We spotlight the hootches of *every*one who lives off post — just to keep the *cao bois* off the roofs, if nothing else. Hell, Mr. Quinn, it's S.O.P. with troopers of the 716th."

The CID agent tried to force a smile but it would not come. Instead, a fine layer of sweat was coating his body. *He could feel it!* Something was wrong. Upstairs. In his apartment. Something "terrible bad," as Schultz would put it, had gone down while he was away. He was almost afraid to climb to the top of the stairs. He wanted to ask Richards to clear the flat for him, while he waited outside for the bad news.

"Lemme have your key, Bob," the Decoy Squad sergeant whispered as the four men reached the door to apartment thirty-two.

"No need for one." Bryant had his boot against the door. Silently, he pushed it inward.

With an eerie creaking, the door opened further, revealing a dark living room.

"Aw, shit," Bryant muttered under his breath. No one missed the anxiety in the involuntary whisper. Quinn felt the sinking feeling swirl through his gut as the thumb safeties on three .45s clicked off.

With a silent, three-fingered gesture, Richards motioned Thomas in through the doorway. Automatically, and without pausing to seek guidance, the Spec. 4 darted into the dark, gun arm fanning left to right, seeking intruders.

"She kept it locked," Richards stated quietly, knowing a cop's wife would, but deciding he had better make it a matter of record — just to be on the safe side.

"Always," Quinn whispered back.

A second later Bryant, focusing on a movement several feet inside the room — perhaps Thomas waving him in without looking back — followed his partner and best friend into the unknown.

"Any problems recently?" Richards kept his voice low, so it wouldn't carry past the doorway.

Richards frowned. If it wasn't the cons in the stockade, it was the hairball deserters living underground — too cowardly to turn themselves in for AWOL, but always "brave" enough to send anonymous notes to MPs who had busted them in the past for stealing or robbing or dope . . . arrests that started them on that downhill spiral to bad discharge papers and hard time on the rocks. "I mean domestic stuff, too," Richards said. "You guys been getting along OK? Could she have packed up and, well, split with the kids for a while?"

A mask of disbelief flashed across Quinn's face. "Xuan? No way, Gary. We've been getting along just fine — always have!"

"Graveyards can screw up the most storybook of romances, Bobby-san. Just look at Stryker and all his pussy problems."

"Naw, not Xuan, buddy. No way. Everything's Code-4 in this bungalow, OK? Believe me."

Richards' mouth opened again, but before he could speak, lights in the apartment flashed on.

"All's clear on the inside, Sarge," Thomas announced. "Nobody's home."

Quinn rushed past Richards.

The investigator raced about the apartment, searching for clues as to what had happened to his family, expecting to find puddles of blood in the children's room, or his wife's head sitting in the refrigerator, a kitchen steak knife through her temple and eyes frozen open in horror—like so many of the anonymous notes promised. *I'll rape your old lady when I get out, pig! I'll ram your favorite nightstick up her cunt, then burn down your house! Your little bastard kids go to school, don't they? You can't watch them all the time! One day they won't come home,* papa-san! *One day they won't come until your pig buddies notify you their heads have been found in a maggot-infested rain forest grave! You'll have to disembowel every lion at the Saigon Zoo before you find the rest of them, oinker! And by then, they'll just be so much cat shit in the corner of a stinking cage! Payback is one hell of a motherfucker! So screw you, Screw!* But the apartment had not been disturbed. Everything appeared to be in its place.

Bryant opened a closet. It was still filled to overflowing with clothes.

"Will ya look at all the *ao dais*! Thomas was amazed. "Brighter than a rainbow, Mr. Quinn! You're really into the local culture, aren't you?"

"They belong to my wife," he said dryly, with a straight face, astonished with himself for being able to attempt a joke at a time like this. Bryant laughed on cue, but Thomas just cast him a "nice try" smirk.

"Could it be she just packed up a few things for the weekend?" Richards persisted as he bent over and examined the door hasp for signs of forced entry. "And didn't tell you? You know how these Oriental women can be when they get a hair up their ying-yang—something you didn't even realize you did might have ticked her off."

"Like forcing her to give you some head or something." Thomas produced the most serious expression Bryant had ever seen on his partner. "Is she Buddhist? You know them Buddhists don't go for none of that sixty-nine stuff. But now the Christians are a different thing. The Christians—"

"Xuan wasn't like that." Quinn ignored Thomas and answered Richards, growing irritated. "*Isn't* like that!" he corrected himself hastily.

Failing to find any damage, Richards glanced up at Thomas and threw a thumb over his shoulder. "Canvass the corridor outside," he directed. "See if you can come up with a neighbor who might have seen or heard something."

"It's getting pretty late." Thomas hesitated, checking his watch. Interviewing Vietnamese in the middle of the night—on *their* turf (not downstairs, on the street)—was not exactly his idea of eight-and-skate.

"Just *do it,* dildo-breath!" Bryant slapped him on the back of the helmet, guiding him toward the doorway.

Quinn's eyes fell to a footstool in front of his favorite rattan lounger. It was lying on its side—the

95

only thing in the room that *had* been disturbed!

He wanted to walk over and examine it, and at the same time he wanted to rush back downstairs to the Jeep to get an f.p. brush and jar of fingerprint powder. But his feet would not move. He was frozen to the spot. Tonight he didn't want to confront the evidence. Or face the music. A file photo of Jeff Rodgers flashed in front of his mind's eye, and he felt suddenly nauseated, convinced he was about to lose it. The picture had been taken at the morgue.

"So whatta ya think, Bob?" Richards was up beside him again. "What's your gut feeling here tonight? We'll handle this anyway you wanna handle it."

Quinn stared down at the footstool. Richards followed his gaze, locking onto the small piece of furniture and immediately realizing its significance, but he did not say anything. It could have been anything—or anyone—who upended it. Little Mang was always running into this and that. Quinn was just thankful the boy was forever breaking the furniture or kitchenware, and not his bones.

Perhaps Xuan *had* taken the kids somewhere. To her sister's, or maybe the car had become disabled, and she was sitting down at some VNP stationhouse, waiting for a *canh-sat* patrol to bring word to him. They didn't have a phone.

He didn't want to make a big scene over nothing—not in front of the men. They were still young—they'd never understand all this fuss over a missing female. Most MPs *prayed* to Buddha they'd come home from work to find their wife gone. "Marriage" was not in the younger enlisted men's

96

vocabulary at all.

"I'll just wait it out, Gary," he finally decided with a soft voice, listening to jets race their engines at the airport and a helicopter gunship circle the Saigon docks, dropping flares. Night sounds in the big city at war. Noise that sent his adrenalin pumping even off duty, and kept him in love with the Pearl of the Orient—when Xuan and his family were safely inside their home behind a bolted door, his pistol on the nightstand inside the hollowed-out Buffy elephant statue. When they were all off the street, safe. But now, with curfew falling, a hostile curtain of dark had fallen across his home. The sounds all around were suddenly alien and menacing—not exciting. "I appreciate your help, guys. I'm sure everything's all right. I'll just wait it out."

"But keep me posted." Richards adjusted his squelch knob so loud static suddenly flooded the room. "Fucking government batteries," he muttered, patting the radio pak-set on his web belt lightly. "I'd hate to have to call for help with one of these pieces of shit." His grin was apprehensive; he had done just that so many times in the past already.

"No one's answering their doors out there," Thomas reappeared in the doorway and reported, "except for some old *mama-san* down the hall who says she didn't hear nothing—and she looks like she's blind as a bat, if you ask me."

"I thought she was deaf too," added Quinn, nodding his appreciation to the Spec.-4. "Well, I'm sure you guys have more important things to—"

Static crackled across Richards's pak-set again,

and he shifted his hip around to get better reception. "Fucking government batteries," he muttered again.

But the twist in position afforded the necessary adjustment for better reception, and the second transmission came across crystal clear: *"MP needs help!"* An almost inaudible location followed as the field unit's power faded again. "Code Zero. Shots fired! WACO, can you read me?" The desperation in the patrolman's voice was accented by rapid discharges in the background. Quinn listened for another transmission, but all any man there heard were the creaking movements behind doors along the corridor as the Vietnamese tenants scurried about, pressing their ears against keyholes, hoping to hear what all the excitement was about.

"Let's beat feet!" Richards directed, Quinn's suspicions suddenly frivolous compared to the Ten-100. But Bryant and Thomas were already gliding down the stairwell, five and six steps at a time.

"Christ, Anthony!" Sergeant Richards nearly fell out of the passenger side of the patrol Jeep as Thomas cut another corner on two wheels, siren blaring and red roof lights twirling frantically. Richards grabbed the notebook that had just flown from his hands off the vehicle's floorboards and thumbed back to the appropriate page. "Okay, hot dog—" he glanced up the road, eyelids squinting as blue smoke and mist drifted through the maze of tenements spreading out before them—"you take a left at the next intersection, then hang a right on Nguyen Van Thoai!"

As they were almost upon the intersection in question, three MP Jeeps flew by, mere yards in front of them, right to left—a blur of green steel, crimson beams and grim expressions. M-16 barrels hung out the sides, poised for contact. Sirens sang their mournful cry against the uncaring night.

"Motherfuckers!" Thomas gritted his teeth as he swerved in behind units driven by Reilly, Raunchy Raul and The Uke. All three jeeps were loaded down with troopers, and Uhernik's had a Hog-60 mounted in the back. "No way are you gonna beat the Decoy Boys on scene!" He downshifted into second gear and let the clutch fly. The front of the Jeep dipped abruptly—the bumper nearly scraping the blacktop—and then the engine recovered, roaring loudly against the strain. Slowly, it began gaining on the other units.

"Ease up, Ants!" Bryant called from the back seat, a genuine look of concern on his face. "We're not gonna even get there if you blow the motor, cunt lips!"

Up ahead, striking a dip with its undercarriage, Jeff Reilly's Jeep threw a spray of sparks back at them as if adding an exclamation mark to Tim's comment.

Richards tapped the bottom of his rifle's clip with the palm of his hand, making sure it was firmly seated, then pulled the charging handle back and let it slam forward, forcing a round into the chamber. But the maneuver was not even heard above the clamor of knocking engines and squealing tires. "The moment of truth," he muttered more to himself than anybody around him. Then, louder, he added, "Should be just up around the corner, gentlemen."

Thomas took the final corner on two wheels again, easing by the other three Jeeps across a sidewalk on the inside. "Ready on the right! Ready on the left!" the rookie crouched beside Bryant yelled eagerly, the adrenalin rush throwing his eyes wide and sending shades of pulsing red all about his cheeks and ears. *"Ready on the firing line!"* Bryant felt like slapping the kid upside his head, but he refrained — it hadn't been that long since *he* was racing like Ghost Riders into his first street gunbattle.

Thomas doused the headlights, but kept the roof strobe flashing as he cruised up to an MP Jeep that lay in flames on its side in the middle of the intersection. Sergeant Stryker was crouched beside it, returning fire with his pistol at a rooftop sniper across the street. Shocked by the sudden arrival of so many reinforcements, the whites of his eyes lit up as Thomas skidded toward him, nearly crashing into the burning Jeep. Stryker frantically waved the Decoy Squad back out of the line of fire, but a slug crashed through their windshield, showering Thomas and Richards with shards of glass, and the men dove from the vehicle just as a string of tracers rained down from the rooftop, stitching the chassis with hot rounds that sent the unit up in a fireball of green flame and billowing black smoke.

As he rolled up beside a cement lamppost, Richards glanced about, assessing the situation in a fraction of a second. Stryker had been the first MP on scene after the call for help went out. The sniper had lucked out with a front wheel hit as the sergeant was turning, and the vehicle flipped onto its side, ejecting the ex-Green Beret uninjured. A spray of tracers slammed into the vehicle, exploding the fuel tank just as with the Decoy team's Jeep. Stryker's rifle and the several bandoliers of ammo mags every MP carried were destroyed before they could be retrieved. Thirty yards away, parked beside an abandoned ARVN troop lorry, another MP Jeep was barely visible through the floating pall of dense gunsmoke. Crouched beside it were the two men who had originally called for assistance. Their vehicle was filled with several hundred bullet holes, and all four tires were flat, but it had not caught fire though the stench of gasoline fumes was heavy on the warm, sticky air—it would only be a matter of time before the snaking pool of fuel found its way to Stryker's burning unit or a stray tracer bounced across it, lighting up the night with another brilliant fireball or two. And behind Richards, Reilly's and The Uke's Jeeps were skidding up beside the protective cover of a leaning tenement, safely out of the direct line of fire.

Sergeant Schultz's vehicle roared past within inches, driven by Crazy Carl Nilmes, and after Raunchy Raul tossed a fresh supply of magazines to the besieged MPs taking cover under the bullet-riddled Jeep parked beside the troop lorry, Nilmes swung around in a tight circle and Schultz leaned out the side, firing an M-60 cradled in his arm. Blinding white flames burst forth from the heavy machine gun's glowing barrel as the notorious lady's man sent five- and ten-round bursts up at the sniper.

Glass in fourth- and fifth-floor windows shattered as a couple dozen misplaced rounds fell short of the rooftop, raining down on the men in the street.

"Go get 'em, Raunchy Raul!" Bryant stood up and fired an entire clip on rock-and-roll, driving the sniper to seek cover. "Tear that building down, boy!"

"Jesus," Stryker muttered to himself as he watched tracers from the M-60 ricochet off the windowpanes of several top-floor apartments and bounce about haphazardly inside the dark rooms. He hoped all the tenants were prone on the floor. "WACO," he reached for his pak-set and called to the dispatcher over the air, "this is Car Niner. Better get four or five ambulances rollin' this direction. Something tells me some Victor Novembers might need med-aid after the show. Over."

"Already en route," the dispatcher advised. "Your Ten-5's will be standing by at Nguyen Va Thoai and . . ." The cross street was drowned out by another shower of lead from the rooftop across the street. ". . . Until you lift the Code Zero. Over."

Stryker sprung up from cover and unleashed a half magazine of rounds at the sniper, then ducked back down just as a tracer zinged off the hood of one of the MP Jeeps, missing him by less than a yard.

"Christ!" Bryant yelled, as the hot slug arced wildly between the two of them, then bounced off the blacktop, back up into the night sky.

"*He* had nothing to do with it!" Richards called out from his position a few feet away, lying prone beneath a second bullet-riddled Jeep. His left eye was closed as his right squinted against the long-range sights. The Decoy sergeant was sending single shots up at the flashes along the rooftop, but he had yet to score a direct hit on the gunman.

Stryker tensed as a sharp pain lanced through his head from the back, then rapidly travelled down through the curve between his shoulder blades. Paralyzing him for only a fraction of a second, he shook the irritating sensation off, and sent the rest of his banana clip blazing up at the top of the building. "Fuck my luck," he muttered as the pain, not unlike a stray sliver of lead ricochets often delivered, tapered away, only to return moments later like echoes of a forgotten nightmare after awakening. He pulled a fresh magazine from his web belt and slammed it into place, sent the chamber clapping with his thumb, then pulled a wad of cotton from his front pocket and stuffed it into his right ear. Another migraine had arrived. He loved it when they came out with the M-16 rifles—they were the first weapons he could blast away with without hearing protection that didn't pound at his ear drums. The discharges were even soothing, in open areas—almost sexually arousing, when the dull, muffled blasts were combined with the licorice taste of cordite. But the sniper was using a Chinese AK assault rifle, and *they* delivered a sharp crack that—perhaps psychologically, he often admitted to himself—always brought on the sudden waves of nagging discomfort. And now a couple of men from Delta Company had skidded up and were popping caps with their loud .45 automatics—a useless response due to the distance. The sniper was out of range of handguns. That's why he had holstered his.

Sergeant Schultz circled around for the third time, letting loose with his Hog-60, adding to the dull crescendo of deafening reports. As the echoes bounced back off the tenements towering up all around, Stryker fought the urge to clamp the palms of his hands over his ears. Like an enraged jungle spirit, drawn from the depths of the rain forest by all the discharges, there came a sudden beating of powerful wings above the scene of the gunfight. Dust swirled about, and the sky erupted with flickering light after Richards brought forth his pocketful of miracles, sending a hand flare up—and the beating "wings" became distinguishable. Rotors from a hovering gunship! Light from the flare sparkled across the metal and fiberglass blades, then the downblast deflated the silk parachute, casting it aside, and darkness again engulfed the Huey before the sniper could align his sights on the craft.

Stryker watched the helicopter's tail swing to the side as the pilot whirled around, zeroing in on the gunman's muzzle flashes. But the Huey's nose cannon did not erupt with a lethal reply, as the ex-Green Beret had expected it would. Instead, aware that innocent civilians still resided in dwellings below the roofline (and this was no free fire zone— *yet*!), the crew chief guided the craft closer in a sideways glide that saw the landing skids miss the edge of the rooftop by inches.

"Why, if it ain't that crazy Egor!" Richards had his folding binoculars out now, and was focusing on the huge soldier leaning out the gunship's open side hatch, swinging the butt of an M-14 carbine at the black-pajama-clad Vietnamese running across the rooftop.

"Egor *Johnson*?" Bryant let out a proud war cry and swung his fist at the sniper as he emerged from the cover of an overturned jeep. He wondered why the medevac ace was riding a heavily armed gunship instead of a lightweight slick.

"He's gonna have *your* ass for sending that pocket flare up at him like that!" Stryker pointed a finger at Richards, laughing, as he waved the other hand at Bryant and Thomas, motioning them to follow him to the building's ground-floor stairwell. It was time to *get* that VC with the AK-47!

"How the hell was I supposed to know it was Tom?" Richards groaned at the prospect of the husky Dustoff NCO coming down hard on him after the engagement debriefing. "The crazy dudes never did have on no landing lights!" he complained, well aware no sane pilot would mount a surprise attack with them on.

The helicopter was swerving from side to side now as it slowly followed the zigzagging Vietnamese about the rooftop—the whole time Egor swinging his carbine stock at the sniper's head. Stryker saw the butt connect with a scrawny shoulder once, before they moved away from the edge of the roofline again, and he and his MPs disappeared into the first floor of the apartment building.

When they burst out onto the fifth-floor fire escape and scurried up to the roof two minutes later, the Huey was still chasing the gunman about—the pilot obviously toying with the Vietnamese before the kill, cat and mouse fashion, as the craft's nose dipped and prodded, tail boom up in the air like some giant airborne predator.

The sniper, his AK still clutched in one hand, sprinted past the emerging military policemen without even seeing them, and stopped at a protruding roof abutment with a door in it that led down into a service attic. The man pulled on the handle desperately several times, but the door was securely locked. The downblast from the rotors overhead pasting his hair down flat and adding to the wild, cornered expression on his face, the sniper aimed his rifle at the knob and fired off a short burst. Tracers ricocheted skyward and into the roof, and a round or two tore into the door, splintering it, but the lock still held.

The Huey ascended slightly as one of the glowing green tracers struck a rotor and showered back down onto the Viet Cong in a floating umbrella of sparks.

His chamber locked open above an empty magazine now, the man abandoned the AK and turned to run back toward the fire escape.

Instead, he came face to face with a squad of angry law enforcers, the white letters on their bobbing MP helmets glowing like the ghosts from a bad memory.

His eyes wide with horror now, the communist knew his fate was sealed—or so he thought. But he had no way of knowing the military policemen were trained to take him into custody for questioning— not throw him off the rooftop to a messy demise five floors down. Despite their fury at being sniped at, they would not inflict jungle justice on him the way warriors in the rain forest would. His hand went to his belt.

And came up with a grenade!

"Wait!" Stryker brushed aside Bryant's rifle barrel as the MP poked it out at the VC. In the background, barely visible through the hazy swirl of excitement and emotions clouding their judgment, the helicopter had descended again and was hovering behind the guerrilla.

Perhaps sensing their hesitation, the grenadier whirled around to confront the approaching gunship. And was knocked flat on his back!

Sgt. Tommy "Egor" Johnson's burly frame somersaulted over the flattened communist and came to rest at Stryker's feet — only to spring back at the Viet Cong, fist raised and a razor-sharp commando knife between his teeth. But Bryant was already rolling past the NCO. He delivered a stunning body block, and the Vietnamese was catapulted backwards off his feet.

The grenade flew up into the air and returned to ground as if in slow motion — Stryker heard it bouncing across the rooftop between himself and Thomas before his eyes actually sent the picture to his brain.

He saw two things happen simultaneously after that. The Viet Cong guerrilla flew back to his feet, a second object in his hand; and Thomas dove onto the grenade that had come to rest a few yards behind the squad of military policemen.

"Fire in the hole!" someone was yelling at the top of their lungs, the insane beating of the helicopter rotors nearly drowning out the words.

Still rolling to the side, Bryant hopped into a crouch, his automatic extended at arm's length, and pulled the trigger twice.

The renewed look of shock on the sniper's face illuminated by the discharge flashes branded now into his memory, Stryker jumped to the right and grabbed Thomas's boot—jerked his entire body up off the rooftop and threw him clear of the grenade. Thomas landed on his side, groaning, several feet away, and Stryker scooped up the grenade in his left hand.

A deafening blast erupted behind him, slamming him prone across the clay shingles. A pain under his belly told him he had just collapsed a sturdy television antenna. Rising to his feet again, Stryker glanced over his shoulder to see the helicopter drifting backwards, nose up and tail down. And then it seemed to lose power and drop down beyond the edge of the roofline—to the street below, rotors still flapping frantically but seemingly drained to the danger point. The guerrilla's second grenade had exploded instantly when one of Bryant's bullets slammed into it. The other round impacted against the Asian's forehead, leaving behind a gaping crater in front and an empty skull in the rear—where the hollow point exited in a bloody spray. Smoking fragments of shrapnel had showered forth from the grenade, shattering the front windows of the helicopter cockpit.

Imagining he was back on his Old Timer's baseball team during the summer break from elementary school—oversized blue socks drooping to his ankles—centerfielder Marky Stryker threw the baseball with all his might, high as he could, envisioning the distant opposing-team player sprinting for home plate. Stryker wrenched his shoulder, so hard did he throw.

The grenade exploded with a blinding white flash far overhead. Though the MP sergeant had tossed it outside its lethal kill range, a rain of fragments still fell across the rooftop, stinging those men they hit. Blood was drawn, but no one was killed by either detonation.

Except Mr. Charlie.

Stryker did not ponder why the grenade Thomas had jumped on proved to have such a long delay in its fuse . . . Had it really been that long? Or did everything transpire in the blink of an eye: the dropped grenade, Thomas leaping for his Purple Heart, Bryant rolling after the body block, a pistol discharging, an explosion, the chopper drifting backwards, seemingly on its tail as it dropped from sight? Instead, he glanced back at Bryant.

The man was still standing in a low crouch, pistol extended—a puff of smoke drifting in front of the barrel. The blank look on his face was a mask Stryker had seen a hundred times before. Quick kills often left you frozen in time, lost in limbo.

Until you were touched by one of your partners, coaxed back into reality.

Stryker glanced to his right. Thomas was rising off one knee, about to start toward his buddy. The Viet Cong was lying face down at Bryant's feet—the blast from the grenade had hurled him forward when the MP bullet wanted to throw him backwards. Even in death, he didn't know which way to rabbit. Egor Johnson walked between Bryant and the sniper, ignoring the soldier's gun, and booted the VC in the belly. "Lousy commie lucked out and downed one of my birds with a cheap frag shot!" he grumbled. "It ain't right, I'm tellin' you!" He booted the Cong sniper again, then turned to face a dazed Timothy Bryant. "Put your piece back in your pants." The emotion was slowly draining from his voice. "The show's over. Chalk up one more bad boy for the body count, partner."

Stryker rushed over to the edge of the roof and peered down at the street five stories below. Belching smoke, the crippled helicopter swooped down between two apartment houses, began another ascent, then drifted backwards again, losing power. The pilot fought with the controls as MPs in the street scattered for cover, but the best he could do was bring the Huey down in the middle of an intersection for a mild crash landing. A skid bent under the harsh impact, tipping the craft awkwardly to one side, and a rotor clipped a lightpole. Glass and spintered fiberglass exploded across the block, and the intersection was plunged into darkness.

"Holy fuck!" Richards appeared beside Stryker as they watched the flight crew bail out of the helicopter moments before an electrical fire lit up the inside of the cockpit like a lightning storm. More smoke spewed forth from the open hatches and further spider-webbed windshields, but the craft did not explode. Two MP jeeps, rooflights throwing red beams of light through the pall of smoke, moved forward cautiously, securing the scene — protecting civilians from the wreckage, and the wreckage from civilians.

"Another hot night in Saigontown," Stryker muttered under his breath as he watched additional military police units coast up almost every side street, forming the required containment perimeter. The distinctive wail of fire engine sirens could be heard in the distance.

"Huh?" Richards slipped his rifle sling over his shoulder. Empty ammo brass crinkled under their boots.

"Nothing." Stryker slipped the magazine from his .45 and replaced it with a fresh clip, then began thumbing loose rounds down into the empty mag. "We'd better get back down to the ground. Thomas can handle this abortion up here till MPI rolls their Shoot Team to the scene."

Their race down through the building stairwell was again four and five steps at a time — hysterical tenants, also rushing for the deceptive safety of the street, leaping out of the way or cringing low, intimidated by the strange intruders' towering size. In the middle of the night, uniforms meant little. Even after you were wide awake, it was often hard to tell the good guys from the bad. This was Saigon.

"What the hell was the original unit responding to, anyway?" Richards asked as they flew out the ground floor doorway, onto the sidewalk crowded with spectators. An ammo box inside the gunship exploded due to the intense heat, and in the midst

111

of a dozen tracers arcing skyward in different directions, a piece of the cabin roof, smoking and twirling end over end, drifted through the air lazily and landed at the sergeants' feet, sending the crowd back like a school of startled fish. A woman somewhere screamed, then an eerie hush fell over the people and they surged forward again, drawn by the scent of battle, fear, loss and triumph. It was a sensation even the children of Saigon knew all too well—the war orphans especially—an emotion protected and pampered youth back in The World might go a lifetime without experiencing.

"Another suspicious package call," Stryker finally replied, after a second belt of 7.62 tracers erupted out at the night like a string of firecrackers magnified tenfold.

"But no bomb went off this time."

"Right." Stryker routinely scanned the faces in the crowd. He believed he could spot a communist a mile away. They were always watching *him*, or the MP helmets, when the rest of the crowd was watching the fireworks. *Bargirls don't count*, he would muse to himself. *A stiff cock is always more important to them than the show. And bedding down one of my boys from Bravo or Charlie Company is a challenge most of them can't resist.*

"Damn!" Richards slapped a hand across his elbow as a piece of glass tore into it. Then the windshield of the MP Jeep parked in front of them shattered and collapsed completely.

Both their heads turned toward the chopper automatically, but all the tracers were shooting straight up, then arcing out. The roar of continual discharges was deafening. Instinctively, both MPs dropped into a cautious crouch behind the vehicle's engine block.

Richards glanced down at his bleeding arm, then back at Stryker. "A ricochet?" His eyes had that wild look in them, but the expression below the white orbs was calm.

"Something tells me that's a wrong guess!" Stryker answered, *his* eyes scanning the rooftops across the street now. The Vietnamese crowding behind them didn't seem to notice Richards's wound, and only a few backed away when the windshield disintegrated.

Then he spotted it. Atop the seventh-floor rooftop of a warehouse across the street: the muzzle flash of a second sniper!

6.

Smaller Than a Breadbox

Quinn stood on his balcony and watched the MP Jeeps scream past three flights below. The units were but a blur—he didn't recognize any faces, saw only the shiny tops of black helmets shooting by. Sirens in the distance mingled with those of the closer units. The city was coming alive. Everyone with wheels responded when an MP called for help. The beat cops nearby ran.

But then all the noise began to fade. The action was moving away, leaving him behind.

Quinn, hands braced on the balcony railing, arms rigid with elbows locked, focused weary eyes on a distant string of bright yellow flares, floating along the edge of the city, several miles away. The lights were always there, it seemed, swinging back and forth under their giant parachutes, wispy trails of smoke marking their sluggish descent. He couldn't imagine life without them, without being able to step out on his balcony and find them dancing beneath the twinkling Big Dipper, or the Belt of Orion.

Star light . . . star bright . . .

A gunship, rotors slapping at the hot, humid heat of the tropical night, cruised past low above the skyline of tenement rooftops across the street, but he paid it little attention.

The string of flares vanished, and he found himself searching out the real stars above his precious Asian world.

First star I see tonight . . .

The bright planet appeared as his eyes adjusted to the absence of the flares. Xuan always insisted it was just another star, but he knew differently. Was it Venus? Or Mars perhaps? The glowing, pulsating globe always reminded him of the week he spent in P.O.W. escape-and-evasion training back at The School. When he had used the planet's position in the sky to guide him across the marshes and through the dense Georgian forest. The memory made Quinn chuckle lightly to himself. Those damn DIs had nearly caught him, but he had made it back to friendly territory without being captured.

I wish I may . . . I wish I might . . .

Quinn's eyes fell to the open-air restaurant across the street. It was closed now. Bums slept in its dark doorways. Militiamen perhaps sixteen years old at the most manned an oil drum filled with sand in the intersection at one end of it, fanning a fire to keep warm as they neglected their duties and ignored those that passed by in the dark. Their shadows danced about the tenement walls behind them, bringing a smile to Quinn's face. Little Lien always snuck out of her bed late at night to watch the soldiers below. She would imitate the shadows with her tiny hands against the Chinese lantern's dim light, creating her own figures on the wall. He whirled around, thinking he heard her voice. But it was only one of the neighbor's children crying faintly across the hall, and he felt the depression closing in on him, pressing him down as if a great weight had been lowered onto his shoulders. *Lien*, his mind called out against the silence all around. *Mang, where have you all gone?*

The restaurant reminded him of Xuan. It was where he first saw her, dining with her girlfriends. He sat across from them, several tables away actually, now that he thought about it—but he watched her every move, memorized every detail of her face . . . everything about her, as he sipped his baggy of ice coffee during the fifteen minute short-7 break away from the street.

She had been a beauty queen in one of the local festival parades, and he had worked curbside security against VC terrorist attacks, along with a hundred other MPs who never really appreciated the beauty of her entourage except to gauge the size of their breasts. Quinn had locked eyes with her as her flowered float passed, thinking she would frown and look away. But she didn't.

And two weeks later, after he appeared at the open-air restaurant seven times, precisely as she and her friends arrived, Xuan cast aside centuries of tradition, the warnings crying out in her instinct, and the disapproving murmurs from her girlfriends, and walked over to his table.

He could still remember the first words out of her

mouth. "What do the letters on your helmet stand for? Are they your initials!" That beautiful, flower petal mouth, with lips so soft and full, beckoning him with their moist, rosy surface, always beckoning.

Now they had two children.

A car raced past below, and he returned to the balcony, but by the time he looked down to the street, it was gone. Probably some fool trying to beat the curfew, he decided, checking his watch and noting it was already an hour and a half past midnight.

He spotted a falling star out the corner of his eye, and the flash, elusive and haunting against the silence of midnight, reminded him of their many nights spent watching the stars on the balcony.

She had laughed the first time he told her she could wish upon the stars. "Such a silly American tradition," she told him.

"Only the first star," he corrected her gently as he held her in his arms and they watched the galaxy swirl about over their war-torn world. "You can make a wish only on the first star you see each evening after sunset."

"We Vietnamese believe the stars are our dead relatives," she protested with a smile on her lips before kissing him hungrily, not in the mood for debate. It was the only thing he didn't like about Xuan. Politics, world events—they meant nothing to her. Only her man, and now her family, were all she cared about. "Or some of us believe the stars are soldiers who were killed in the fighting."

"Then that's all the more reason to wish upon—"

"Then you believe my talking to my dead relatives is not so silly after all," she had interrupted him,

118

remembering some crazy argument they had had weeks before. Xuan was like most Vietnamese women. She might forgive you, but she never forgot anything.

"I never said—"

"Can I wish for anything?" she had asked innocently, staring up into his eyes as the flares drifted on the hot breezes beyond the balcony railing.

"Well, this *is* Vietnam," he fumbled for the words. "Anything . . . within reason."

"Is a long and happy life too much to ask for?" She batted her eyes up at him in that playful, typically Oriental fashion that always aroused him beyond control. "A long and happy life with *you*?"

"I think that's rather reasonable, woman of my dreams." He ran the tip of his tongue along the edge of her cheek—something that drove *her* wild.

"And children?" she persisted. "Someone to carry on your name? We wouldn't want to have the great name of Quinn die after you and I leave this undeserving earth, my soon-to-be husband."

"I have brothers back in The World," he replied, wincing at the phrase after it came out, hoping she wouldn't catch the disrespectful comparison to her homeland. "Three to be exact. Let *their* children carry on the family name. Let *their* wives go through the pain of childbirth. Let *them* put up with the crying through the night and the—"

"I think two would be just right for us," she cut in again. "One boy and one girl."

"What?" he feigned a mixture of shock and horror.

"A *son* to follow in the footsteps of his legendary father."

"Not quite so legendary, Xuan."

"A son!" she sighed as another falling star streaked across the skies. "We could name him—"

"I thought you didn't like my being an MP, *dear*?"

"Well, he wouldn't have to follow *exactly* in your footsteps, honorable husband." She bowed to him in Japanese fashion, mocking his seriousness.

"Ahhhh-*so*!" He threw a weak karate chop at her but missed and she scrambled away, stopping to dangle precariously against the balcony railing. Her eyes searched the stars until she found the large one that had first conquered dusk.

"Please give me my wish!" she pleaded to the heavens softly, tiny hands clasped against her heart. Her chin seemed to strain toward the twinkling star hanging motionless beneath the bottom point of the crescent moon.

Have the wish I wish tonight . . .

Quinn felt his breathing stop, startled, when a small black bird landed on the balcony railing a couple feet from his left hand, but he did not move. The bird, some species of crow that escaped him, stared up into his eyes, its head cocked to one side. It was shaking, feathers ruffled—as if it had just flown down from an advancing storm cloud. Thunder rumbled in the distance, and the bird shivered more violently at the menacing sound, but did not take its eyes from Quinn's.

"Where are Xuan and my children?" he finally asked after several silent seconds. "Can you tell me where they've gone, little bird?" But the crow flew away without even pausing to contemplate his words, or offer a "sign" that he hoped for. Something, *anything* to help him solve this dilemma.

He watched the bird fly off into the night. He watched the storm clouds advance across the sky, until they gobbled up the moon and the stars, and then he went back inside and sat down on the bed.

Quinn listened to the sporadic shooting that answered the thunder, several miles away, but he did not wonder about the military policemen working the street so far away. Instead, he examined, visually, all the objects within the room, hoping to come up with an explanation, a clue, a possibility.

He stared at Mang's toys, and Lien's little doll collection from Thailand and the Philippines, but nothing came to him. Only visions of his children at play, abandoning their "priceless" possessions whenever he walked in the door, home from work. Lien would always reach his arms first, eager to tell him about her day's activities or what Xuan had cooking in the oven, hoping to surprise him. Mang would stand in the background, arms folded bravely across his chest — the little man of the house, patiently waiting his turn for his sister to be done with her foolish girls' talk. Then he would brief his father on the latest TV exploits of Friday and Gannon.

The vision of his wife entering the room, all smiles as she brought them a platter of split coconut and slices of salted pineapple, faded as the thunder grew closer, and he remembered he was in a cool, dark bedroom, completely and terribly alone. A breeze swirled in from the balcony, tearing one of Lien's watercolor paintings from the wall where it had been tacked. The creation flew nearly to the ceiling, then dropped abruptly as the wind retreated from the apartment like a ghost confronted by candles. Lightly fluttering from side to side, the painting came to rest on the bed, only inches from his leg. He picked it up, feeling the tears well up in his eyes as rain began to tap at the windows in intermittent sheets. The painting showed Quinn wearing an MP uniform and standing beside a marked patrol unit. Girls in bright umbrellas and colorful *ao dais* floated behind him. Palm trees lined the background, shading all the smiling subjects. Quinn smiled back, a tear racing down his cheek. He hadn't worn the arm band in years, but to Lien he would always be a line MP.

He laid the painting down and reached for the pile of Vietnamese cassettes leaning precariously against a shelf inside the headboard. He carefully pulled a Thanh Lan tape from the bottom, and the others spilled over onto the pillow in protest.

Quinn slipped the cassette into a recorder on the night table and depressed the Play button before brushing the other tapes aside and laying back into the huge satin pillow.

This morning I walked down to the spring for cooking water, the song began, in Vietnamese. Soft and soothing, like the rain tapping against the other side of the walls.

But Quinn's eyes flew wide when he stared up at the ceiling.

I surprised a tiger, taking his drink, and the great beast roared, but I did not run away.

Attached to the ceiling was a crudely drawn note. It was written in lipstick, or red water colors, and it was in little Lien's handwriting, but ragged — like her tiny hand had been forced along the paper. Quinn reached over to turn off the tape recorder, but he could not find the correct button.

Thunder behind me sang along with the angry cat, but I ignored them both and filled my pail with water, then slowly walked back to my hut.

He glanced about, terror in his eyes, searching for some other clue he must have missed, some other piece of evidence that would lead the mystery in another direction. Something, *anything*! Quinn jumped up on the bed, knocking over the night stand, but the cassette continued to play its sad, sad song.

I returned to find a VC bomb had destroyed my humble home. Soldiers in black pantaloons stood atop the rubble, grinning. Their bayonets stirred the ashes. "It is all a mistake," they told me. I said nothing, only dropped my eyes in mourning, silent grief. My tears fell into the pail, mingling with the spring water of my precious homeland.

Heart pounding, Quinn tore the note down from the ceiling and read it again.

I HAVE THEM NOW, MISTER C.I.D. AGENT. BREATHE DEEP THE MEMORIES LEFT FADING IN THIS ROOM, FOR YOU WILL NEVER SEE THEM AGAIN.

"My God," he sighed, drained of all energy, suddenly weaker than he had ever been before in his life. Thunder pounded outside the walls, and a sheet of rain lashed at the balcony railing. The storm chased a warm breeze in through the balcony curtains, fanning

123

them with ghostly fingers, and Quinn felt an ominous evil lunge awkwardly about the house, then vanish just as abruptly.

Drenched in sweat, he stepped back down to the floor and started for the front door, folding the note and sliding it into his shirt pocket absent-mindedly. The landlord down the hall—*he had to use her phone*! Call Richards and the others back. They would know what to do! Right now, he couldn't think straight.

He pulled the latch and deadbolt back and stepped out into the dimly lit corridor, basking with mild relief in its familiarity. He was back in the outside world again. Away from the intense swirl of emotions closing in on him inside the apartment.

And the lights went out.

Quinn whirled around, ran to the window at the closest end of the hallway. He watched lights fade in building after building down the entire block until the whole neighborhood went dark.

The usual weekly power outage.

Breathing heavily, he returned to his apartment and slammed the door shut, headed for his bedroom closet as skillfully as a blindman, never pausing to feel his way about the dark.

And he tripped over one of Mang's toys the little boy had left out.

Before he was snatched away from Robert Quinn. *Before that bastard stole my babies!* He collapsed across the red metal wagon and broke down, sobbing. "Xuan!" he called out, but his only answer was another wave of rolling, uncaring thunder.

The bastard! But who? Which one? The note had

been unsigned. Which one had—

There came a tapping at the door. "Mr. Quinn! Mr. Quinn, are you alright? Mr. Quinn, what happened you?"

It was the little girl down the hall—one of Lien's playmates.

"Mr. Quinn!" Then, out of desperation, perhaps seeking to switch to something she was comfortable with, "Can Lien come out and play, sir?"

"Later, honey." He stumbled back to his feet and staggered for the bedroom. "Later. I'll bring her over myself. *I promise you!* he thought to himself, biting his lower lip determinedly.

Quinn rushed into the room and slid on his knees up to a closet. He slammed the doors back and jerked a heavy footlocker from behind Xuan's wardrobe of colorful *ao dais*. The combination lock was broken off, but still hanging in place lopsidedly.

He felt his heart begin to race again. His throat swelled up. He thought he would not soon be able to breathe.

Quinn whirled around, a terrifying presence pressing in on him from behind, but there was nobody there.

He rolled across the room to his bed and pulled the .45 automatic from beneath a pillow, then rushed throughout the apartment, searching. But he was still alone.

He returned to the footlocker and opened it. Three brown metal file boxes appeared untouched inside, but atop the middle box was another note.

Again, it was in Lien's handwriting. But this time smoother, unhurried. And in blue water colors instead of the crimson-red lipstick.

A VERY NICE MAN CAME OVER TO-
NIGHT, DADDY. HE SAYS HE KNOWS YOU
FROM A LONG LONG TIME AGO.
MOMMY IS CRYING BUT HE SAYS THAT
IS ONLY BECAUSE SHE IS SO HAPPY TO
SEE HIM. THEY PLAYED, AND HE
RIPPED HER DRESS A LITTLE BIT, BUT
IT IS FIXED NOW. MISTER MERLIN SAYS
IT IS TIME TO GO NOW. HE IS TAKING US
TO THE MAGIC KINGDOM. BUT HE SAYS
YOU WILL COME VISIT US SOON,
DADDY, SO DON'T BE JEALOUS. IS THE
MAGIC KINGDOM ANYWHERE CLOSE TO
THE IMPERIAL CITY OF HUE?

Quinn felt his heart shudder. He actually believed
it stopped beating a moment because of the shock,
only to resume again with an irregular pace. He felt
faint, like he was going to collapse again — like all his
strength had been drained from him by this terrible
incident.

Mr. Merlin? Who the hell was Mister Merlin? He
racked his memory banks as he began pulling the
heavy file boxes out. They had all been pried open.

The first box was full of souvenirs, valuables and
important papers. All the citations he had amassed
over the years. A plastic bag with his "longevity"
medals sealed inside. Some small jade statues, an
ivory carving of an elephant from Hong Kong,
Xuan's seven intricately carved traditional Vietnamese bracelets of twenty-two-karat gold, which she

stopped wearing the day they were married. He dumped the items across the bed. They appeared to have been left alone; the contents — all his valuables — were intact.

The second box was crammed with files. That was one of Quinn's weaknesses; he kept copies of everything. And he filed them accordingly. Promotion, transfer and travel orders. Letters from family. Letters from friends. Outgoing copies of letters that were important, such as bank transactions or credit references. A file containing his high school grades and diploma. A tattered yearbook from back in The World. And a perfectly preserved copy of the latest 716th MP's yearbook. One file containing all the pamphlets and booklets they gave him at Camp Alpha during in-processing. Another with unique articles or magazine pictures he had come across downtown. Newspaper clippings of his street unit in action, and now stories about the CID group he was assigned to. Envelopes containing negatives for over a thousand photos of Xuan and the kids. A file with lists of civilian companies in Saigon he might someday apply for a job with. One folder containing lists of his favorite songs and movies.

Every month Quinn picked a favorite song and had a relative back in the states send him a cassette of it. Then he'd splice the songs together at the end of the year and announce them himself as they began, pretending he was Casey Casem introducing the Voice of Vietnam's Top Fourteen. June and October were his favorite months, so they got two records, thus fourteen favorites. Once a year he announced a favorite singing group or recording artist too. This year it was the Moody Blues. Of course, he kept this little hobby a secret — even from Xuan. One of his dreams since his teenage days was to become a disc jockey. This was his private little way of living out that fantasy. There was no need for his family, or the men, to know about it.

The third box was a collection of police reports from cases he had been involved with over the last several years. Injury traffic accident photos and diagrams. Crime scene investigation sketches. Suspect profiles and mug shots. Rap sheets. Xeroxes of every important arrest he had ever participated in. A list showing the location, date and circumstances surrounding every apprehension he had made since graduating from the Military Police Academy. And files on *them*.

The lunatics out there on the street. The murderers, robbers, rapists, arsonists, con men, psychos, thieves and perverts he had had the misfortune to come in contact with during several Tour 365's in the Nam of Indochina.

The files were all numbered. Several appeared missing, but his desktop was piled high with them, so there was no telling — yet — if the madman had taken any. Quinn would have to conduct a rapid inventory.

He would have to . . .

Quinn paused. Thunder clashed with the jungle gods overhead. The building shook under the roar. Rain beat at the walls unceasingly. There was a constant clamor outside from the storm. Even between blasts of lightning, there was a never-ending rumble of rolling thunder in the distance as the angry heavens pressed down on Saigon. But Quinn remained frozen in that uncomfortable squat, listening. And then he heard it again.

Someone was knocking at the front door!

"Xuan!" He leapt to his feet, nearly breaking a leg as he vaulted over a chair in front of his wife's dresser.

He rushed through the living room but skidded to a halt several feet before reaching the door. He could *feel* it. His wife was not outside the door. He could *sense* the uniforms—the policemen waiting outside for him. Their tall, leaning shadows pressed against the doorway of his mind and he felt his head ache uncontrollably.

Thunder crashed overhead and a fist resumed beating against the door.

"Mr. Quinn! Mr. Quinn, you in there? It's me, sir, Thomas!"

Fearing he might look a million years old, Quinn moved forward and unlocked the door anyway. He slid back the latch and pulled the door inward, motioning the young MP closer.

"No time for that!" Thomas threw him a rain poncho and grabbed his forearm in the same movement. "Sergeant Stryker needs you down in Sector Six, Mr. Quinn!"

"What happened to you?" Quinn pulled away and stepped back, startled by all the blood on the front of Thomas's uniform.

"Oh, nothing." The MP brushed passed him into the apartment. He flicked a light switch a couple times, checking to see if the power was out, as he suspected. "Caught a piece of a chickenshit ricochet trying to bail Gary's ass out of trouble again. Don't even rate a Purple Heart, I guarantee you! I already checked!" Thomas laughed loudly. "Got your gun? Probably should take it along. The streets are really rowdy out there tonight — don't ask me why."

"What's so important that you gotta roust me out of my—"

"Another bombing, sir. Well, kind of. Stryker and Richards knew you'd want in on this one! We got hit by another sniper — the whole bit. But this time the bomb didn't go off, Mr. Quinn."

"Didn't go off?"

"No, sir — and we got one of the snipers," Thomas announced proudly, abandoning his search for any of the CID agent's service weapons. He pulled his snub-nosed .38 back-up revolver from a boot and handed it to Quinn.

"*One* of the snipers?"

"Yeah, I guess there was two of them — I don't know. They're still trying to figure it out down at the scene. Stryker just told me to get your ass — I mean, your butt, sir — downtown ASAP."

"Well, yes, I guess I'd better come along, but what about . . ." Quinn looked like a bewildered old professor who had just been wakened from a deep sleep.

"Oh, we already told the men on the street to be on the look-out for Xuan and your kids. Stryker put it out over the air in a way that made it sound like they were probably having car trouble or something."

Quinn took the rain poncho from Thomas and wrapped it around himself. "But what if I'm not here when they get back," he muttered under his breath as they started out of the room and into the hallway. He was talking more to himself than to the MP at his side. "What if—"

"Sergeant Richards detailed a man in a Zulu unit to stay parked downstairs, sir, in the event they didn't find a hotel along the way somewhere to spend the night. You know, weather out this storm. Gary's got all the angles covered, so don't you worry, OK?"

Robert Quinn gently closed the door to his apartment and took special care to lock it securely. Along the edge of the doorframe, beside the deadbolt, was a smear of blood screaming back at him, and though his eyes focused on it for one horrified moment, his mind refused to see it.

"This should only take a couple hours." Thomas patted him on the back as they started toward the stairwell, thunder pounding at the roof overhead. Outside, the gutters were filled to overflowing with rainwater. Quinn watched debris from the sewers merge with the swollen current on its way downhill toward the river, then he climbed into Thomas's MP Jeep, staring straight ahead as the engine roared to life and they headed for Sector Six.

Quinn swallowed hard—his throat had gone dry— as Thomas rounded that last corner and they rapidly approached the scene. MPs were still crouching behind their Jeeps and staring up at the rooftops cautiously (though the sidewalks seemed overflowing with Vietnamese spectators, despite the curfew) and that could only mean trouble.

"How many men injured?" he asked, forcing confidence into the words, as Thomas brought the vehicle up behind the Duty Officer's with a dramatic skid.

He chained the unit up—wrapping the thick links around the brake pedal shaft and the steering wheel—and stepped down onto the street, killing the engine but leaving the red lights flashing, before answering the CID agent.

"Just three or four minor scrapes, Mr. Quinn." He suddenly dashed across the open kill zone to the building where two MPs stood guard, holding his helmet in place until he got under the roof overhang. "But no Purple Heart wounds." Glancing at the dark roofline, Quinn rushed after him, barely noticing the grins of the military policemen standing in the doorway with their M-16s at port arms. Two young Vietnamese women pressed slender, shapely bodies against one of the troopers as they ran their fingers through the hair on his arms.

Inside, Sergeant Stryker was talking to a squad of men fresh off an Alert Team V-100 assault tank, which sat restlessly rumbling outside.

"I want you to circle this block counterclockwise on foot," he was saying. "Leave Thor behind," he said, referring to the tank with the four balloon tires and .50-caliber machine gun. Bristling with M-60's, too, a colorful mural of Thor was painted across the front of the beast. "If the dude is still around, and I seriously doubt that, he'd hear you coming. So work your way out counterclockwise, extending a block each time you complete a circle, and check in with WACO every one-five, got that?"

The men nodded understanding and were quickly led out by Sergeant Greenlee, who added, "And let's not get trigger happy—you've all got the description. There can't be that many seven foot tall white giants running around Saigon with their heads shaved bald."

"What ya got here, Mark?" Quinn stepped forward after the Alert Team filed out of the room.

Stryker smiled a greeting and pointed to a small box barely visible between two oil drums filled with gasoline.

"I still haven't pieced it all together, Bob, but it seems we got sniped at by two separate entities tonight who had nothing whatsoever in common."

"Happens in the Nam now and then," Thomas said sarcastically, and Stryker shot him an irritated look.

"First, some of my boys get shot at by a rooftop asshole across the street. Richards and the hot dog here beat feet up there and take him out rikky-tik but—"

"Tim dusted the dude, actually," Thomas cut in again, "with the help of that crazy Egor."

"I take it that's what the smoldering Huey is all about out there."

"Yeah." Stryker nodded with a frown. "So just as we're about to secure the area and start checking buildings for bombs, some other cat on the top of *this* building—" he waved his arms around to encompass the room they were in—"starts blasting away."

"Your KIA is a national?" Quinn scratched his chin in thought.

"That's affirm. Hard-core type, from up north. The stupid fuck had papers on him, the whole bit— even a goddamned diary talking about his trip down the Ho Chi Minh trail."

"Which doesn't really exist," Thomas remained sarcastic, "according to the bleeding-heart press

133

corps."

"Bunch of fucking commies," Stryker muttered. "Anyway, the suspect that was poppin' caps topside eluded us."

"To put it lightly," Thomas added, rubbing a bruise on his cheek.

"And we began a floor-to-floor search of this building and the one across the street, and came up with that device tucked away there within the first five minutes."

"E.O.D.'s on the way?" Quinn stepped closer to the bomb, but remained a good five feet away as he went down on one knee.

"I don't think we're gonna need the bomb squad, though," said Thomas.

"And why is that?" Quinn took Stryker's flashlight and directed the powerful beam at the device.

"Richards already checked it over and—"

"He what?" Quinn's eyes went wide. "Without waiting for E.O.D.?"

"Aw, you know how Gary is. Anyway—"

"Richards found that a critical component was left out of the bomb," Stryker took over. "The minute hand on the watch was missing."

Quinn stared at Stryker silently for a couple seconds, then moved forward and picked up the bomb. Someone had already disconnected the wires leading from the dynamite's detonator to the battery-operated timepiece. "Doesn't make sense," Quinn muttered under his breath.

"It's the same kind of device used in the other explosions," Thomas said. "According to the E.O.D. report I read yesterday, anyway. Same brand of watch — cheap, made in Taiwan. The dude, whoever he is, musta bought a batch."

"Which means we can expect a lot more carnage around town if the maniac isn't brought in soon." Quinn shone the flashlight about on the floor, vainly searching for the missing minute hand. But as he feared it was nowhere to be found.

The watch had two wires running from the battery and detonator soldered to its face. One was connected to the hour hand. The other, was fastened across the "12," so that when the minute hand made contact with it, the electrical current was completed and the explosive detonated. Such a device had a maximum sixty-minute time delay. It was crude and simple, but very effective, providing the bomber with ample time to effect his escape before the building was demolished.

"What's your hypothesis on all this, Mark?" Quinn looked up at Stryker.

The ex-Green Beret paused a moment as he searched the man's eyes for the cause of his obvious depression. Quinn always glowed with energy, eager to tackle the mysteries his line MPs threw at him, but tonight he was sluggish, dragging along. Hardly taking an interest in the case. *Perhaps it's lack of sleep*, Stryker decided, *Or a heavy caseload*. He hadn't heard about Quinn's personal crisis yet. "I'm not sure, to tell you the truth — I'm still trying to get the five layers of gunsmoke out of my nostrils. We really went to town out there with those scumbags."

"In my opinion," Thomas offered his best educated guess, based on the facts they had at hand, "the dude finally got sloppy, that's all. The glass is missing from the face of the watch—"

"Of course," said Quinn. "He'd have to take it off to attach the wires."

"The guy's a rocket scientist." Stryker grinned, referring to Thomas's deduction.

"I'm impressed." Quinn smiled finally, giving in to the game every cop played to keep his sanity on the street.

"Can I continue?" Thomas asked indignantly.

Stryker bowed slightly and waved his hand in front of his stomach, left to right, palm up, Arab style. "By all means."

"The asshole obviously bumped into a brick corner or scraped against a fire escape on the way over here," he explained. "Tore the minute hand off without noticing. Simple as that."

"Naw," Stryker began, shaking his head.

"He would have noticed the missing minute hand when he planted the bomb and bent down to set the time delay," Quinn interrupted.

"You're a damn good street cop, Anthony." Stryker folded his arms across his chest and leaned back slightly on his heels. "But you'll never make MPI coming up with stories like that."

"Well, fuck *me*!" The enlisted man turned and walked away, only to return as he began pacing the room in frustration.

Quinn scratched at the stubble on his chin again as he stared down at the bomb. "For some reason, the suspect did not want this bomb to go off, Mark." He glanced back up at Stryker. "You have any theories at all?"

As Stryker began to answer, the doors burst open

and all three men turned around, expecting the bomb disposal crew. Instead, an excited MP private rushed up to Stryker, who automatically checked his portable radio's squelch switch—he had obviously missed out on something transmitted over the air. "Fucking government batteries," he muttered as the man skidded up nose to nose with him.

"Twenty-two-Echo's got a chase, Sarge!" he reported. "On Le Van Duyet, heading toward the airport. *And they think it's your bomber suspect!*"

7.

Moose On The Loose

Pvt. Nicholas Uhernik didn't like shooting .45 automatics with his left hand. Though the pistol was his favorite handgun, it packed a punch that pretty much made forming a sight picture impossible when the vehicle racing along beneath you was hitting every pothole in sight and travelling in excess of sixty klicks an hour. Striking a target while your feet were firmly planted on mother earth was a lick, but shooting at a fleeing felon while the suspect was also melting rubber off his tires, was—or so the drill sergeants back at The School maintained—bordering on the impossible.

But he leaned out the left side of the Jeep again anyway, popped off two quick rounds as his right hand struggled with the steering wheel, then laughed uproariously as his ears picked up the faint sound of lead smacking against car metal. *Such job satisfaction!* he decided as he took to steering with both hands—the pistol still clutched in the fingers of one—when they screeched around a corner on two wheels. *The fucking job satisfaction is outrageous—there oughta be a law!* "If only Sergeant Kip could see me now!" he yelled at a startled militiaman that appeared at an intersection then vanished in a blur, but then the MP they called the Uke remembered Mather was dead. And so was Hoa. And so was the dream they shared for so long. And he returned all concentration to his pursuit driving, more determined than ever to run this hairball into the ground.

"Hairball?" He laughed aloud again at his own thoughts. "Now that's a lick on me!" The man frantically swerving in and out of curfew roadblocks in front of him had a large head shaved down to the skin. His crown shined beneath the moonlight.

"WACO, this is 22-Echo," he called into his radio mike, ever-conscious of the dozen MP units in his rear-view mirror, racing to catch up with the chase. "Still heading northeast along Le Van Duyet." He paused as he strained to focus on the first street sign he had seen in over a mile. "Now passing Hien Vuong, over."

"Ten-two-four, 22-Echo," the dispatcher answered with an unemotional drone. "Repeat your suspect vehicle description, and gimme a plate, over."

"Vehicle is a red Peugeot, WACO." The MP wiped sweat from his brow with the edge of the hand holding the pistol. "License number taped over. He's got a souped-up engine under the hood, too—any chance we can get the chase car in on this, over."

The "chase car" was a powerful 1967 Plymouth with a stateside police package under *its* hood.

"Chase Car's Ten-12 at the Saigon Docks at this time," WACO announced. Ten-12 was radio talk for "out of service."

"Some *cao bois* 'borrowed' its tires," an anonymous informant came over the air. "It's sittin' on blocks at this time."

"The chase is all yours, 22-Echo," WACO confirmed no supercharged assistance was on the way to help out. "What's your current fourteen? Come on, Nick, talk it up."

"Just passing the traffic circle at Yen Do," 22-Echo advised in a calm voice. The odds had shifted to his side. Uhernik could see gas pouring from the undercarriage of the Peugeot. *If only I had a flare gun*, he decided. *Or better yet, a tracer!* He stared briefly down at the M-16 chained to the support bar which usually had a swivel-mounted Hog-60 resting atop it. There was no way he could free it and drive at the same time — all those hot dogs gaining on his tailbumper would zip by and claim the glory.

"WACO, this is Car Niner-Charlie attempting to intercept from the Tran Quoc Toan side!" The sergeant's dual electronic sirens nearly drowned out his transmission as he approached from the west. Five streets met at the Yen Do intersection with Le Van Duyet. But that was not what worried Uhernik. He floored the accelerator, tired of seeing NCOs muscle in on his pursuits with the newer units.

Flashing red lights sparkled in the corner of his eye as he roared past another squad of startled checkpoint sentries, barely beating the sergeant from Charlie Company through the intersection.

He was still in the lead!

A disagreeable odor reached his nostrils just then as it appeared he was finally gaining on the Peugeot, and he felt the sweat saturate his back. He recognized the smell immediately: burnt oil. His engine was burning up! If he kept up this rate, he'd blow a rod within the next four or five miles.

He let up on the gas pedal, allowing the oil—what was left of it—to circulate for a second or two, coasted through the dips at Hoa Hung, then floored the accelerator again.

"WACO, this is Car 37-Alpha," a disappointed voice cut in on the transmissions when he should have stayed off the air. "I'll be Ten-12 at Le Van Duyet and Pha Thanh Gian—my unit just tossed its rods through the hood, over."

"Fucking rooks," The Uke muttered, forgetting the short time he himself had been with the 716th, as he waited for the transmissions to cease so he could call in his latest cross street.

"WACO, this is Car 36-Bravo. Preparing to intercept at Bac Hai, over."

"This is 36-Delta," another excited voice crowded the net, "coming eastbound up Tu Hien Thanh. Should be able to intercept at—"

A three-toned scrambler blew the private off the air as the dispatcher at the International cleared the frequency. "All units *Code One*!" he directed. "Twenty-two-Echo, what's your Ten-14 at this time, over?"

But The Uke was too busy trying to keep up with the suspect and force the steering wheel hard to the left at the same time without dropping his .45 pistol. Finally, he holstered the automatic, freeing both hands — they had turned west down Tu Hien Thanh and were re-entering a heavily congested residential area. Stray rounds could mean hard time at Leavenworth back in The World.

"WACO, this is 22-Echo!" He finally got back on the air as they started down a straight stretch of road again. "Now proceeding westbound Tu Hien Thanh, approaching Bac Hai. Better start a couple Ten-5's this direction because — "

His windshield shattered as the suspect turned and unloaded an entire clip of pistol rounds at the MP Jeep. Swerving to the right, The Uke sent the vehicle bouncing roughly over the sharp edges of a vertical curb — bamboo and teakwood from an abandoned vendor's wagon were crushed beneath the spinning wheels and cast aside in a spray of splinters. He floored the gas pedal, practically standing up in his seat now, and sped along on the sidewalk for the rest of the block.

When the MP Jeep swerved back into the street, it was only a couple feet behind the sputtering Peugeot.

Uhernik rammed the sedan. Twice. Then a third time. The driver with the shaved head turned to fire again, and The Uke rammed the car's rear end a fourth time.

The impact caused the gunman to lose control as he was knocked to the side of his seat, pulling the steering wheel hard to the left. The right front wheel locked and collapsed under the strain, and amid a terrible grating of folding metal and flying glass, the Peugeot flipped end over end off the roadway and crashed through the storefront of a jewelry shop.

"We've stacked it up into Numba seven-one-four Tu

Hien Thanh, WACO!" he reported into the radio mike, feeling the adrenalin rush as the entire building collapsed onto the sedan rocking back and forth on its top. "Better rush me some cover cars. This guy's big as a moose, over!"

But even before he had dismounted from his jeep, gas leaking from the Peugot ignited, and within seconds, the tiny shop was engulfed in flames.

Gun drawn, Uhernik rushed forward, but the heat was so intense he could not get closer than the sidewalk. With his gun hand, he shielded his face, feeling the edges of his eyebrows singe away. The sirens on MP Jeeps rolling up behind him brought a dreadful, ear-splitting chorus to the crash but, head cocked to one side, he strained to listen past the crackling flames and popping glass. Someone inside was screaming beyond the dancing wall of fire.

An explosion threw debris and flying metal out at the military policemen suddenly, and as they moved back, a glowing fireball ascended into the night sky and a pall of inky smoke drifted out to settle over the street. The desperate screams stopped after echoes from the rumbling explosion died away.

Overhead, the heavens thundered back, and a heavy downpour was unleashed upon the Americans, but even before they could break out their poncho liners, the storm had passed, to be replaced by a warm, fine mist that became a sizzling cloud of steam when it touched the growing fire. The rainfall had little effect on the flames, and when the Vietnamese firemen finally arrived they didn't even pull out their hoses. It was too late. They just stood around, watching the structure burn itself to the ground.

"Maybe you men could break out a couple hoses and at least spray down the adjacent shops," Uhernik recommended impatiently as another fireball erupted into the sky. It was greeted with applause and laughter by the growing crowd of *cao bois* who had filtered in from the back alleys.

The fireman smiled politely and bowed his head in the affirmative several times before walking back to his red and white sedan. Then he got in and slowly drove away.

CID agent Robert Quinn sat at the small desk in his modest apartment, feeling the ghosts of his family pressing in on him from behind, but he ignored the uncomfortable sensation. *They were not dead!* He kept telling himself that. A week had passed since he discovered Xuan and Lien and Mang missing and he had received no word from them or their captor. And this was Saigon. By all rights, considering the odds, their bodies should have been found by now.

Those would be his thoughts, anyway, if he were working any other kidnapping case. *But this was his family, by God!* He clung to the desperate hope Buddha would see them through this. He thought of Stryker, and the stories the ex-Green Beret had told him about the mysteries and power of the rain forests, and he walked over to the window — feeling the ghosts swirl away from him in apprehension — and stared out at the edge of the jungle, many miles away.

"Please," he spoke to the ominous darkness rustling about under a distant string of floating flares, "if there is a power lingering out there greater than all of man's gods, as Mark claims, please help me now. Please see my wife and my children safely home."

One of the flares broke free from its nylon parachute and plummeted to earth, leaving the hissing string of lights far behind. Quinn took it as a sign. An omen. A terribly bad, depressing omen. Thunder rumbled in the distance. Or was it artillery, blasting away, on the edge of the city?

He returned to the desk and sat down, stared at the framed photo of his family for a long time, then dropped his face in his hands and trembled. He wanted to sob, to release the grief and the pain and the uncertainty, but the tears would not come. Instead, a queasy feeling took hold of his gut, and he became very light-headed.

Quinn leaned back in his chair and took several deep breaths, then slid the top drawer of the desk open and dug through a small stationery box that held pictures of his relatives back in The World. They all sat in the living room of a modest house in Montana, a piano—his mother's pride and joy—in the background. Montana. Cold, cold Montana. He flashed back to the days of his youth when he would holster his BB pistol, pack a lunch and thermos, and hike six miles through the snowdrifts to a cliff at the foot of his favorite mountains. There he would talk to the spirits which, according to area legend, inhabited an immense, solitary oak tree. They never talked back, he reflected now, smiling at the memory, but he had enjoyed the hours spent mapping out his future hopes and dreams.

He would climb up into the outstretched branches, protected from the icy wind swirling down through the valley, and carve his initials into the bark — apologizing the whole time to the old oak, for he, back then, truly believed the plant world had feelings too.

Quinn smiled again. Back then? Perhaps he believed it even more now. After taking trips up into the Central Highlands following a fierce firefight. The jungle, its trees riddled with bullets and oozing sap — plant blood — took on an angry atmosphere. Sometimes, even when the wind died, the trees seemed to sway about, such pain were they in. Other times, it was so mournfully silent, one couldn't help but feel the sadness all about. The *pain*. The emotion — was it emotion really? — and ominous "presence" in that smoke-laced stretch of rain forest. Most grunts he met in the field didn't care. They hated the jungle. It had never brought them anything but a world of hurt. They *wanted* the trees to suffer. Sometimes they fired off entire banana clips just to see how many palm fronds they could shoot down. Payback was a bitch. What goes around comes around. They claimed it was revenge for the jungle rot.

Quinn flipped through the photos, but he couldn't shake the memory of the old oak tree. The one-sided conversations he had had with it. Back when, because he was just a goofy kid, such sessions were permissible. Just so long as the tree didn't start talking back. And not that he ever told anybody about the little talks he had with nature anyway.

Not Mother Nature. To him, so many years back, the old oak was like a big brother he never had. The branches were always there to protect him from the harsh winds, the driving snows. The trunk, with its weird knots and loops that sometimes looked like sad, understanding eyes, was always there to listen.

But here in Asia it was different. The jungle was a bitch. Nature was fierce. There was something definitely feminine about the spell the rain forest held over men like him. He would never be able to explain it. Men who served in the Nam understood already. Those who didn't could only go there to find out for themselves.

He often talked to the old oak about a girl. A woman, actually, who he dreamed of someday finding. It was a strange fantasy he confided in the ancient tree, but she wouldn't be like the girls in high school. And though she would have the inner strength and confidence, and the outer beauty of the Indian maidens he read about in his wilderness novels, *this* woman would be even more exotic. She would be from another world. Another place and time. He didn't know where. He didn't know when. He had no idea how he would find her. Sometimes he prayed she would just appear at the base of the cliff, naked beneath the branches of his beloved tree, but she never did. The old oak just fluttered its leaves in reply.

And then he had met Xuan. And she showed him a world and a life more wonderful than any of the fantasies waiting for him in his books.

Since coming to Saigon, he had never opened another paperback.

Quinn kept returning to the picture of his first, back-in-The-World family. He had never been one to fool around with a camera, but when his father learned he had volunteered for duty in "that crazy little Oriental fiasco," he bought his son a fancy new pocket camera. "Take plenty of photos, Rob. I'll send you all the film you need. And take notes, too. Before you know it, you'll have so many photo albums in your duffelbag you won't be able to remember what or where or why each picture was taken. Hell, keep a journal. When you get back, I'll talk to a friend of mine about getting it onto the racks. Start setting aside some bank allotments, and if nobody'll buy it, we'll publish it ourself." Quinn had just laughed. He took the photo at a big family reunion the day before he shipped out.

They didn't stock film for pocket cameras, he found out shortly after arriving at Camp Alpha. And his father never sent him replacement cartridges.

He stared at the expression on his mother's face: a forced smile beneath sad, apprehensive eyes. He would always remember her that way. *Why did you have to pick the army, anyway?* he could still hear her. *You could have joined the Air Force like your brothers and gone to Greece or Italy.* Beside her, his father stood in his proud my-son-is-going-off-to-war stance, arms folded across his chest, Republican pin in his lapel, sparkling a brilliant red, white and blue.

In the foreground, his five sisters posed on their knees, all looking bored and restless—only one actually staring at the camera. He laughed to himself, wondering what kind of trouble they were all getting themselves into at this very moment.

On the wall behind them all, their family coat of arms. He had never been told its history, or what it

149

stood for. Now, suddenly, he wished he knew. He would have to write, asking.

In front of his oldest sister sat the dog. Snow white fur marking the most colorful spot on the photo. Eyes wide, an evil tundra green. Tongue hanging over the edge of its lower jaw. *Wolfman.* His mother had named it some faggy French name, but that didn't fit an Alaskan Husky. His brothers never called it anything but Wolfman. He could still remember when he'd sleep in his back yard in the summer with his buddies Mike and Bill. At dawn, his mother would let Wolfman out the back door of the house, and they would pretend they were being eaten alive by their sleeping bags. Wolfman would go crazy, trying to save them, leaping from bag to bag, playfully biting into the fabric—somehow knowing it was really *them* inside, yet still going into a panic over the animal-thought his human brothers were being attacked.

Again, Quinn smiled at the flood of memories a single old and faded photograph brought back.

But he became suddenly aware of the intense silence in the apartment. No Mang running about, knocking things over. No Lien singing lightly to American tunes on the TV or radio. No Xuan, banging pots and pans in the kitchen, cooking his meal—*their* meal—sending that shrimp and rice fragrance throughout the house. It smelled so good, birds flocked to the balcony railing at the same time every evening, joining Lien in song, performing for a handout little Mang always somehow provided when his mother wasn't watching.

Quinn looked back down at the photograph and

examined it more carefully until he found the parakeet perched on the rim of the large blue popcorn bowl. The bird was captured by the camera slightly off balance as it swung back and forth on the edge of the plastic container, head cocked to one side—eyeballing the fluffy kernels below. The bowl sat in front of Quinn's youngest sister—a look of amusement on her face as she anticipated the bright blue bird's next clownlike move.

"Gus," he muttered under his breath, remembering now the time it flew out an open window, only to be terrified by the sudden freedom. And it flew straight to the top of a pear tree in the back yard, where it stayed all afternoon, shivering in the fall breeze, until his uncle arrived with a long two-by-four, and coaxed the bird aboard, then slowly lowered him back to the ground.

Quinn chuckled at the memory. The parakeet seemed so happy to see them all again. "That's what I need," he decided, "to liven this place up a little."

He pulled his shoulder holster on and slid the oiled-down .45 into it, then started out of the apartment into the dimly lit corridor.

He paused with his key in the lock as the sound of children running up the stairwell reached him—a shiver of anticipation raced through him. But then he heard their voices, and they appeared—a young brother and sister from down the hall. Billy and Carol. American names, in preparation for that eventual journey to the Big PX stateside. Their father was an Air Force mechanic, their mother a Vietnamese seamstress with a flair for tailored uniforms.

They slid to a stop in front of him and bowed

reverently without saying a word. "And what are you two doing up so late, if I might be so bold as to ask?" Quinn made a show of checking his wrist watch.

"Not late yet, Mr. Quinn." The boy reached up on tiptoes, touched the butt of his automatic protruding down from its holster, and produced an ear-to-ear grin. "Only ten o'clock! Father work overtime, airplane garage!"

"And mother work late too!" his sister chimed in, and Quinn saw little Lien's face flash before him. "Downstairs!"

And then they vanished, in a scampering whirl of chatter and laughter.

Papa-san *working a double shift*, he surmised, *out at Tan Son Nhut. And* mama-san *putting in another eighteen hours at the sweatshop down the block*.

Quinn breathed in the warm, humid night air that met him at the bottom of the stairs as he came out onto the street. The tropical heat, ever-present, even after the fall of darkness, always invigorated him — as opposed to the way it usually fatigued and depressed most Westerners arriving in the Orient.

He watched a cyclo, loaded down with boisterously laughing bargirls, sputter past — one of them threw him a kiss laced with a suggestive lick of vulgar lips — then started down the sidewalk toward vendor row. Chinese lanterns, gold and red, swung gently in the warm breeze above rickety stands loaded down with black-market goods and pornographic magazines.

He paused briefly in front of a pile of flyboy sunglasses and Japanese radios, examined a price tag or two, fought the urge to bargain, then homed in on the sound that had always beckoned him in the past but which he had never had time for—chirping. Like twangs of memory from his childhood.

He started toward it, jerking his arm away from the female hawker behind the stereo equipment who wanted him to stay longer. A half block between the highly stacked layers of rattan baskets, then left down a narrow alleyway a couple feet, and they appeared. Bamboo cages six feet high, crowded with a collage of ricocheting colors. *Parakeets!*

"You like, Joe?" An old *mama-san* tugged on his elbow after he examined one cage for several minutes.

"How much, madame?" he asked in pidgin Vietnamese.

"For you, Joe," she kept to English, "only twenty-five hundred *p*, OK?" She flashed a hand at him five times, all her withered and dark fingers extended.

Quinn frowned. "Five dollars? For *one* lousy bird?" He feigned a look of incredulous disbelief and started to walk away, but the old crone stepped in front of him, her black, betel-nut-caked smile a stop sign.

"Two thou *p*!" She reduced the asking price a dollar.

Quinn shook his head in the negative. "Five hundred piasters, madame." He folded his arms across his chest, feet braced apart in the classic street stance. "And not a dong more."

The old woman waved a bony, gnarled finger in his face. "You numba ten GI! You cheap Charlie for sure, Joe!" Then she made a dramatic show of considering his proposition, chin cupped in hand.

"Fifteen hundred *p*!" Her optimistic smile returned.

Quinn held out two greenbacks to whet her appetite — he knew she sold the parakeets to Vietnamese for a quarter apiece — and the old woman snatched them up, then turned away from him, shoulders hunched over, head lowered as she scurried to her money box, annoyed with the transaction. "You cheap Charlie for sure, Joe." She slid the bills into a secret slot and returned to the cage, muttering under her breath.

Quinn stooped to examine the birds closer. Half were lively, clutching to the sides of the cage with their talons as they peered out at him — no doubt starved. The others stood perched atop one leg in the back of the cage, heads twisted around and resting on their backs, sleeping through the din of whistles and chirping.

"You take this one!" The old hag reached into the cage with lightning speed and grabbed a healthy-looking parakeet by the head. Talons kicking, the bird flew into a frenzy, screeching. The others darted about the cage, terrified.

But Quinn had moved to the next cage beside the vendor. His eyes had found a frail-looking blue parakeet that stood perched on a middle bar, using both feet. It stared back at him, trembling, refusing to blink — perhaps hoping the human would go away if it stood perfectly still, invisible.

Quinn knew this was the one. He would nurture the poor creature back to health. Show it trust. Kindness. Compassion. Friendship.

The way you showed your children? a voice entered his mind, and he felt a bolt of guilt arc through

154

him at the things he had never done for Lien and Mang.

"I want this bird." Quinn pointed weakly at the pale blue parakeet in the middle of the cage.

The old woman, obviously annoyed, scampered up beside him. "That one is sick." She pointed too, and the poor bird ruffled its feathers at all the attention, finally blinking as it shifted its balance back and forth, uncertainly.

"I don't care," Quinn insisted. "I want *that* one."

"I tell you already, Joe, she is *bookoo* sick. She is — "

" 'She' is a he," a seductive voice sounded behind them and the CID agent whirled around to find the woman who had been following him for so long before their encounter at the bombing scene a few weeks earlier.

"*Chao Co,*" He bowed his head slightly, unable to ignore the swell of flesh beneath the fabric under her throat. "And how are you tonight, Lan?"

"You can tell by the color of its beak." She moved forward confidently, and the old *mama-san*'s frown deepened disapprovingly as she backed up, out of the way.

"Very well," the vendor muttered, unlocking the cage door.

"I'll do it!" Quinn did not want to see the bird handled roughly.

Shrugging her shoulders, the woman moved again, rolling her eyes skyward for their benefit.

Curiously, the parakeet did not put up a fuss, but merely emitted a nervous caw as Quinn gently took hold of him around the shoulders. Nibbling at his knuckles in protest, it nevertheless failed to bite.

The vendor provided a small box with air holes, then motioned the three of them out of her life as if she had no further time for them. "Go away, cheap Charlie." She shook her head back and forth. "Go away."

"What shall you name him?" Lan asked as they walked back toward his apartment.

His mind pausing while his feet moved mechanically up the stairs, Quinn considered for a moment, then said, "Gus . . . Gus *III*."

"Gus the Third?" She looked up at the back of his head quizzically as she followed him. "It is American, no?"

"It is American, yes," he imitated her French accent playfully. Then, reaching the second flight landing, Quinn lost his smile and stopped. Xuan used French during foreplay.

"Better to have a Vietnamese name for a Vietnamese parakeet." She halted obediently behind him and bowed, smiling. "Perhaps Nguyen the Eskimo." She stole a twinkling glance up at him, but the tall CID agent did not seem amused with her play on words. "Or maybe Tu Do," she amended her choice. "It means 'freedom,' you know. Free as a bird taking flight."

Taking flight, Quinn mused as he stared down at her voluptuous body, its young, firm curves beckoning him—her virtue his for the taking, obviously, now that she had followed him up into the bowels of his home. *Taking flight.* Her words made him recall the dreams that had come to him during a night of restless, fitful sleep the evening before. He had labored through nightmare after nightmare in which he saw the fall of South Vietnam to the communists. President LBJ had finally succeeded in pulling American troops from the quagmire, and a month later Ho's fierce fighters swept down across the DMZ like seven-headed dragons, catching Thieu's commanders with their butterflying pants down. Quinn himself had been caught by surprise too—while he was TDY to Bangkok assisting Thailand's 281st MPs with a gun-running and narcotics investigation, and in his vision he saw the North Vietnamese soldiers marching his wife and the wives of all the other American policemen naked down the streets, bayonets in their backs, rivulets of blood trickling down to the smooth swell of their haunches as the crude blades scratched skin with each footfall. His children had been beheaded and hung upside down with all the other Amerasians in the public square at Le Loi—after the victors tore down the statues of Arvin soldiers that had loomed protectively over the park for so many years. The dreams always ended abruptly with news media footage of President Thieu alighting from a helicopter aboard a Navy ship at sea and the sailors pushing the crippled Huey overboard. Its rotors tearing into the water and snapping apart—barely missing a sinking vessel of boat people nearby as they sliced past through the air—always woke him, drenched in sweat.

"OK." Lan cocked her head to one side as she moved a few steps closer, draping her arms around his neck. "How about Little Joe. Or maybe . . ."

Quinn thought about her earlier suggestion as she tightened her grip on him, eyes moist, lips slightly apart, seducing him, drawing his face magically closer to her in that dimly lit stairwell. Her earlier suggestion: Tu Do. Freedom. It had been the same name Bryant gave *his* parakeet. A flood of pain swept over him as he remembered the investigation he completed, exonerating Thomas after the accidental shooting. They had been fighting with cat burglars in the canal behind Bryant's bungalow. Thomas fired shots at one of the suspects as he was about to plunge a knife down into Bryant's back . . . and the hollowpoints had passed through the bastard, and through the walls of Bryant's humble home, and into his wife's belly, ending her pregnancy in its sixth month. One of the bullets decapitated Tu Do-san as it stood perched helplessly in its bamboo cage, terrified by all the gunfire outside.

Feeling a shiver race down his spine as Lan's breasts brushed up against him, Quinn gently pushed her away without releasing her. "I don't think you better proceed any further," he decided, patting her hand as a disappointed look glazed the sparkle in her eyes. "The neighbors would talk."

"But we wouldn't —" she began.

"Even if we didn't do anything, they would talk. It wouldn't be fair to Xuan . . . if she ever returns." The last four words left him as a whisper of dread.

"We could enter silently," she coaxed him, refusing to let go of his hands. "No one would have to know."

"The way my luck's going —" he forced a smile — "someone would leave his apartment just as we entered mine." He stared down at her silently for several seconds. "It would be all over the building before the next noon. And Xuan has many friends here, Lan. As do my children. The cruelty they would suffer at the hands of their peers would be even worse than the humiliation my wife would experience. She might survive. *They* would never forgive me. It is just not worth it."

A Phantom jet, flying low across the rooftops on its approach to Tan Son Nhut, rattled the ceiling, and the parakeet in the box scratched its claws against the cardboard nervously as it sensed the giant predator pass over.

"You need a woman by your side tonight." Lan caressed his forearm with the back of her hand, and Quinn felt a stirring in his loins.

He pulled his hands away slowly. "I do not wish to be disloyal to my wife." His words were firm but gentle. He turned and started up the last flight of stairs, alone.

"I will wait five minutes, then tiptoe to your door," she whispered after him, the ruthless smile plainly evident in her words. "Be sure to leave it unlocked."

The tiny bird in the box uttered a soft wolf whistle in reply.

Lan smiled at the complimentary noise and nodded to herself as she checked the reflective blue face of her narrow Seiko. She tried to ignore the dark, cold eyes that stared back at her, silent reprimand radiating from their depths, scolding her for trying to seduce this married man. She listened to Quinn's footsteps fading away up the stairwell, and another chirp from the bird reached her ears. *A brave, defiant whistle*, she decided. *We shall name you Tieng Sam: Angry Thunder.*

Lord, help me remain strong. Quinn looked up from the files of paper on his desk when he heard the door creak open. *Why did I leave it unlocked?*

The door closed softly a second later, and he listened as the hasp was slid into place. A vision of Xuan passed in front of him, but he knew it was *her*.

"You forgot this." Lan appeared beside his desk, smiling—carrying a tall bamboo cage. "You cannot expect Sam to live in that tiny box all his life!" She waved a finger at him, and Quinn thought of the old hag in the marketplace, and would Lan ever lose her beauty? Xuan seemed to be growing even more sensuous with the years, and he wondered when the change came. *When we lose our men*, a tarot-card reader had confided in him once.

"Sam?" He looked up at her finally, a tight smile of resignation on his lips as he set his pen down and closed a file with several large glossy black-and-white photos—mug shots—in it. "I was thinking of a Vietnamese name. Pham Bam, or Nguyen-Charlie, or Pleiku Paul."

Lan laughed at the third choice, but said instead, "Nguyen-Charlie? You insult our pet?" She walked over to the box sitting on the nightstand, lifted it up, and shook it gently. The parakeet slid about on its sharp talons and chirped in annoyed protest. Quinn listened to it ruffle its feathers.

"Yet you would name it Sam?" Quinn feigned astonishment. "In honor of Uncle Sam, no doubt— patriotic coattails and all." He felt suddenly disgusted with American involvement in Vietnam and he couldn't explain why.

Lan placed the small box against the open cage door and slid a wall of cardboard away, coaxing the parakeet through the exit with a tapping of her finger against the opposite wall. "Tieng Sam," she said, as the bird flew into the larger cage and bounced about from side to side for several seconds. "Vietnamese words for thunder." Feathers shot about through the wooden bars, then floated lightly to the floor.

"Yes," Quinn sighed in agreement as he slid a drawer shut. "The little tike did create a fuss all the way home."

"To Sam," she spoke in defense of the parakeet, "this is not home, Robert." She trilled the 'b' in his name, and the sudden intimacy made him uneasy. "Not *yet*." She watched the bird settle down and find a perch — again halfway between the top and bottom of the cage as when he had first seen it — before turning to face him, smiling. She had been bent over, palms resting on her knees, and he had tried not to stare at her enticing curves, but she caught him. Quinn blushed, and she straightened up, smile growing with the first minor victory. "And what is all this about?" She motioned to the pile of papers on his desk, conceding a small stretch of ground politely with the change of subject. "Anything an uneducated Vietnamese waif could help you with, sir?" She kneeled beside him and rocked back on her haunches, thrusting out her breasts for a moment as she swung long, black hair back across submissive shoulders.

Don't kneel, Quinn heard his conscience pleading in the depths of his mind as it rapidly seemed to cloud with emotions he did not understand, yet knew all too well from working the street so long. *Please don't kneel like that!* The fragrance of clean sheets drifted across the bedroom to his nostrils, and he saw Lan naked across the satin, legs spread, delicate hands drawing his buttocks in harder as his pelvis grinded against hers, pumping in deeper and deeper. "They are files." He felt the harsh fabric of his crotch stretch tight in protest as he grew hard beneath the protective covering of the desk. "Notes I have kept through the years."

"You try to decide which of your enemies has stolen away your family." She sensed it immediately, gauging the look on his face, and her accuracy stunned Quinn.

"Well, yes," he admitted. "Sometimes, in this profession, this job." He switched to smaller words for her benefit, wondering if he even had to. "We make enemies who . . . hold a grudge." He strained for the Vietnamese word. *"Thù bạn oán thù."*

"I understand." She smiled appreciatively. "Do not all policemen make such enemies?"

"Yes, I believe so." He had never really thought about the other men's problems in this light. It was sort of like having to wear flak vests in the heat or contend with crotch rot out in the boonies—you didn't waste time worrying about the other men's discomfort.

"But it is rare when they actually retaliate after making threats during the heat of an arrest," she surmised, and again he was amazed at her comprehension of the situation faced by MPs the globe over.

"It is rare," he agreed, fighting to keep memories of the murder scene at 541 Thanh Mau street out of his mind, but visions of a raped and tortured Le Thai Mai filtered back to haunt him.

"He has left you notes boasting of his crime?" She glanced about the desktop then frowned with disappointment.

Quinn pulled a sealed plastic envelope from a desk drawer and handed it to her as she shifted into a more comfortable Asian squat. He watched her thighs flare slightly and a passage from some long forgotten book came to mind. "Years of squatting instead of sitting on Western-style chairs leave these Indochinese maidens with magical legs their Western sisters can never hope to imitate in the bedroom."

"You can read and write English?" he asked—automatically surprised at his own question, wondering why it mattered at all.

"Sometimes." She smiled up at him with those sensuous eyes again, arcing her back so he could see down her blouse if he chose to. The top three buttons were open, and her nipples were taut against the thin fabric, straining to be free. *To be sucked!* he decided, fighting the passion racing through his entire body now like wildfire. *To be sucked and squeezed and swallowed and sucked even harder until her breasts burst and I have devoured her.*

"You found no fingerprints?" She turned the packet over and over without opening it.

Quinn's eyebrow jumped slightly at the latest question. He was impressed. "I had it treated chemically at the lab," he revealed, wondering if she knew the meaning of all the words. "No latents whatsoever. But then again, I knew there would not be. The sonofabitch is a pro. He is an expert at—"

"Yet you know who he is," she interrupted. "And he *wants* you to know."

"Yes," he sighed softly, lifting three files from the pile on the desktop.

She visually counted the manila packets and puzzlement clouded her eyes. She sensed that each packet belonged to a separate suspect — an individual case. "Yet you have a problem deciding who is behind the pain and uncertainty you now suffer."

Quinn took the notes from her, placed them in a drawer, and spread the mug shots out in front of her to view. "Yes, Lan. There is conflicting evidence. The clues just don't fall together like they should."

She rose to one knee to better examine the photos. "Please explain, agent Quinn." Her eyes took on an eager, excited cast as she absorbed the visual features of each suspect without touching the glossy prints.

"The handwriting on the notes somewhat matches thi man's." He pointed to an apelike grimace etched across the features of a gorilla with a head shaved bald. Below the jutting chin was the name BOARD-CHEK in bold letters.

"How many notes, total, have you received?" She stared at the photo without looking up at him.

"Four, total, now," Quinn said. "The first two were in my daughter's handwriting — he no doubt forced her to write them." He swallowed, bowing his head at the thought of her and Mang in this maniac's custody, and Lan reached over and touched his shoulder.

"I am sorry," she said, reading his thoughts. "It must be very painful." She paused as he fought to compose himself, then said, "I have never been close to someone as you seem to be to your family. It must bring you a very warm and pleasant feeling."

"He probably told her it was all a little game." He fought back the sobs climbing his throat, and tightly closed his eyes. "Probably said they were just playing a little joke on Daddy."

"I am sorry, Robert." She clasped his fist with both her hands, but he looked away.

Quinn pulled a notepad from a drawer and read copies of the latest two notes. Sealed in envelopes with his last name scrawled across them, they had both been slipped under his door while he was away. "This first one says, simply, 'It's a waiting game, Quinn. You are beginning to learn what it's like.' "

"And the second?" She returned her concentration to the photo of Boardchek.

" 'A few more months of waiting, screw, and you will be ready for the first clue.' " he read from the notepad, then set it aside, hands trembling.

"This term he uses," she spoke with a serious tone, deciding not to take advantage of the dual implications. "It has another meaning—a slang expression prisoners would only use?"

"Yes," Quinn said. " 'Screw' is a convict's title for guard, or any cop for that matter, I guess."

"I see." Lan glanced at the other two photos, but kept returning to Boardchek's.

"In my daughter's note—" he looked down at the yellow legal pad again, and then the sealed packet of originals—"she calls him Mister Merlin, and makes reference to the Magic Kingdom."

"That was my next question," Lan said, and he surmised she read through the plastic container and understood English writing after all.

"But none of these three assholes uses that AKA." He motioned to the files.

"AKA?" she repeated the three letters.

"Sorry." Quinn reddened again slightly. "Cop talk, Lan. Also Known As. Aliases. None of these jerks uses an AKA anything similar to Merlin."

"That could mean nothing," she replied dryly.

"You believe that?" he challenged her.

"This is Saigon, Mister Robert Quinn." She drew his eyes to hers. "The rules of the other world do not always apply here." He thought she would wink at him then but she did not. "You should know that by now."

"Yes."

"What did you arrest this man for?" Lan dropped an accusing finger across Boardchek's ugly likeness.

"They are all—" Quinn swallowed hard again but forced the question out—"I arrested all three of them for child molestation," he said. "Back in The World."

"Why do you use that expression?" she snapped suddenly, jerking her head toward him, fire in her eyes.

"What?" Bewilderment flooded his own expression, but he automatically knew what she was talking about. Xuan scolded him about the same thing often enough. The mock mask was not convincing.

"Back in The World!" Her lips became a thin line as she gritted her teeth. "Why do you Americans always leave Vietnam out?"

He wondered how many GIs she had slept with just then, how many American erections she had aroused only to suck limp.

"Why do you hate this land so much?" she continued. "Why do you hate it so much as to do this disservice to it? Words are powerful in the Orient, my friend!" He thought she might get up and leave then and there. "This is a beautiful land! I hear your great United States is cold and barren and windy and lonely—with boring people who stare the other way when you pass them in the street!"

"I am sorry. I didn't—"

"You choose a Vietnamese woman to be your wife!" She waved a finger at him menacingly. "You choose to have children with her, to make your home here! Yet you speak so lightly of this land—like your life *here* is only temporary."

Lan's eyes grew very sad, as if she had been betrayed.

"I'm sorry," Quinn said. "I meant nothing by it. It's just an expression all soldiers have drilled into them their first tour here, and it—well, it sticks, I guess, though Xuan's tried to rid me of it often enough with her frying pan." He glanced into the kitchen, thinking he heard her cooking his favorite Vietnamese meal, but the sound was only the parakeet hissing at the darkness and their argument that kept him awake.

A tense silence followed, lasting for several minutes, and neither of them moved.

"Never say 'Back in The World' again, Robert." She dropped her eyes to the floor, and her features softened. "Please."

"I promise." Quinn leaned forward and kissed her lightly on the forehead, but she failed to respond. "I'm sorry, Lan. I meant nothing by it. You know, we Americans are brusque and clumsy when it comes to things . . . *cultural*. We soldiers, anyway—"

"Robert?" She stared at her knees several more seconds, then looked up at him with a questioning, puzzled expression. "What means 'child molestation?' "

Quinn's smile faded, and he looked away.

"It is bad," Lan decided softly, regretting the question. "It is something terrible bad. I understand now. I am the one who is sorry. I understand now why you are so . . . obsessed by this. Why you do not let the other investigators handle the case."

"It is *my* family involved," Quinn said, stroking her hair gently until his hand brushed her shoulder and she grasped it. "I have not told the other agents at my office."

"They are already overburdened with cases, no?" She moved his hand lower until it covered her breast.

"They would not have the time to devote the work necessary to solving this." He tried to ignore the erect nipple scratching his palm through the thin fabric of the blouse.

"You do not feel any of them are competent enough to catch this madman," she corrected him. "You feel only yourself possesses the skill and experience necessary to trap and capture the thief who stole your family."

"Something like that." Quinn smiled uneasily. Lan squeezed his fingers against the swell of flesh under her blouse, and she sighed, dropping her head back. The movement pulled another button loose, and the blouse opened wider, revealing the top halves of her full breasts. Quinn watched her skin, smooth as amber silk, throb slightly with each racing heartbeat.

168

"I shall go back out into the night and find the information you seek." She returned her eyes to him, leaving the lips apart after the last word as the dreamy glaze remained in her jet-black pupils. "I will return in the morning with some sort of answers about this bastard, to help you with your investigation." She rose to her knees again and reached for his belt, loosening it expertly.

"But we do not even know which suspect it is, for sure. We do not even know . . ."

Lan unfastened his belt with her right hand, then slid the zipper down as her free hand slid across the photograph of Boardchek. "This is the man we are looking for, Robert. This man Boardchek is the one who steals away your loved ones."

"And by what evidence do you reach that conclusion?" He ignored her probing fingers, curious why he no longer countered her advances, no longer felt any guilt. *It's just a working relationship. It's all purely business. What she chooses to do with her mouth is no act of disloyalty on my part.* The demon inside him broke into hysterical laughter.

Lan's left hand slid across the glossy print in circular motions as her head dropped back again, eyes tightly shut. Her other hand had found him, and she seemed immersed in a sudden pool of anticipated pleasure. Her left hand froze over Boardchek's ugly countenance, and the long, slender fingers seemed to clutch the two-dimensional bones of his skull in a powerful vise. "This is the man you are looking for, Robert," she repeated quietly, experiencing a shiver of revulsion course through her body, chasing the words out. "I . . . *feel* it in my soul!" Her head dropped forward again, limp, and beads of perspiration formed on her forehead. "This bastard holds the mother of your children."

At the same time he became aware of an oppressive "evil" lurking in the room, Quinn noticed her hand was gently stroking his erection. Exposed now, the enlarged head of his penis protruded up through the flaps of his trousers like an uninvited intruder.

He stared down at it, then a few feet over at Lan, her head tilted back again, lost in some supernatural vision, lips moist and pursed to take him in if he so desired. And Robert Quinn had never yearned for anything so much in his life as he desired her mouth in his lap just then. *You evil wretch!* his mind called out as he gently took hold of her head by its sides and guided her down onto him. *You irresistible enchantress! What spell is this you've cast on me? What curse?*

At the moment he felt the warm, hungry sensation engulfing him, there came an impatient pounding at the front door.

8.

And All The Other Things Little Girls Are Made Of

Quinn took hold of the doorknob, hesitated, glanced back over a shoulder—waiting for her to close the closet door securely—then took in a deep breath and pulled.

Sgt. Mark Stryker's towering, stocky frame appeared before him, hands on hips, blocking the dim light down at the end of the hallway.

Stryker laughed when he saw the CID agent, a pained look on his face but relief flooding his eyes, and let out the lungfull of air he had been holding. "Didn't mean to interrupt your evening, old boy!" Stryker produced his best British accent, remembering the POW officers in the movie *The Bridge on the River Kwai*, which was playing at the MACV outdoor theater that week. A pleasant, familiar fragrance drifted up to greet his nostrils and the ex-Green Beret's thoughts shifted to the beautiful Thai maidens who doubled as freedom fighters in the

171

same film. The white letters on his black MP helmet, which was tilted smartly down to where it just barely rode the bridge of his nose, glowed down at Quinn. A lesser man would have been greatly intimidated, which was often the desired effect.

Quinn forced a similar chuckle in response. "Oh, no, no, Mark." He motioned the military police sergeant in with the wave of a slightly trembling hand, but Stryker didn't seem to notice.

"That's a big negatron, my friend!" he said, himself wondering why he was in such good spirits — so energetic. Perhaps it was the ice coffee he had downed on the ride over from the International. "I'm afraid this visit's official. You gotta get yourself a phone, Quinn. Can't be wastin' the Green Machine's petrol runnin' around ol' Saigontown chasin' down homebodies like you every time the alert goes out."

"Another bombing?" Quinn tightened his belt, returned to his desk while Stryker stood in the doorway, and slid the pile of papers into a file box.

"Well, not quite. Another *bomb*." Stryker glanced about, removed his helmet, and combed back his sweat-slick hair with broad fingers. Quinn noticed the knuckles were all covered with scars.

"It didn't go off," the investigator surmised.

"Correct." Stryker pulled at his left ear lobe. The one with the bullet hole in it.

"Where was it this time?"

"In the basement laundry room of a flophouse over on Thong Nhut, about a dozen blocks down from the embassy. Covered with piles of gasoline-soaked linen. The chambermaid who discovered it freaked out, tripped backwards over a crate, and miscarried on the spot before passing out. The janitor who discovered *her* ran screaming through the lobby that there was a murder—what with all the blood and all. Hell, thought we had a bitchin' crime scene for a while."

"When all you had was a boring bombing that failed to detonate." Quinn slipped on his shoes and threw a jean jacket over his shoulder holster.

"Something like that." Stryker noticed the parakeet in the hallway and entered the apartment for the first time, just as Quinn was ready to leave.

"Just something I picked up tonight," the CID agent said, sounding embarrassed. "To liven the place up—you know . . . "

Stryker leaned forward and whistled a few lines from *"Lonely Are the Brave,"* and the bird, which had been cowering in the back of its cage, trembling, moved forward a few inches and craned its neck to listen to him.

"Looks like you've made a friend," Quinn said, stepping outside—a signal for Stryker to do the same. "You're welcome to drop by anytime you want. You and Sam can party till the sun comes up . . . "

"You named the poor thing Sam?" Stryker raised an eyebrow at Quinn. His expression told the investigator it was just about the worst choice anyone could make.

"I'll explain it to you later," Quinn said, glancing back at the bedroom closet before they both stepped out into the hallway. "It's a long story."

"I'm afraid I got some bad news," Stryker announced as he coasted up to the crime scene—an old, dilapidated hotel ringed with MP Jeeps. Armed sentries stood at the front and rear doors. Down the block, a firetruck and several ambulances were parked, waiting for something to go wrong.

"It's about Xuan." Quinn closed his eyes tightly as he stepped out of the vehicle and felt blood rush to his head.

"No! No, Bob," the MP sergeant rushed to correct any mistaken implications. "I'm sorry—I didn't mean *that*. It's about that chase Uhernik had couple days ago."

"Uhernik?" Quinn reached for his pocket notebook only to find he had left it back at his apartment.

"The Uke."

"Oh, of course," Quinn remembered the private immediately. "The Uke." Nicknames came to him more readily than proper ones.

"Well, Christiansen and a couple other men from your office went through the ashes where his suspect stacked it up, and all they came up with was the body of the female shopkeeper through whose store the chase culminated."

"Female shopkeeper?" Quinn stopped halfway through a step, and Stryker urged him the rest of the way up the stairs into the building.

"Yep. Seems the screams everyone heard were hers."

"You'd think they'd be able to distinguish between male and female screams!"

"Yes, you'd think so." Stryker led him through a maze of hallways to a rear stairwell, where they started down into the basement. "But maybe the bald fucker in the Peugeot yelled a couple times to throw some confusion into the whole show."

"You're telling me the bastard escaped the fire?" Quinn asked incredulously. "That he made it through that crash unscathed, Stryker? I don't believe it!"

"Christiansen went through the debris with a fine-toothed comb," the husky NCO maintained, "like he always does. And he didn't come up with anything — not a legbone, not even a charred molar. The dude beat feet on us, buddy — I'm afraid that's all there is to it."

They came across a squad of military policemen lingering at the bottom of the stairs, M-16 rifles slung over their shoulders upside-down. All the fire-power was a sight that brought pleasure to Quinn. It reminded him why he stayed in law enforcement. Why he refused to give up the badge. Even when times got rough, like this.

"There she be." Stryker pointed down to the wrapper of dynamite protruding from the layers of white linen.

Quinn ignored the device, and stared at the large blood smear on the cement floor instead. "The woman?" he asked.

"They Code-threed her to the hospital," the MP in charge of the scene cut in. "She'll probably make it — these Asian women are tough cookies. But she dropped the kid right here." He motioned toward a small lump under a sheet that was soaked in blood. "Male, I'd say," he surmised, swallowing loudly, so that everyone in the room noticed but acted like they hadn't. "About five months gone."

"So that makes it murder." Quinn came across as if asking a question more than making a statement. He dropped to one knee in the puddle of blood and drew closer to the bomb.

"Looks that way," a sergeant beside Stryker said confidently.

Quinn started to touch the device, then hesitated — not really concerned for his own safety just then, but that of the men gathered all around him. A training scenario replayed itself in his mind. A DI back at The School screaming at raw recruits, *"Never bunch up! Never gather like this! One lousy Chicom grenade'll take out the whole lot of you!"*

He locked eyes with Stryker. "Is it safe?"

"Code 4." The NCO beside Mark nodded.

"Missing one slightly vital component," an enlisted man added. "The blasting cap!"

"I'd call that slightly fucking vital," Quinn agreed, rising to his feet. He ignored the blood-soaked fabric clinging to his knee.

"Yeah." Someone's portable radio crackled with static in the background.

"Our shaved-head suspect?" Quinn turned to face Stryker.

"I don't think so." He moved forward from the semicircle of troopers confronting the man from CID. "That was something else I was meaning to bring up on the ride over here. Richards and Schultz got together yesterday and triangulated a bunch of stats. It looks highly unlikely the dude Uhernik chased is the same one involved in the sniping a few minutes earlier."

"And why is that?" Quinn folded his arms across

his chest in an impress-me stance.

"Because there's too much distance and too little time between the two incidents. The guy would have had to be an Olympic track star, for starters. And even then, what with Saigon traffic and all—"

"What about the description?" Quinn cut in. "The shaved head?"

"Don't mean nothin'." The sergeant beside Stryker spat a wad of chewing tobacco down on the floor, ignoring the sacrosanct atmosphere at a homicide crime scene. "This is the Nam, Mister Quinn—you, of all people, should know that. Bookoo lifers running around with their hair shaved off. Hides their bald spots."

"And it's good for promotions," Stryker added, his tone revealing the jest.

"So we're back to square one," Quinn concluded.

"Kinda looks that way." The sergeant standing beside Stryker produced an apologetic frown.

"What about tonight?" Quinn persisted. "No sniper topside this time?"

"Tonight, we played dirty," Stryker admitted, shaking the tension out of his wrists as he walked closer to the disabled bomb. "An anonymous tip to the Dispatch bunker warned there was going to be trouble at this hotel and that we'd better bring in the troops if we didn't want all hell to break loose."

"Male or female?" Quinn thought of Lan for some reason, but no—she had been with him the whole time.

"Male. Thirties to forties. Sounded Caucasian, according to Schell."

"Ethnic accents can be phonied easy enough,"

Quinn countered.

"Whatever."

"I'll want to have a listen at it—how soon can you arrange it?"

Stryker grinned, already anticipating the request. "I've got Farthing transferring the twenty-four-hour tapes to cassette right now."

"So anyway . . . "

"So anyway, we get this call in tonight, and Slipka decides to send in Richards and his Decoy crew instead of a marked unit."

"Good move."

"Yeah. Thomas and Bryant cruise up in one unmarked Jeep, stumble about, looking drunk, and bounce into the hotel's ground floor restaurant—"

"Which hasn't served anything but *Saigon tea* for the last five years," the man beside Stryker joked. Several of the men in the room laughed along, but Quinn remained stone-faced.

"Richards and the new man to the squad, Nilmes, coast up from a rear alley, and the four of them beat feet up to the roof."

"But there was no sign of him," Quinn deduced, anticipating the end of the story.

"On the contrary." Stryker's smile grew, though there was mixture of irony and disappointment flashing in his jungle-green eyes. "The rooftop above—" he made a thumbs-up gesture, indicating the top of the building they were standing in, several flights up—"was deserted. Not so much as a pile of rat shit. But that goofy Nilmes spotted a man with a rifle atop a building across the street, running away."

"Could he describe him?"

"Naw, the guy was too far away—except to say he was a Caucasian male."

"He obviously had no problem spotting your men before they spotted him."

Stryker ignored the insult and cocked his head to one side instead, puzzled. Why was Quinn so on edge—so irritable towards his own comrades? They were all on the same team, damnit!

"We put out a BOLO," Stryker told him sheepishly, "but—"

"But the suspect got away."

"Correctemundo, pal. Had the whole sector ringed with enough firepower to blow away half of Saigon. I don't know how he did it—I honestly don't know how. Sometimes I'm beginning to think we're dealing with a fucking phantom here." The grin remained in place, but Quinn did not smile back when he looked up at Stryker.

"Vietnam is full of ghosts, Stryker," he said coldly. "You should know that by now." Using the last name that way made Mark pause before responding. It was the first time he ever heard the CID agent sound hateful. He hoped the man was just mad at the world, or at his career—that it was nothing personal. And at the same time he wondered why he even cared. Stryker's golden rule had always been: Don't fall in love with the local women, and don't make best friends among the troops. It was the only way to go. And look where that route had taken him. Look how many times he had ignored his own advice. Visions of Lai and Kim and Wann flashed before him. And he thought of Quinn's children, and Xuan's cooking. He thought about how Mang always jumped up on his lap to show him his GI Joe toys whenever he came over. And how Lien always called him "Uncle Mark."

And he knew why he let himself get into these predicaments. It was all part of life. All part of growing old and experiencing fate and the hard times that chased it along. There was nothing he could do about it — it was far more powerful than him. It was best to just leave it all alone.

"Yes," Stryker muttered, shaking the visions from his head slowly, "Vietnam is full of ghosts, Bob."

Quinn glanced around at the men standing in the room. "Put in a call to MPI," he said. "I want this chickenshit excuse for a 'bomb' dusted for prints. *They* got some new people aboard, who need the experience — let's put the rookies to work."

"Soon he will trust me." Lan knelt in front of the parakeet's cage patiently. She was tempting the bird with bits of seed balanced on the underside of her fingertip when he entered the apartment, but when the door opened so suddenly, Tieng Sam scampered back into the shadows of his cage.

Quinn was surprised to see she was still there. Naked except for one of his long-tailed shirts around her shoulders, she jumped energetically to her feet and took his jacket for him. He watched her shapely bottom sway from side to side along the edge of the shirt as she whirled around and headed for the closet. "I thought you would be long gone," he said.

"You are disappointed I am still here?" She slowed in her skip across the room, losing her smile. Quinn decided the look of hurt in her eyes when she turned to face him again was genuine.

"I must admit that I am somewhat . . . relieved you remained here during my absence, Lan."

"You have been gone nineteen hours and *twenty* minutes!" She assumed the expression of a suspicious wife, checking her wrist watch, then broke into a smile. "Only kidding!" She hung up his jacket and swiftly returned to his side. Tugging at his shoulder holster, she said, "So heavy. I take it for you."

"I missed you," he said, handing her the .45 automatic, secure in its trap of camouflage-design leather. "It's nice to have someone around to talk to."

"I have a surprise for you." She embraced his arm, rubbing her body against his side, teasing him. Then she skipped away again—her breasts bouncing up and down firmly with each footfall—and stopped in front of a box on the nightstand, wrapped in bright colors, complete with a red ribbon.

"A present?" Quinn frowned. He was not in the mood for surprises. He was not feeling optimistic, or cheerful. He felt like a dead rodent some vicious tomcat had dragged in from an alley sewer.

Lan set the holstered weapon gently against the box, then moved the ribbon back and forth with her knee. Bending her leg brought the edge of the shirt up over her hip, and Quinn felt an aching in his loins when he saw the strands of pubic hair rise from the mound where her thighs came together. "You have three guesses," she announced.

Quinn couldn't imagine what it was, but he was obviously going to have to play the game. "Why don't you put on some pants," he said. "I'm sure you

181

can fit into something Xuan has hanging back there." He motioned toward the bedroom closet.

"You're no fun," Lan protested. "Come on, *guess*!"

For some reason Quinn thought of Raunchy Raul Schultz. Did he actually smell one of the man's exploding cigars in the apartment? "An inflatable doll."

Lan laughed loudly — and from her heart, like an innocent schoolgirl. "A *what*?" she asked. Quinn was glad when she lowered her ankle back to the floor.

"OK, a deluxe box of multi-colored Army-issue rubbers one of the town patrols dropped off as a joke." He frowned again, sorry he said that the moment it came out of his mouth, but he just could not take his eyes off her jutting breasts. She was standing sideways, and they strained against the chest of the shirt, full and upturned, nipples rigid. Ready and waiting, it seemed, to be fondled.

"You're getting warmer." Her smile grew as she drew the last word out for several seconds, excitement dancing in her eyes.

"OK, how about a —"

Suddenly a bell began clanging away within the brightly wrapped box, and Lan's eager smile dissolved. The first thing that came to mind for Quinn was a timer signaling a bomb was about to go off, but then, with a weary expression growing on her face, Lan pulled the bottomless container off, revealing a telephone. "*Voila!*" she said sarcastically, little enthusiam in her tone.

The phone rang a second time, and she folded her arms beneath her breasts, refusing to answer it.

182

"A telephone?" Quinn just stared at it too. "Why the hell did you get me a telephone, for Christsake?"

"I did not deliver it!" she said defensively. "Some MP with bookoo stripes on his arm named Raul Schultz brought it by. He said the men chipped in and got it for you. He said they wanted you to be in closer touch with WACO, what with all this problem surrounding your family. He said—"

"Enough," Quinn cut her off, holding a hand up. The phone rang a third time.

"You in a piss-poor, shitty mood today, Robert." She trilled the "b" in his name again. The phone rang a fourth time.

"Now I *know* Raunchy Raul was here today—just listen to those words you're using. Why don't you try talking like a lady again." Quinn changed subjects as the phone rang a fifth time. "Did he behave himself?" He looked at her curiously, hoping to gauge her truthfulness.

"He has a tongue longer than an anteater's!" she snapped defiantly, rubbing her crotch. "At least *he* doesn't ignore opportunities that *arise* unexpectedly."

Fuming, Quinn nevertheless decided not to play her game. "No, I'm sure he doesn't. Who would that be calling?" he demanded. "Who the hell would have my number already? *I* don't even have it, for Christsake!"

"How the fuck would I know?" Lan lashed back at him, waving her small fist. Quinn watched her breasts sway back and forth with the effort. How he wanted to drag her into the bedroom, throw her down on her back, and pump her till she split apart or burst! "Maybe it is Raunchy Raul himself!" She

183

produced a wicked smile, concocted to inflict pain.

"Then answer it!" he yelled back, realizing for the first time his neighbors were probably hearing every word they were saying.

"Alright, *I will*!" Lan picked up the receiver. She placed it against her head upside-down, and listened.

"Well, say hello!" Quinn's frustration showed through before he realized she had probably never used a telephone before.

Lan threw him a this-is-all-new-to-me frown, then said, "Hello?"

They both paused a few seconds, and she said it again. "Hello?"

The room had gone deathly silent, then, even at this distance, Quinn could hear the connection break, the line go dead, then a harsh dial tone return.

"Nobody speak," Lan said.

"I know," he said. "I heard." His tone softened, and he moved across the room to her as she hung up the phone.

"How you hear when nobody speak?" She switched to pidgin English, her habit when times turned tense.

"I'm sorry, Lan." Quinn took her hands in his. "You have become my very good friend. I have no right to yell at you. Xuan will enjoy meeting you when she returns. I'm sorry. I have not had much rest."

"You are very tired." She ran her hand over his forehead, wiping beads of perspiration away.

"Yes. Very tired." He sat down on the rattan loveseat alone. "How 'bout if I take you out to the Caravelle tonight?" He hoped the suggestion would light up his own eyes, but he sensed they remained dull and lifeless. "For some dinner."

"And a movie afterwards?" Lan sat on his lap like an eldest daughter, and Quinn felt another shiver course through him.

"Yes, of course, dear. A Chinese kung-fu epic down in Cholon perhaps."

Lan hugged him. "That would be wonderful," she said, but then her own eyes lost some of their color. "I have information, Robert."

"Information, Lan?" Intense sadness seemed to settle over Quinn as he remembered how theirs was to be a purely businesslike relationship.

"I spent the entire day in the library," she revealed. "The English section."

"And?" Quinn had never felt so tired in his life.

"This man your daughter calls 'Merlin' . . ."

"Yes?" He felt an inner tug at his heart.

"You are not sure whether or not he is the same man in the photo labeled 'Boardchek.' "

"Unfortunately, I am not sure," he conceded, lowering his head to defeat after defeat in the battle to solve the most important investigation of his life.

"Is Mr. Boardchek's first name Marlon by any chance?"

Quinn straightened up in his seat. "How did you know that?" He locked eyes with her.

"It is then?" She seemed to be growing more excited with each passing moment.

"Yes!" He grabbed her shoulders and started shaking her. "But why? *Why*?"

"The AKAs fit now, Robert!" She pulled a folded Xerox sheet from her shirt pocket and dropped it in his lap. "I checked the directory of names!" she announced, as he unfolded the paper to find a copy of a page out of some faded archives. It contained a list of male names beginning with 'M,' and ran in alphabetical order.

"Look!" She pointed at one in particular, which she had circled with red ink. MARLON jumped back at him, in big, bold letters.

Below the name was the following caption:

(Old French), meaning "little falcon."

A common form of Merlin. Also, Marlin.

"Look on the other side," Lan directed. Quinn frantically turned the sheet over, nearly ripping it in two in his own excitement now.

Also circled in red, so that it stood out from the other names, was MERLIN:

(Middle English), From Arthurian legend,

a famous wizard. Means, literally,

"falcon." Also, forms of Marlin,

Merle, Marlon.

Quinn emitted a triumphant howl from the pit of his gut and rose to hug the woman standing before him.

And the phone rang again.

He reached down and picked it up immediately, feeling no premonition whatsoever about who might be on the other end of the line.

"Hello?" he said, a jubilant smile forming on his lips.

"Father!" a little boy screamed into his ear before being roughly dragged away from the phone.

"Mang!" he called out, shocked. He dropped the Xeroxed paper. In the background, he could hear a man cursing angrily, and then a sobbing woman being dragged toward the receiver. "Mang!" he called out again.

"Robert," a crying, helpless voice silenced him, and he cupped his free ear so as not to miss a single word. It was his wife.

"Xuan! Yes, Xuan, honey—*I'm here*! I can hear you, baby! Are you alright? I love you honey! *Are you alright?*"

"Robert, I need you so bad!' she sobbed into the mouthpiece, and he could feel her wince under pressure. Someone was pulling on her hair and physically restraining her in the other direction at the same time. "Robert, please come and help us! *Please!*" And then she was torn away from the phone and thrown roughly across the floor.

Lan's little stint of investigative work had been unnecessary. He recognized the harsh voice on the other end of the line the moment the man spoke.

"Greetings, *asshole!*"

"Boardchek! You lousy slimeball sonofabitch! If you harm one hair on their heads I'll—"

"You're hardly in the position to dictate terms to *me,* pig motherfucker!" the escaped convict screamed back with an insane, high-pitched laugh. "Because I've got the goods, Quinn! *I've* got the goddamned merchandise, Okay?"

The CID agent, seeing the alarm in Lan's eyes, forced himself to calm down. Boardchek, for all his arrogance and defiance, was right.

Quinn took a deep breath and slowly let it out, the entire time listening to his children crying in the background. He heard the man holding his family captive kick little Lien, and he broke into a cold sweat over his entire body, helpless to do anything to help them. "What is it you want?" he asked. A strange, sucking noise could be heard on the other end of the line now.

"Your old lady gives the worst head jobs in town, Quinn," Boardchek erupted into laughter again. "Can you hear her going to work down there?" The sound of Xuan gagging and sobbing at the same time sent Quinn into a fury—he thought he would rocket up through the ceiling at any second. "But then again, I guess *quantity* is more important than *quality*, now isn't it bitch?" The strength of his voice faded somewhat—the man was obviously lowering his demented head to pose the question to the woman he had in a stranglehold. Quinn found himself praying it was all just a terrible joke—a horrible prank, sound effects and all, to make him think his wife was being forced to do such a thing.

"*What is it you want?*" he demanded again, raising his voice impatiently—hoping the words would somehow end the degrading, obscene act taking place on the other end of the line.

Boardchek laughed again. Quinn could hear him throw Xuan to the floor and kick her aside. He wondered if she was naked, if the maniac had violated his children. "I want one fucking million dollars, CID agent Quinn," he revealed boldly, his tone swollen with confidence. "Do you hear me? *One million!*"

Quinn forced a nervous chuckle. "I'm in the United States Army, for Christsake, Boardchek—I'm a lousy warrant officer in a low-paying CID assignment. You know that! I don't make that kind of money."

"One fucking million dollars, Quinn," Boardchek repeated. The man sounded adamant.

"Jesus, I can swing five, maybe six thousand. Maybe even seven thousand, with some help from the men in the battalion."

"One fucking million dollars, Quinn."

The investigator sensed the convict on the other end of the line didn't care about the ransom. Knew Quinn couldn't raise a fraction of what he was asking for. The man was harassing him—toying with his brain. Mindfuck, the men in the field called it. The opposite of jungle justice and sanity: *mindfuck.*

"If you'll give me another week, maybe I can even come up with—"

"One million fucking dollars, Quinn," the madman's voice took on a deadly serious tone. "By eleven o'clock tonight—one hour before the curfew you screws have bolted down across the town. Well, now see how the rules feel when they work against *you*, asshole! Just feel what it's like to have the ring of concertina, the long arm of the law," he slurred his words sarcastically, "closing in on *you*, disrupting *your* life, dropping a stink bomb into *your* party!"

The man went rambling on insanely. After listening silently for over a minute, Quinn asked to speak with his wife again. "We love you, Daddy!" he heard Lien cry out in the background before being slapped viciously across the mouth.

"One million fucking dollars, Quinn. Or you'll never see your family again. We've already packed our bags for a trip to the Magic Kingdom. And when it's all over with, after you've buried them and grieved over their tombstones — if you ever find their bodies — you'll still have me to contend with! *Me!* Out there in the dark somewhere, Quinn. Watching, waiting, prowling."

"Don't do it, Boardchek. You'll never get away with it. *You'll never get away with murdering my family!*" The phone receiver was slick with sweat in his hand. "I'll hunt you to the ends of the earth, you sonofabitch!" *Do you hear me?*"

"One fucking million dollars, Quinn." The maniac laughed defiantly. "By eleven o'clock tonight."

There was a scuffle, and he heard strange, guttural sounds flow from his wife's throat as she tore at Boardchek with all her might, trying to get near the phone again. She screamed at the receiver in rapid Vietnamese. "Don't pay it, Robert! Don't pay *anything*! He is going to kill us anyway."

Still helpless, *always helpless*, he listened to Boardchek slam Xuan's frail body into the floor before kicking her several times in an attempt to silence her.

Then the line went dead.

The powerful might of the thousand-man-strong 716th Military Police Battalion was brought to bear on the seething Saigon underworld shortly after Robert Quinn received the phone call from escaped convict Marlon Boardchek, but five hours later, at ten-thirty p.m., they had still not located the CID agent's wife and children.

"I don't know what else to do." Quinn sat beside the phone in his apartment, a quiet, consoling Lan at his side. "I've exhausted every lead I had. Everything has bottomed out. All the clues ran into dead ends. I have no idea—absolutely *no* idea where he's keeping them. They could be *anywhere*! Do you realize how big this city is, Lan? Do you realize?"

She ran a hand along the bridge of his back gently. "All we can do is wait, Robert. The story was on the TV tonight. Now the whole city knows. Saigon is three millions of people. Vietnamese love rumors and talk more than sex, I think. They will be watching. Someone will see this man Boardchek. Someone will hear something. They will call the *canh-sats*."

Quinn rubbed his eyes until tiny stars swirled around inside the lids. He was exhausted, and still tormented over the decision to release the story to the news media. Had it been the right move? "The Vietnamese don't talk to the police, Lan—you know that. They keep to themselves. They don't want trouble, and to them the *canh-sats* are trouble, all corrupt."

"But they know this is a special case now." Optimism coated her words but did not make him feel any better. "It involves an American cop, Robert. To them, an MP. Remember the slogan all your rooks use: Pride, Intergrity and Guts. Vietnamese watch the TV. The cops on *Dragnet* never accept bribes. The Vietnamese, they are impressed. They like the thought such a police department might exist somewhere."

"It is only television, Lan. The Vietnamese are not so naive. This is war, after all. This is—"

"The TV is still new to them, Robert. Take advantage of that. Think positive. They like the image of the American cop—an image represented by MP Jeeps cruising Le Loi or Tu Do or Nguyen Hue. I feel it in my heart, Robert. Someone out there, some Vietnamese will help you. It is only a matter of—"

The phone broke the tense conversation with its sudden ringing. Quinn nearly knocked the nightstand over in his rush to answer it.

"Hello?" he said.

Watching intently, Lan saw his features soften as the investigator listened to the voice on the other end for several seconds. Nodding slightly, Quinn finally said, "Thank you, Sergeant," and hung up the phone.

"Who was it?" Lan demanded.

"Sergeant Schell, over at the International," he replied, as if rising from a drug-induced trance, back to reality. "Just reporting PMO received teletypes responding to the queries I sent out last week, back to Leavenworth."

"Queries?" Lan frowned at the unfamiliar word.

"The 95-Charlies back at the stockade confirm Boardchek escaped several weeks ago. He killed two prison guards and a fucking attack dog."

"My other two suspects are still in a maximum security lockup. Christ, Lan, he killed a police dog with his bare hands." Quinn's face dropped into his hands, but he fought back the sobs silently. "And now he's got Mang, and little Lien."

"How the hell did he get a passport to leave the states?" Lan remained firm. Strong. "How the hell did he get a visa to South Vietnam, for Christsake?" Her tone was an exact imitation of his own frustrations, and Quinn looked up at her, almost smiling at the insanity of it all.

"The maniac's a genius. A pervert, a scumbag and a sonofabitch, but a fucking genius. A genius with a cause."

"A cause?"

"Revenge."

Three flights below Quinn's balcony, a black, unmarked U.S. Army Jeep sat concealed in a dark alleyway halfway down the block. Two men in civilian clothes reclined in its front seat. One drank ice coffee from a moist baggy. The other sucked on a Blue Ruby cigarette. Both were armed with well-oiled, precision-sighted "sterile" weapons.

"How long you think this thing is going to go on?" Anthony Thomas turned away from the string of flares floating along above a distant rooftop and stared unblinking at Tim Bryant.

"No telling," the senior MP answered, rubbing the cool barrel of his submachine gun. "I don't have a whole lot of fucking experience with hostage negotiations, bicycle-seat-breath."

Thomas frowned and resumed watching the flare show drifting against the night sky over the eastern edge of Saigon. The men joked about them—speaking with a phony Japanese accent when they compared "flare shows" outside with the "floor shows" taking place inside Mimi's Bar or the Queen Bee. Both provided performances of near-orgasmic proportions, according to Sergeant Brickman. Thomas missed The Brick more and more each day. A starburst of green flares exploded somewhere over Tan

Son Nhut, and he sighed at its beauty.

Bryant coughed, and lit up another Blue Ruby. He wasn't a smoker. Thomas didn't ask why he bought the pack at the same stand where he stopped to purchase the ice coffee. It didn't matter. It wasn't his business. It was the Nam.

"You guys are pretty close?" Thomas asked his partner.

"Some." Bryant inhaled a lungful of bitter smoke, then slowly let it out, watching the blue cloud obscure the stars overhead as he leaned back in his seat.

"Tighter than you and me?" Thomas glanced over at him again.

"Naw, Ants." Bryant shot Thomas a reassuring grin. "His old lady and my old lady and The Uke's old lady get together couple times a week to play cards and listen to Angi's police monitor. That's all."

"The Uke gave her a fucking radio?"

"Yeah. I'm sure he regrets it by now. Probably started out with the usual macho syndrome. 'You can listen to me chase the bad guys around Saigontown.' you know, that sort of crap."

"Fucking rooks."

"Yeah."

"I'm sure he regrets it by now."

"I *know* he does." Bryant laughed.

"Speaking from personal experience?" Thomas produced the wry smile this time.

"Yeah."

A cold hand clamped itself across Thomas's wrist, and he practically somersaulted out of the Jeep. He stumbled across blacktop, regained his balance and footing, and whirled around, weapon braced against his waist, ready to fire from the hip.

A short, frowning shoeshine boy barely nine years old stared up at him with hands on hips. "Hold your pants onto, Joe," he muttered, holding his hands out, palms up. "Me no VC, for sure. VC numba ten. Me numba one *baby-san*! You want shoeshine? Fifty *p*!"

The kid set down his shoeshine box, but kept a second, brightly wrapped container under his arm.

"What's in the box, son?" Bryant pointed to the one with the gold ribbon on it, suppressing a chuckle over Thomas's reaction.

"Get the fuck out of here, ya little rug rat!" Thomas rebounded, waving the butt of his weapon menacingly as he wiped spilled coffee from the front of his shirt.

"You guys cops?" the boy stared wide-eyed at the submachine gun.

"*Di di mau*, asshole!" Thomas waved a fist this time as he approached. "*Di di mau* or die!"

Scooping up his shoeshine box, the small Vietnamese youth darted away, laughing tauntingly. Bryant watched him slow down as he reached the rear doors to the apartment building.

"One, two, three, motherfuck MP!" The boy directed an upraised finger at the two Americans.

"And your sister!" Thomas yelled back, checking his watch as the youth disappeared into the complex. "Near enough curfew, Tim. I shoulda wasted the little bastard!"

"He'd just come back to haunt you in your nightmares, Ants," Bryant muttered without emotion, sounding bored.

"But I still shoulda smoked the little dude." He blew on the wet stain spreading across his chest.

"Forget it." Bryant forced a light chuckle. "Don't mean nothin'."

"Do me a favor and save that grunt slang for the boonies, OK?" Thomas took his frustrations out on his partner.

"OK, pal."

"Shoulda dusted the fucking punk." He flipped the safety back on before resting the weapon between his legs, out of sight.

"Yeah, maybe you should have. Now shut the fuck up!" Bryant lit up another cigarette and blew smoke in Thomas's face. "Just shut the holy fuck up, OK?"

"OK, Tim." He took out a rolled-up *Playboy* magazine, tore the centerfold free, and began eating it with a straight face.

Robert Quinn sprung from his seat when he heard cardboard slide against teakwood outside his apartment door. He flung the door open, but there was nobody there. Down the hallway, light footfalls could be heard rushing down the stairs.

Quinn stared down at the brightly decorated box. He was frozen with indecision. Should he chase after the mysterious caller, retrieve the box, or slam the door shut and phone the MP desk? The word *bomb*! flashed through his mind over and over.

"Who was it?" Lan brushed past him and stooped to pick up the box.

"No!" Quinn yelled, visions of a terrible blast erupting in his head now, but she already had the container in her hands.

"What a pretty ribbon!" She ran her fingers along its silky texture.

Lan tilted the box to one side, searching out its seal, and her eyes went wide as a crimson liquid gushed forth, coating her arms.

She screamed and dropped the container, lifting her blood-soaked fingers in the air in terror and confusion. Quinn caught the box before it hit the ground. He ripped it open and dropped to one knee, nearly fainting, when the contents were revealed. The veteran policeman let out a long, painful sigh and held out the box for the gods' inspection.

A young girl's tiny arm, severed just above the elbow, held a blood-smeared envelope out to whoever opened the "present."

When Lan looked down and saw the savagely shredded limb, she went hysterical and fell to her knees beside Quinn, screaming at the top of her lungs. She held her hands out away from her body as if trying to forsake them—to discard them. To renounce them. The sound of a half dozen sets of jungle boots could be heard rushing up the distant stairwell, headed in their direction.

Quinn gently set the horrible box down, feeling the sobs tear from his insides like razor blades. He ran down the hallway in a desperate sprint, plowing through the squad of MPs that appeared suddenly at the top of the stairs.

"Follow him!" Stryker ordered one of the privates, the directive really saying *I don't know where he's going or what just happened, but he may need help*! Then the ex-Green Beret rushed down the hallway to

Apartment thirty two, his men trailing behind him. One private nearly slipped in all the blood spread across the open doorway.

"My God," Stryker muttered, as he gazed down on Lan, still on her knees, shivering, holding her hands out away from her body. Blood dripped from her fingers onto the hacked-off arm lying in the box. She stared straight ahead, at the opposite wall, not comprehending their arrival. A door opened behind Stryker, and the neighbors looked out, gasped, then slammed the door shut again. In the distance, a siren wailed its lonely, mournful song.

Quinn took the stairs five and six at a time. Midway down the last flight, he stumbled, badly spraining an ankle. The MP private was immediately behind him, helping him up, but he resisted and broke free to continue down to the ground floor, pain lancing up through his leg with each footfall.

Outside the front doors, he skidded to a stop, chest heaving, lungs ready to burst. Sergeant Richards and Private Nilmes, in civilian clothes, were detaining a young Vietnamese boy, shoeshine box slung over his shoulder. The youth was jabbering in rapid Vietnamese, and pointing down the street. In the distance, taillights faded in the mist as tires squealed and a car sped away.

"There's a checkpoint down that direction!" Richards motioned Nilmes over toward their Jeep radio, a few feet away. "Get on the horn and tell them to hold onto all sedans for us!"

Then he slid his handcuffs from a pouch on his belt and secured the boy to a wire grille covering a ground floor apartment window.

"Come on, Mr. Quinn!" Nilmes yelled, as the two Decoy MPs jumped into the Jeep and the engine was fired up. "Maybe we can catch his ass!"

Quinn ran for the Jeep as it pulled away, glancing up over his shoulder when a window grated open and Stryker leaned out a third-floor hallway opening, a questioning look on his face.

"Get someone down here to keep an eye on that little hoodlum!" Richards called up to him. And then they disappeared in a cloud of smoking rubber, exhaust fumes, and flying dirt.

9.

Storm Clouds Looming On the Horizon

Lan had recovered somewhat.

She knelt in front of the parakeet's cage, her hand partially through the tiny opening, unmoving. She was trying to get the bird used to its presence. Her eyes worked at coaxing him onto a forefinger.

Quinn stood on the balcony, hands clenching its railing. He stared at the rain falling in the distance. Overhead, the burning sun beat down on him, unimpressed with the show taking place on the horizon.

"Soon I will have him dancing on my forefinger," Lan said proudly before whistling a soft song to the parakeet. Dropping its head to one side, the bird listened intently for several seconds, then chirped back uncertainly, bringing a bright smile to Lan's lips. She was to the point where she could speak in front of Tieng Sam without frightening him.

"I love the clouds that float over Saigon," Quinn

whispered in awe from the balcony. Lan was not sure if he was talking to her, or himself. "They shoot straight up, jagged at the edges — like great white cliffs."

"Come say hello to Sam." She began worrying about him again. He was at his worst when left alone out on the balcony.

"You should see them from the air." He ignored her, though his words remained polite. "Descending down through them is like entering a fairy-tale land — it's so beautiful."

"I have never been in a plane, Robert," Lan said.

"From the air, they look like castles. Giant castles, built to protect the cloud dwellers." His expression took on that faraway look again as he watched heat lightning crackle in the distance.

"Protect them from what?" Lan slowly closed the bamboo cage door and glided to his slide.

"From the dragons," he snapped, shocked that she would ask such a foolish question.

"A storm is brewing." She watched the dark wall of clouds move across the edge of the city, dropping sheets of rain in its wake. A collage of shifting rainbows formed, vanished, then appeared again, only to be devoured once more. By the dragons.

A cool breeze swirled up through the balcony railing, lifting Lan's skirt to her thighs, and she pulled a shawl tightly around her shoulders. "Come inside, Robert," she said. "You will catch a cold."

Quinn returned his gaze to the black-and-purple horizon. Two gunships lifted off from Tan Son Nhut, several miles away, climbed the skyline, and abruptly disappeared into the advancing cloud-bank. "I think I love the rain even more than the clouds," he decided, a grin forming. "Perhaps someday, after I retire, I might open up a bar on Tu Do street. How does that sound, Xuan?" He glanced back over his shoulder at Lan, not even realizing which name he had used. "I could name it the Monsoon nightclub, hang glittering streamers from the ceiling and fill the corners with plants, the walls with vines. Make it look like a genuine rain forest!"

Lan returned to the living room and sat down on a chair. She watched him silently for several moments, but did not say anything in response to his off-the-cuff remarks about making her the "head hostess." She listened to him giggle then apologize — something about the job title must have been disrespectful.

She glanced at the front door and felt a shiver rush through her as she flashed back to the bloody box three days earlier. She looked down at her hands and sighed, relieved. They were not coated in blood.

She lifted her eyes to take in the balcony entrance, and the man standing out there. Why did she stay with him? He was on the edge — was today sounding like he might have taken that last step off.

Her loyalty surely had nothing to do with love. Or lust. He never held her passionately. At night, she slept on the harsh rattan sofa.

Lan bit at a fingernail and pulled her hand away, scolding herself for staying. But she could not leave him. Without her, he would destroy himself. The grief would kill him. She had never seen a man —

American *or* Vietnamese—so dedicated to his family.

They never caught whoever was in the speeding sedan two nights earlier. They knew in their gut it was Boardchek, or someone he hired to drive the shoeshine boy to Nguyen Cong Tru street, but the driver made good his escape.

The Vietnamese youth produced a five-dollar bill a "white devil" had paid him to deliver the box. He later picked Boardchek's mugshot out of a photo lineup. But he could not lead investigators to the escaped convict's safehouse—the boy steadfastly claimed the bald man had cornered him in a back alley off Tu Do and threatened to cut off his privates with a pair of gleaming scissors if he didn't accept the task. And the kid eagerly took the job. You didn't see five dollars until you spit-shined an awful lot of combat boots. The *canh-sats* still had him locked up in an isolation cell. For protective custody more than further questioning.

CID agent Christiansen had removed the blood-soaked box from the doorway before Richards brought Quinn back to his apartment. After assuring him his co-workers at Division Office were doing everything possible to bring Boardchek to justice, the stocky, red-haired investigator handed a bracelet over to him.

Christiansen had worked hard at removing the blood stains from it, but small specks still remained here and there when Quinn returned from the brief chase down the block. "It's against the book, as you know," he had whispered so none of the MPs standing around could overhear, "but after we got all the photos we needed, I removed it. I knew you would want it at home, where it belonged, and not stored away in some dark, moldy evidence locker."

Composed of thin, tightly wrapped strands of Vietnamese gold, the bracelet had two tiny bells and a small heart-shaped locket attached to it. He had given it to Lien at her fourth birthday party. Quinn still remembered the event fondly, with moist eyes. All her little girlfriends had arrived bearing stuffed animals and baskets of food, but she had enjoyed the bracelet the most. It was her first article of jewelry. He would never forget the way she hugged him around the neck, rubbing her nose against his cheek without touching her lips to him — a Vietnamese-style kiss. He could still hear her affectionately breathing in his fragrance — Lien loved the Old Spice aftershave lotion. Xuan had scolded her once for pouring an entire bottle over herself. Mang collected the empty containers — he liked the ships on them.

Quinn had turned away from Christiansen without thanking the man. He staggered into his bedroom, clutching the damaged bracelet, and shut the door. He didn't come out for two days.

Lan patiently waited in the living room, expecting the shot at any moment, but it never came to that.

Afternoon drifted into dusk, car headlights began their evening pattern of zigzags through glowing haze, three flights below, gunships on the edge of the city began their routine flare-dropping duties, stars appeared where storm clouds had loomed on the horizon, and Robert Quinn remained on his balcony surveying it all, silent, unmoving, a sculpture in frustration and helplessness.

Lan waited patiently for more words from him, but the only sound she heard was the constant crackle of codes and military jargon from the MP radio he had installed in the bedroom, and the honks from traffic in the street below.

She rose to prepare them a meal—knowing full well he would sit at the table and just stare down at it instead of eating anything—when the faint cry of a distant siren reached her ears.

Saigon was a constant hum of warning signals and human emotion, but she paused when she heard this particular wail. She was to the point where she could distinguish between MP and fire sirens, ambulances too—even between those on the military police Jeeps and their Vietnamese counterparts. An MP patrol was slowly growing closer, engine straining to a roar as it swerved in and out of the heavy traffic congesting Nguyen Cong Tru.

She thought her heart would stop when the vehicle skidded up in front of their building. She started toward the balcony, but Quinn flew past her, knocking her aside as he dashed out the front door and into the hallway.

Lan ran into the bedroom, grabbed his shoulder holster and service weapon off the nightstand, then started for the stairs after him.

When she caught up to Quinn, he was beside Sergeant Stryker's MP Jeep in front of the main entrance to the compound's courtyard. The big NCO's partner reached for his .45 when he spotted the Vietnamese woman in the tight hot pants and loose, swinging halter top running up with a holstered pistol, but Stryker motioned him to back down. Lan slid up and handed the CID agent his automatic.

"I think you better come down to the docks with us," Stryker was telling the investigator. "Nothing positive, mind you—and it doesn't look good—but I thought you'd better be there to see for yourself when they get it out."

"Get it out!" Quinn leaned forward nose-to-nose with Stryker. "What the hell do you mean 'Get it out!'"

Lan also moved nearer to hear the details, but the two uniformed MPs were urging Quinn into the back of the patrol unit, and then they were pulling away in a deafening squeal, leaving her behind in a cloud of burnt rubber.

Disheartened—she had slammed the apartment door shut, and Quinn had yet to give her a key—Lan sat down on the steps to the front entrance, frowning, and watched the speeding Jeep, its red roof lights throwing bright beams through the misty gloom, fade into the night.

Her narrow, almond eyes shifted to a bright star hanging on the horizon, and she wished him well. Thunder suddenly rumbled overhead, and a heavy sheet of monsoon rain dropped into her painful world, saturating the entire block within seconds.

Penniless, with no place to go, she just sat in the rain. Water soaked her hair to her features, accenting her high cheek bones and dark eyes. Her full breasts shone through the halter top, nipples erect from the cold. Her shapely legs trembled as a fierce

207

wind swept down between the leaning tenements across the street, and she wrapped her arms around her knees, weathering the fury of the storm.

A cab driver pulled up to the curb, ten feet away, and, smiling, motioned her closer as he opened the passenger side door. His hand stroked an erection that was in plain view.

Lan flipped him the finger and dropped her forehead to her knees, ignoring him. The cabbie muttered a choice obscenity in rapid, disappointed Vietnamese, and sped away, never noticing her tears for all the raindrops on her face.

Quinn felt his hopes crumble as the MP Jeep pulled up to the Saigon docks. Stryker had not said anything during the high-speed, Code-3 trip—he was too busy driving. His partner—a newbie rook with shiny new fatigues and too little time in-country to even be allowed behind the wheel yet—stared straight ahead the entire time.

A dozen other patrol Jeeps cluttered one ramp where a fishing boat was docked. Twenty military policemen were gathered around the rear of the vessel, where workmen were trying to free a tangled net from a propeller.

"Oh God," Quinn sighed as he jumped from the Jeep, releasing a lungful of air he had been holding for an eternity without realizing it. "Oh my God, no."

"Got it!" a Vietnamese dockhand announced cheerfully, smiling ear-to-ear, as he jerked the last of the net from beneath the water.

Faces grim, the MPs rushed toward the seaweed-covered object that splashed forth and bounced across the wooden planks of the loading ramp.

"No!" Quinn screamed as an MP private unwrapped the thick green strands and little Lien's savagely tortured body—its arms and legs brutally hacked off—rolled to a stop in front of the investigator's boot. Several soldiers rushed to restrain him, but Quinn flung them aside and dropped to one knee beside the mutilated corpse. Stryker raised a hand, holding the surprised men back.

"The gods in heaven!" he cried, as he raised his baby in shaking hands. Her face was covered with burn marks and unrecognizable. A water buffalo's torn and shredded scrotum had been stuffed into her tiny mouth, making her cheeks bulge grotesquely. *Why?"* Quinn ripped it out and threw it to the side, incensed.

His .45 automatic dropped from its unfastened holster and clattered across the loose planks of the dock but did not discharge. The noise of metal sliding against wood reminded Stryker of a demonstration a drill sergeant had once given back at The School. *"This here .45 pistol packs a punch. It'll take a man's arm off."* Stryker stared down at Lien's bloody torso, caked with river-bottom slime. *"But it's also the safest weapon you'll carry. So long as you keep this here safety in place."* And the DI had flipped the thumb safety on and threw the pistol across the floor after chambering a live round into it. The recruits had watched in awe as the .45 bounced off the far wall of the classroom without discharging.

Another siren wound down as an ambulance pulled up to the dock, and several of the men turned around to glance at it. Stryker contemplated waving it off, but he didn't.

"Maybe it's somebody else." A young private stared down at the touching scene as Quinn, on both knees now, rocked back and forth slowly, his child clutched to his heart, sobbing silently. "Maybe it's not Mr. Quinn's kid at all."

"There's floaters turning up in the Saigon River every day, Sarge," another MP agreed quickly.

But Stryker just nodded his head slowly from side to side and turned to stare at the swiftly moving river, sampans loaded down with goods destined for the open market gliding past on it. "It's her," he sighed, dropping his eyes for a private moment of silence. "It's little Quinn Thi Lien."

Lightning spider-webbed through the black night beyond Tim Bryant's bungalow window and Stryker stared at the haunting show for several seconds before moving across the room to Quinn's side, whiskey bottle in hand. "Have another." He poured the dazed American his fifth shot.

"Nice to have the old lady away for a while," Bryant mused as he stared at the porno film flashing against one wall of the dark living room. He regretted making the remark the second it came out. *Quinn's* wife might never make it back. But he kept talking, hoping additional words would smooth over the error. "Lets us men get down to some real raunchy entertainment." The sound of the Swedish flesh flick was turned down. Suggestive music from a sensuous Khanh Ly blared from a cassette tape player.

Bryant's wife, Hue Chean, had left town a few days earlier to visit her sick grandmother in Vung Tau. She was due back in the morning, and Bryant had decided one last choir practice before the "tyrant," as he lovingly called her, returned was warranted. Additional troopers were due to arrive as soon as relief shift got off.

Quinn was not watching the movie. Instead, he stared into his liquor, searching for something. Stryker watched him closely, wondering if perhaps Bryant's decision to show a confiscated X-rated movie at the spur of the moment was a mistake. The CID agent didn't need to watch a blond whore with a size-forty chest get lubed by five well-endowed lumberjacks and a collie that looked like Lassie. But the investigator had been intoxicated ever since they dragged him away from the morgue, complaining about police procedure and a postponed funeral because the evidence had to be preserved until this whole mess was settled. Thomas saw to it the man was drunk long before he reached Bryant's bungalow. Stryker doubted he could see three feet in front of his face.

"Can you believe the gall of that sonofabitch?" Quinn waved a hand out at them, slurring his words. Bryant was sure he was talking about Boardchek, but he wasn't. "My fucking honcho down at the office had my heels locked in front of his lousy desk just yesterday, the ball-less bastard! 'Quinn, you gotta get your ass into gear! Quinn, you can't let this hostage business get you down—ya got cases to solve. You're my best damned investigator! Quinn, I got bomb devices turning up left and right and no suspect behind bars—I can't spare you at a time like this! Quinn this, and Quinn that!' "

"Did he give you a promotion as an incentive to fucking forget your family is missing?" Thomas was beginning to feel the effects of the alcohol also. Stryker shot him an irritated glare.

"Fuck no!" Quinn produced the first half smile of the evening. "This ain't the Air Force, lad! We're in the ever-lovin' Green Machine!"

"Tell me about it," Bryant muttered.

Quinn's expression softened as he tried to focus on Tim's face, perched atop a swaying body on the other side of a coffee table littered with booze and stale pretzels. "I want to thank you for letting me unload on you guys like this," he said. "I feel like a goddamned fool, the way things have gone down to this point." Quinn paused for a moment, cleared his throat, downed the last of his drink, then continued. "I want to apologize for crying like a baby a half million times since my Xuan and Mang and Lien disappeared." He barely got Lien's name out as sobs fought to rise from his chest through his throat. "But . . . I . . . never . . . knew . . . I . . . loved them so . . . much."

"Hey, don't worry about it." Bryant got up, stumbled around the coffee table, and sat back down beside his friend. He stared down at the teakwood floor as he draped an arm around Quinn's shoulder, and his eyes found a ghost of a stain from where his own unborn child had died so many months ago. His mind froze as memories rushed back at him as he saw Hue Chean lying there in a pool of blood, clutching her swollen belly, legs drawn up to her breasts in the fetal position.

"But men aren't supposed to cry." He successfully kept the tears in. "Especially cops."

"Now look." Bryant shook the depressing vision from his head and downed the last of his own glass. His eyes came to rest on Thomas but what he saw was Anthony standing in the doorway several more feet away months earlier, a smoking .45 in his hand, eyes wide in terror, mouth agape, unable to speak. "You and me been buddies a long time. This town's one mean sonofabitch, Bob. Sometimes it goes after you personally—with a vengeance."

"Saigon's a *lady*!" Thomas raised a whiskey bottle to his lips, kept it there for several seconds, then tipped over backwards out of his chair and blacked out face-down on the floor.

"Sometimes the city becomes too much for the best of us to handle." Bryant ignored Thomas's antics and glanced at Stryker for moral support.

"Right," the ex-Green Beret said, nodding solemnly, drifting back to another time, another place. "Vietnam's a bitch in heat, Quinn. People like you and me—we come here accidently and decide to stay because we like what we see: the constant storms, the feisty women, the food, the climate, the action and excitement of a big city at war, seething with elbows and assholes. Everyone and his mother packs a piece and you never know when your number's gonna come up."

"When your ticket's going to be cancelled," Bryant agreed.

"When your pecker's gonna rot away and fall off!" Thomas rose up on one elbow, saluted with a clenched, defiant fist, then collapsed again.

Stryker glanced at him, nodded in resignation with a tired frown, then said, "People like you and me are cursed, Quinn. We're too stupid to leave here after our first tour and return to a normal life back in The World. No, we gotta be gluttons for punishment. Masochists, if you will. We see all this death and destruction and suffering every day and we grow accustomed to it, hardened—like the sharp edge of a fine survival knife. The constant turmoil becomes addictive. We receive cards and letters from buddies who have rotated to vacation or resort duty in Europe or the states, and they try coaxing us into joining them, but there's something about us, something deep in our gut which we got no control over that makes us stay. And those of us that *do* break through the spell and flee aboard that freedom bird find that they've been forever changed. They're never the same. They return to The World and all they can think about is the Nam. Those are the guys who, when they're *here*, talk about nothing but their round-eyed cunts stateside, suckin' on cucumbers, waitin' for them to get home to Mama! But they're never the same, Bobby-baby. They take back a souvenir with them, some little chunk of jade from Tu Do street, or a dried VC ear from the Central Highlands—any fucking little memento—and the ghosts of Vietnam follow them home, pal, haunting their souls forever."

214

"I knew this dude who was *really* pussy-whipped," said Bryant, pouring them all another round and belching loudly with applause as the cassette came to an end. "Some red-headed rich bitch back in Memphis or somewheres. Ragged him about dropping out of college, ragged him about getting drafted instead of running with his tail between his legs to Canada, ragged him about getting laid-off from a factory job two weeks after his discharge and their honeymoon, ragged him about re-enlisting when he couldn't find another job, ragged him for leaving her behind when Uncle Sammy sent him to the Nam for a second tour, ragged his silly ass ragged!"

"What happened?" Quinn sat up in his chair slightly, curious about the outcome.

"They met in Honolulu on his R&R, she started raggin' him about his short hair and the unexplained interruption of monthly allotments from his paycheck."

"What did the wimp do?"

"Punched her lights out, returned to Saigon on the next flight, and married his Vietnamese lover."

"Saigon'll do that to you," Stryker muttered.

"Whatever happened to them?" Quinn rubbed at bloodshot eyes.

"A VC rocket took out their bungalow in Gia Dinh back in '65," Bryant revealed somberly.

"Bummer," muttered Stryker. "Numba ten dream come true."

"A mishap of the worst degree," Bryant concluded.

A phantom jet swooped low above the rooftops

215

overhead, rattling the windowpanes as the men allotted memories of the unnamed couple a moment of silence, then Stryker threw his glass against the opposite wall, smashing it into a shower of sparkling pieces.

"Fuckin-*A*!" Quinn tossed his after it in reply. It bounced off a tapestry of a tiny Vietnamese girl playing on the back of a swamp-bound water buffalo without breaking and rolled across the floor, striking Thomas in the nose.

"You guys are bums," Bryant protested their table manners quietly.

"I had this rook ridin' around with me yesterday." Stryker scratched at the bullet hole scar in his left ear lobe. "And I notice the kid is always scribblin' shit down in a pocket notebook after each call we respond to. Well, at first I don't think much about it—first tour's a learning experience, right? Let the newbie take as much notes as he wants.

"But then I notice he's jottin' crap down after bar checks, and when we stop at an open air cafe for Short-7, and when we park down at Le Loi Square to observe the prostitutes trying to reel in a catch." Bryant winced at the choice of words, but Quinn didn't seem to notice.

"So I ask the dumb-fuck, 'Why the hell you always writing in your little diary there, sweety? You're not keepin' notes on Sgt. Mark Stryker's bad habits are ya?' The kid just stares back at me with this innocent, naive expression, and I say, 'The men are startin' to worry about you and your flair for writing. You're making them real nervous.'

"And he says to me, '*Ha!* No sweat, Sarge! I'm just writing about my experiences with the 716th, just all about Saigon.'

" 'A journal?' I say. 'Sort of,' he says. 'A . . . street diary, if you wish. Yeah, a journal, I guess. This place is powerful, Sarge,' he tells me, like I don't already have my own suspicions, you know? He says, 'It's the most intense city I've ever been in.' "

"Kids these days," Quinn laughed sarcastically, imitating the same thing adults had said in front of him for so many years.

"Yeah." Stryker wiped beads of sweat from his chin and glanced up at the ceiling fan. It was twirling lazily but didn't seem to be accomplishing anything except to bully the heat from one side of the apartment to the other. "He says, 'But some-day it's all gonna be gone, Sarge. I can feel it. And I wanna remember. I wanna remember Saigon, Sarge. People aren't gonna be able to come here, not like us, not like we have. But my kid or my grandkid — or my folks, if I don't make it back except in a box — can read about it.' The boy slammed the journal shut in my face when I tried to steal a glance. 'That's the magic of books, Sarge,' he tells me. 'You can take people places they couldn't ordinarily travel — lands they can't buy a plane ticket to. And I guarantee you, Sarge. Someday this place is gonna wash down the sewer. It can't last. Paradise never lasts, Sarge — I read that somewhere in one of my books. The good times always come to an end. It never remains the same, and you can't live in the past. It'll kill

217

you.' "

"Fuck," Bryant muttered, suddenly depressed.

" 'I hope you're wrong, son,' I tell him. 'I pray to Buddha and all the gods in the rain forest that you're wrong.' He just laughs in my face — respectablelike, mind you, but laughter mocking me just the same. 'See what I mean, Sarge?' he says. 'Listen to yourself! You're so into this place, you believe in the fucking goblins that roam the jungle. I love it!' he tells me. 'I wanna capture that flavor, that attitude, on paper. You're the last of a dying breed,' the little runt had the gall to tell me." Stryker flexed a powerful bicep muscle for both of them to see.

" 'It's all gonna change forever someday, Sarge,' he tells me. 'There's no business like show business, but the show can't go on forever in Saigon. Just look at the history of the region. Look where the land is headed. Look at the Vietnamese themselves! Someday the commies are gonna take over, and they're gonna bayonet all the whores and all the embassy workers and all the shoeshine boys up the yin-yang, and men like you who hope to spend the remainder of their lives here *are* gonna end up doing just that. The VC are gonna lop off your rebellious, stubborn heads in a public execution at Le Loi Square. The commies are gonna run the Arvins into the ground,' he tells me. 'Gonna run them into the ground till you can't hear the pitter patter of little feet, the Arvin army in full retreat no more! They're gonna invade Tu Do itself, Sarge. Gonna rename the city Stalinville or Marxtown or something. It's all gonna change, Sarge — I

218

guarantee it. I'm not happy about what I'm saying, don't get me wrong—I'm just telling you like it is. Someday you and me and all foreigners are gonna be cast out of Vietnam. We probably don't belong here anyway. And after tempers cool down, maybe the guys from the photojournalism units can come back on a tourist visa or something to see the Ho Chi Minh trail, but the natives won't let 'em stay, Sarge. You'll be able to return to Vietnam for a visit. But you won't ever be able to go back.' "

Bryant and Quinn sat in silence after Stryker finished his story. They stared without blinking as frames of light flashed across the wall from the projector—the movie had ended long ago, but their eyes saw a private little film that would remain with them, sharp and painful, the rest of their lives.

Through the open window, from somewhere down the alley, tender music drifted in, reaching each of them at a different volume, a separate level. Judy Garland was singing *"Over the Rainbow."*

It was still raining when the MP patrol dropped Robert Quinn off in front of his apartment building.

He entered the courtyard gate without turning to wave the soldiers a farewell, and he never noticed the young Vietnamese boys crowding the building's double doors, hands held out silently, expecting the usual wrapper of bubblegum, or five-dong coin. "Cheap Charlie," one of them muttered after him. Quinn didn't hear the words either.

He acknowledged Lan's presence in the third floor hallway with a slight, bewildered nod, then entered his apartment after motioning her in.

Frowning, she headed straight for the bathroom to freshen up.

"How long have you been waiting?" he finally asked after walking out onto the balcony, exhibiting the first sign of concern in his tone.

"Well, I surely haven't been waiting for *you*!" Lan reappeared, towel drying her damp hair. She had the sniffles too. "In all the excitement, I locked myself out yesterday. You never have provided me with a key yet, you know."

"And I've no plans to at this point in time," Quinn revealed matter-of-factly as he stared out at the retreating storm clouds.

"Your gratitude overwhelms me," she said sarcastically, stopping beside the bird cage to confront him in an angry stance, feet braced apart. But when he failed to return her challenge, Lan immediately softened. "I heard talk from the women in the building here," she said. "I'm sorry about little Lien, Robert."

But Quinn replied as if he hadn't heard a word she said. "I can't give you a key, because Xuan and the children will be returning home soon." He finally turned to face her. "And how would *that* look?"

Lan's eyes fell to the ground. She would not be able to take much more of this without breaking down in front of him.

A knock came at the door, and both of them

winced noticeably. Neither made a move to answer it at first, and when the second series of knocks came, the CID agent drew his .45 from its hiding place in the hollowed-out Buffy elephant and stepped past her, reaching for the knob.

A Vietnamese mailman stood outside, an impatient look in his eyes as he struggled to balance several small boxes on a clipboard. His expression changed slightly when he saw the tall American standing in the doorway. "Please hold!" He slid the pile across Quinn's outstretched arms and expertly retrieved the clipboard from beneath it, eager to practice his English. He didn't seem to notice the pistol pointing at him, but only kept nodding up and down eagerly.

"What the hell are all these?" Quinn exploded in rapid Vietnamese. "I didn't order anything!" Behind him, Lan was backing away apprehensively, lips hidden by the tips of her fingers.

The postman frowned with disappointment at the sudden switch of languages and Quinn's inability to get all the tonal syllables correct. "Only *one* for you." He stuck with English, trying to give the American a subtle hint.

"Maybe a . . . Care package from home," Lan suggested, moving back to his side.

Quinn nodded his head from side to side—*those* had stopped coming during his second tour 365.

"Sign here, please." The postman displayed the clipboard to Quinn. Arms full, instead of protesting, he turned and poured the boxes into Lan's arms. She felt a sickening chill sweep through her, but there was no stream of escaping blood like before.

Quinn scribbled his signature across the sheet of paper and handed the clipboard back. The mailman retrieved all his packages except one, somehow tipped his hat to the couple, and backed down the corridor, smiling an ear-to-ear, toothy goodbye.

Quinn closed the door softly and examined the box. It was the size of a large toothpaste container, and was wrapped with brown paper. A string had been tied neatly around it. "Who is it from?" Lan asked, backing away again when Quinn didn't immediately open it.

"There's no return address on it," he said, biting his lower lip.

"Throw it away," Lan snapped, sounding irrational for the first time since Quinn had met her. "Just toss it out the window!"

Instead, the investigator slipped a fingernail into the seal and tore through tape until one side unfolded.

Lan's open hand went to her heart when she heard his sudden gasp. Quinn staggered backwards and dropped the box onto the floor. A woman's severed finger rolled out across the cool teakwood, coming to rest at Lan's feet.

10.

Concrete Beat

Stryker paused as he passed through the double line of half a hundred parked military police jeeps on his way to briefing. A harsh, metallic clacking noise seemed to be coming from inside several of the vehicles.

Hand on the butt of his holstered pistol, he returned to a duty officer's unit, and spotted the dim green light glowing immediately. Someone had left the radio in the back seat on.

The strange clacking noise echoed through the night again, and he smiled, recognizing the sound. His hand dropped from his service weapon. Someone, off in the distant confines of his concrete beat, was bored with the rare moment of inaction on the street — so he was passing the time by forcing the loop of one handcuff across its steel teeth over and over, inches from the radio microphone.

An acknowledging burst of siren yelp from some

MP on the same frequency would no doubt soon follow.

Aware he was frowning now, Stryker ignored a fleet of gunships passing by overhead, and glanced instead at a display of brilliant heat lightning off in the distance. When the silver bolts ceased for a moment, he saw the last of a starburst cluster plummet to earth. By then he was at the stairwell leading up to the briefing room in the rear of the International, and he started up it without pausing to watch the string of flares die out.

Fifty enlisted men were already assembled for guardmount. An NCO had instructed them to form up for inspection. Five neat rows of ten men each greeted Stryker as he entered the room. The white letters on their black helmets glowing at him faintly, every trooper held out his .45, barrel pointed toward the ceiling and slide locked back—ready for the worst.

Folding his arms across his chest, Stryker surveyed their boots. Spit-shined toes gleamed back at him. So much time wasted on muscle work, he decided, visually checking each man's web belt brass. I turned in a suggestion we go to patent leather and chrome months ago, but wouldn't you know it ended up in a File 13 somewhere?

"Take your seats, gentlemen." He smiled broadly. "There'll be no uniform inspection tonight." About half the MPs bent over and grabbed ahold of their buttocks. Stryker's eyes rolled toward the ceiling. "Your *other* seats!" he clarified the directive, not in the mood for any Thomas-led shenanigans.

The men all sat down obediently.

Stryker stared down at them from behind his podium, eyes roving from soldier to soldier, trying to discern what was to come next. Trying to gauge the evening's attitudes. The front row always seemed to be filled with members of the Decoy Squad (he believed they relished the nightly opportunities to find fault with items of interest he brought up at the briefings). The second and third rows of metal folding chairs were usually filled with rookies still in their first month with the 716th, or fresh over from the Camp Alpha in-processing center at Tan Son Nhut airport. In the back of the room sat the vets. Sometimes cocky, often silent—mere observers to the proceedings. Faces grim, hardened, cold. Often leaning back in their seats, eyes closed, bored with the routine of guardmount—eager to hit the streets and dust another *cao boi*. Their eyes—when they were opened—identified them, even to the layman not familiar with the goings-on in old Saigontown. These men lived only for the body count. Each new night was a fresh challenge to go out and *"get some."* Yet, in this case, the game could only be found on sniper row. And the prize was a VC skull.

Stryker tried to remember when his own priorities in life had shifted gears. When had he lost that desire to go out and help people in need? When had the game suddenly become death stats and broken nightsticks? When had the contest become a chase that was judged on who could waste the most bad guys, be the first on-scene to fire the first shots, return the most smoke?

"Hey, *Mark*!" a husky voice boomed from the corner shadows in the back of the room.

225

Stryker rose up on tiptoes and leaned forward, squinting in an attempt to find the owner, but it wasn't necessary—he'd recognize that drawl anywhere. "Why, *Cob!*" He glanced down at his clipboard. "How the hell are you? The old war wound healing up alright?"

Sergeant Carmosino displayed an arm cast that was decorated with signatures in multiple shades of blue and red magic marker. "The clowns at PMO, in their infinite wisdom—" several of the men cleared their throat over that one—"have sentenced me to a month or two light duty on The Desk but I'll be *watching* the way you run things around here, Mister ex-Special Forces." Someone on the other side of the room began whistling Barry Sadler's "Ballad of the Green Berets," and a whole row of rooks applauded.

Stryker couldn't decide who was being sarcastic, and who wasn't. "Anyway, Mark," Carmosino continued, "got a serious question for you before we get into the boring crap like stakeouts and hot sheets."

"Get it over with." Stryker rocked back on his heels, ready for the worst. Carmosino's Italian medallion sparkled beneath a flash of bright teeth.

"So tell me, *honcho-san*, what do the Mafia and a juicy pussy have in common?"

Stryker frowned, nodding his head from side to side in resignation. "I thought you had a legitimate question, Cob," he said. "Christ, fine example you're settin' for the rooks fresh over from Camp Alpha."

"What *do* the Mafia and a juicy pussy have in common?" Thomas stood up, interrupting Stryker. "I just gotta know!"

Sauntering up through the rows of chairs, he said,

"One slip of the tongue, and you're in deep shit!"

The room fell suddenly silent and a paper airplane shot across the room, missing the recuperating sergeant's nose by inches. Carmosino retreated to the back of the room, still smiling.

"So what's the latest on Quinn's situation?" an MP in the second row asked, a serious expression on his face that told Stryker he wasn't amused by Carmosino's antics. The kid looked Italian, Stryker decided.

"We've turned the city inside out. We've rousted all the child molesters on file, and called in our best snitches. Quinn himself just briefed me on the primary suspect—" Stryker scratched at the stubble on his chin—"and, gentlemen, use a lotta code zero if ya come across him, 'cause we're dealin' with a real bad dude here."

"*He's* dealing with a bunch o' bad dudes!" Bryant stood and flexed a powerful arm muscle.

Stryker pulled the cover off a box containing several hundred BOLO flyers, leaned down, and inhaled for the benefit of the men in the front row who had taken to wrinkling their noses. "Ink's still wet," he announced, handing the first dozen Wanted posters down to the closest men. "Name's Marlon Boardchek, guys. Memorize the mug—he's the asshole we're looking for. He's the one who's got Quinn's family."

"I can't understand what all the hoopla's about," a teenaged private in the middle of the room turned and said to his partner.

"Huh?" The Spec. 4 beside him paused from shining his chromed web belt to look up at the baby face. The customized buckle read: SAT CONG!—

227

SORRY 'BOUT THAT!

"I just don't see what the big deal is about some missing dinks! Everybody's makin' this kidnapping into a circus. They're blowin' it all out of proportion, I'm tellin' ya."

"Well, I guess it depends on your vantage point, amigo. Were they your kids or mine, we'd probably feel a lot different about it. Someday you'll ETS out of the Green Machine like everybody else, and settle down and raise a family and get you a decent job and—"

"Now there you go sounding like that goddamned foreign correspondent who's always hangin' around down at the MACV annex!"

"Huh?" the Spec. 4 resumed polishing his belt buckle, but formed a bewildered expression across his features anyway.

"That jerk from UPI or AP or ASS or wherever he's from had the gall to come up to me yesterday— and I was on my coffee break, no less—"

"Aren't you always?" the specialist grinned and polished harder without looking up.

"And I ask him for some ID, real politelike, OK? And he tells me, 'When you gonna go out and get a respectable job?' P.O.'d me to the max, I'm tellin' you. So I think about stickin' his butt, but I decide to launch into a little conversation with the prick and he says, 'Bet you're countin' your days and markin' your short-timer's calendar till you turn into a single digit midget, right?' "

"They all ask that one."

"And I tell him I'm seriously considering extending for another 365, OK?" His partner didn't seem in the least bit surprised. "And he says I must be dumber than I look, 'cause there's no money in a soldier's career. Well, I about bust a nut by now. I unload on the fucker with both barrels, you know? Shit, I'm content, OK? That's what I tell him. Why the hell do I want to be rich? All I ever hear is: Get out there and make a lot of money! Well, hell—you go out and ask them big wigs in their skyscrapers and nine-to-five drag, what's it all really amount to? Christ, they'll tell you it don't matter that they're stuck in a rut and get both migraines and ulcers trying to pull in those big bucks. I've heard it a thousand times. They wanna make a better place for their children. They don't want their kids to have to struggle month to month like *they* had to."

"Yeah, you got a point there. I've heard that a couple times myself," his partner admitted.

"Me? I hate kids."

"You 'hate' them?" The Spec. 4 paused again and looked up, his attention diverted.

"I despise the little creeps. They shit in diapers and smell the place up. They wake you up in the middle of the night and cry till sunrise. You spend a fortune buyin' 'em clothes only to have 'em grow out of 'em quicker than an annual stat report. *Then* they turn into asshole teenagers, and you gotta worry about 'em gettin' into drugs if they're boys, and gettin' knocked up if they're girls. Just don't seem worth it, to me, OK? I mean, I got a fuckin' right to my own fuckin' opinion, right?"

The Spec. 4 broke into another grin. He considered making a comment about his partner's current age, and contemplated asking the kid if he was speaking from personal experience, but he just resumed polishing his belt buckle silently.

Sergeant Stryker tapped the podium with his nightstick. "Awright, OK," he muttered. "Let's knock off the chatter and get back to business." He checked his clipboard and placed an "X" beside a line halfway down from the top. "Who handled that Ten-3 out on Le Van Duyet last night?" He shuffled some long papers about, searching for a TC report.

"Guilty!" A lone hand shot up in the back of the room. Stryker leaned forward slightly, but couldn't make out a face for the sea of helmets.

"Well, you're going to have to do it over again, sport."

A groan drifted forth as the hand sank. "I put in three extra hours just drawing the damn diagram, Sarge," the trooper complained.

Stryker seemed to reconsider. "OK," he said finally. "The diagram's no problem. But you gotta change the classification. This wasn't no auto-pedestrian crash, pal."

"It wasn't?" The MP stood up this time, a genuine look of concern on his face.

"Nope, dope. The real owner of the car that was parked alongside the road came forth this morning. The dude that got crushed to death when he was under the hood of his 'disabled sedan' and a drunk truckdriver drifted off the edge of the roadway and smashed into him head-on was not the driver of the vehicle."

"I don't think I get your point, Sarge." The man scratched at a thick mustache.

"That reminds me." Stryker zeroed in on the man's

230

upper lip. "Trim that womb-broom, soldier. Rumor-control has it that the first sergeant is planning a surprise inspection sometime this week, and I don't want needless gigs on this shift—do I make myself clear?"

The MP nodded, and someone behind him called out, "Get back to the head-on!"

"Oh, right." Stryker didn't seem the least bit disturbed by the EM's demand—on the street he considered them all street cops and equal to himself or the other NCOs. "Well, it turns out the dude who got squished under two and a half tons of speeding metal was a *cao boi*, gentlemen. He was in the process of stealing a battery from beneath the hood when fate dropped its karate chop on his ass."

The room erupted into applause and laughter. Several men volunteered to do the report over for the accident investigator but he declined their offers of help and took his seat. Stryker returned their smile. Stories like this were what kept the men happy, kept them on that tightrope overlooking the pit of depression. The jokes they were all now telling helped ease the stress of the street. Stryker fell silent, giving them their moment of disrespect to the dead. He knew all too well the mood never lasted for long. Here, in the bowels of the Headquarters complex, they were safe. They were, as Thomas would put it, on their own turf. But it all changed once they started out the doorway to their Jeeps. The city lay in wait for them. It was a no man's land out there. And Lady Saigon went out of her way to rain on your parade.

When Stryker remained quiet for several more seconds, a few of the men stood up and headed for the exit, thinking the briefing over. He banged his nightstick against the podium again, catching their attention, and motioned them to return to their seats. "Not quite," he said, turning the clipboard around for all to see. "We're only halfway down, I'm afraid.

"OK, animal carcasses . . . "

"Animal carcasses?" several MPs responded.

"An unknown subject seems to be prowling around Pershing Field and the MACV annex wasting four-legged critters on night shift. I'm talking dogs here, gentlemen. Rovers of the Vietnamese persuasion. Montagnarde mongrels—whatever. I want you to keep an eye out for him. The ambassador's afraid his poodle might be next. But let's not go gettin' trigger happy or—"

"You talking' about all the mutts turnin' up 'deceased' on graveyard shift, Sarge?" a young corporal in the middle of the room spoke up.

Irritated, Stryker stopped in midsentence, stared down at the man for a moment, then said, "Do I stutter, lizard-lips?"

The corporal, embarrassed, blushed cherry red and seemed to roll his head from shoulder to shoulder. "Heck, Sergeant Stryker," he said. "That's just Moorhouser out dustin' some dink dogs. Some four-legged whore gave Bear the doggy clap or something, and now he's pissed at all the mutts in Saigon."

Stryker seemed to consider what had just been told him, then decided not to respond. Tilting his head to one side in an effort to suppress the laugh he felt coming on, he cleared his throat and went on to another subject. "Malaria pills, guys. Some of you

232

are not taking them like you're supposed to. Am I correct?"

Several men snorted in reply, but nobody spoke up. It seemed to be universally agreed upon by all soldiers that malaria pills were good for nothing but loose bowels. "Rumor-control has it we can expect another urinalysis test sometime this week!" a man in the back of the room stated as he bent down behind the man in front of him so as not to be recognized.

"If you aren't shootin' dope into your system or smokin' pot, you got nothing to be worried about," Stryker said matter-of-factly. Several of the rooks in the three first rows nodded their helmets in agreement.

But Thomas stood up. "That ain't the point, Sarge. We're *MP*s, for Christsake. *Cops!* They don't have no right roustin' us with these surprise pecker-pulls trying to find junkies."

"We got no dopers in the 716th!" another man added.

"It's downright degrading," Thomas said. "We put in twelve and eighteen hours a day or night enforcing law and order in Sin City, *puttin' our fucking lives on the line!* And them medic assholes and that righteous major from HHC got the gall to wake me up at four in the morning to piss in their pot!"

"Nobody said this was an R&R port, Ants," Stryker lowered his voice apologetically.

"If ya ain't smokin' it, ya got nothing to worry about." Bryant grabbed onto his web belt and pulled Thomas back down into his chair. "Now shut the fuck up, OK?"

"Radio procedure." Stryker marked off another

233

line on his clipboard. "On the way in here this evening, I overheard some conversation on the WACO net that left a lot to be desired. So let's knock off the crapola, OK? Consider this fair warning: If I recognize anyone who's using profanity or improper codes on the air, it's automatic Article-15 time. Got that?"

The room grew deathly silent. Everyone was guilty of that one time or other.

Stryker examined the ten remaining subjects on his clipboard. Then he glanced at his watch. *Never enough time*, he decided, pulling the paper free and wadding it up. A paper airplane floated up through the muggy air amid applause, missing his nose by inches.

Just as he was about to dismiss them, the rear doors to the room swung open, and Lieutenant Slipka appeared, leading two NCOs and ten privates inside. "At ease! At ease!" The officer motioned the men to remain in their seats before anyone could call the room to attention.

The shiny new fabric of the arriving soldiers' green jungle fatigues immediately marked them as newbies, fresh off the flight from the states. "Bunch o' F.N.G.'s," someone muttered as the lieutenant led the group up toward the front of the room.

"Are we tardy for briefing?" Slipka seemed surprised, checking his watch. He frowned, the minute hand already giving him an answer. "Running late tonight, I see." He frowned in Stryker's direction.

But the ex-Green Beret was visually inspecting the NCOs Slipka had brought with him. One looked vaguely familiar. "Is that you, Pruett?" He stepped down from his podium and offered a handshake to a tall, stocky man with dark, close-cropped hair, and a clean-shaven face.

"Well if it ain't ol' Marky-Malarky!" Pruett's right boot slid forward several feet while his left remained in place, and just as it looked like he was going to execute a "split" drop, he sprung forward, accordion fashion, hand also extended. His Alabama accent brought a smile to the faces of several nearby soldiers who instantly recognized him from a TDY assignment a few short weeks ago.

The two sergeants took hold of each other's fists and tried to outshake the other. Stryker slapped him on back, but failed to knock Pruett off balance. "Well what the bujeegers brings you to South Vietnam?" the ex-Green Beret flashed an ear-to-ear greeting. "Did the Chinese reclaim Korea or something?"

Pruett's smile faded somewhat but he managed to wink at the man in front of him. "My heart skips a beat when you mention the Land of the Morning Calm, buddy." The men all around them crowded closer. "But someday I'll return!"

"Famous last words." Stryker's smile brightened, sensing Pruett was not just here on another temporary duty assignment.

"Not for at least 365 long, hot ones," a private in the tight ring joked, and Stryker motioned the enlisted men back.

"Make way, make way," he said, clearing a path through the green, gold and black arm bands with massive opened fists. "If the Lou's got nothing more for you, hit the bricks! You all fashion yourselves such notorious crimebusters, then get out there and

235

prove it! First one to bag a rooftop *cao boi* gets a six-pack . . . on Raunchy Raul!"

Pruett glanced around, but Schultz didn't seem to be close by to defend himself or negate the wager. His eyes shifted to the lieutenant with blond hair and blue-tint prescription sunglasses.

"I've got nothing for these girls," Slipka admitted wearily. "But some of you NCOs hang around a minute so I can pair the new men off with you. Show 'em the town for a couple hours, but have 'em back here for midnight chow—they've been on their feet all day!"

Pruett joined Stryker out on the veranda overlooking the line of MP jeeps, and they watched as the men performed preventive maintenance and spot checks on their vehicles before heading for their beats downtown. Two V-100 Assault tanks, loaded down with dusty, grim-looking, gun-toting short-timers, rumbled into the compound from Fort Hustler, and several of the senior MPs waved at Pruett. "Welcome back to the Nam, John!" One tank commander, Greenlee, flipped him the thumbs-up. "Here to stay this time, or just back on your thirty-day leave?" The men clustered around the small-statured, jovial Greenlee and laughed along as they clutched the armored vehicle's sweat-slick handholds, and the V-100 was gone before Pruett could yell an answer.

Stryker watched as fifty-some patrol Jeeps came to life, engines roaring as "the cobwebs were blown out." Nearly a hundred red roof lights began twirling lazily as the men checked their emergency equipment. "Pretty sight, ain't it?" Stryker sighed, feigning something bordering on sexual arousal which Pruett couldn't quite pin down.

Stryker glanced over at him when he didn't immediately respond. Pruett looked like he was waiting for something more, and when the troopers all hit their sirens for a short burst, he too exhaled. "An inspiring scene of orgasmic proportions," he whispered, and both men laughed. One after another, the Jeeps began pulling out of their slots on the stone-covered parking lot, and headed for the main gate in front of the heavily fortified International.

"So really, John." Stryker ran thick fingers back through hair that was already soaked from the tropical humidity, and replaced his helmet. "What's your story? Did you bring your wife along with you or what?"

"Aw, some jizz-for-brains major got the ass 'cause I dusted a congressman's doper son back in Seoul, and here I am—the latest career move in a more than illustrious chain of events beyond my control. Thought I'd recon the joint a bit before bringing Kwang-Im over. They say Saigon's no place for wives."

"*Who* said?" Stryker looked amused. "You can take that two ways, I guess. Anyway, your girl'd fit right in here, pal—trust me. We'll line you up with a hooch downtown, show you all the right places to eat, where the markets at—the whole nine yards. I'm sure the guys'll chip in so you can send her a plane ticket. *She'll love it here!*"

"Well, I'm not so sure." Pruett looked somewhat apprehensive. "Don't you people get a lot of rocket attacks around here?" He glanced over at the charred and blackened tenements rising up behind the International.

"Hell, John." Stryker's smile brightened. "It adds spice to your life! Ask Bryant's wife! Ask Quinn's!" But his smile suddenly faded, and he seemed a different person as his expression changed from joyful to tragic.

"What the fuck, over?" Pruett sensed something was terribly wrong.

Stryker bit his lower lip, fighting back the tide of anxiety that always swept in over him when he thought about Xuan. He never saw her face, though, in his thoughts. He saw Lai's, the woman he had lost so long ago. He saw Lai being held captive by Boardchek, and he wondered why. "We'll talk about it later." Stryker motioned him toward the steps that led down to the Jeeps. Pruett's face erupted into an anxious grin again. It was obvious he was being invited for a little tour of the bricks. The in-processing crap could wait.

One of the privates, late for the guardmount and now running behind schedule as far as relieving a static post was concerned, rushed past Stryker, flak jacket, M-16 rifle, steel pot, helmet liner and five bandoliers of clips piled atop extended arms. The sergeant grabbed a handful of shirt, and the teenaged MP sprang back like an accordion without dropping any of his gear. He turned to face Stryker with an angry grimace, but when he recognized the ex-Green Beret, fear glazed his eyes and he swallowed so hard Pruett's smile brightened with admiration. "Yes, sir?" The youth's voice cracked slightly.

Stryker's grin fell into a frown. He never intended to intimidate his men by his size. It bothered him that some of the younger soldiers were so awed by his reputation. "It's *sergeant*, Clementi, not *sir*! Got that, troop? I *work* for a living!"

"Yes, sir . . . I mean *sergeant*!" The E2-with-no-time-in-grade swallowed again, and Pruett almost laughed out loud, but he suppressed the chuckled because he firmly believed you didn't make a man lose face in front of others. It eroded his respect for his superiors.

Stryker punched the private softly on the shoulder and, with his chin, motioned the kid to continue down to his patrol unit. "And Clementi!" He had second thoughts.

The private skidded to a stop again. "Yes, Sarge?"

"Keep in mind what was said in there about radio procedure, OK? I seem to recall some shit last night in the wee hours just about predawn."

"Wasn't *me,* Sarge!" Clementi's chest puffed out and he got defensive without losing the fear in his eyes. But it was obvious he knew *exactly* what Stryker was talking about.

"Something about 'beaming up to the Enterprise now.' "

"I think you're referring to something The Uke might o' said, Sarge."

"No, Clementi, I don't think so." Stryker folded his arms across his chest and rippled the muscles wrapping around his wrists for the slender private's benefit. Clementi swallowed again, and attempted to sidestep the reprimand.

"What's Sergeant Schell's major gripe, anyway, sir? We gots to unwind now and then, you know. Sometimes a little unauthorized chatter on channel two is enough to brighten my spirits and keep me goin' the last six hours of the shift. What can I say 'cept *sorry 'bout that*, OK?" The kid cocked an eyebrow at the two towering NCOs, prepared for the worst.

Stryker's countenance softened with the admission of guilt, even though it came out more as a plea of *nolo contendre*. "Aw, Schell's OK, Clementi. You gotta cut the guy some slack, bic? He's from the old school of broadcasting. Get my drift? His sense of humor is on an entirely different plain. A separate frequency from our own."

"Well . . . " Clementi seemed to contemplate what Stryker was trying to get across.

"You just don't know Schell like I do, pal. You gotta understand how the man ticks inside. He's the kinda dude who puts on the winning candidate's bumper sticker *after* the presidential election, OK?" This time Pruett *did* allow a chuckle to escape. "He's real careful about everything he does. He don't take no chances with his career. Can you blame him?"

"He's got a good rep," Pruett added. "And he's got an obligation to the Corps to protect it. Hell, we've heard of Schell clear over in the R.O.K."

"So get out there and hit the bricks." Stryker patted the soldier on the back and gently pushed him back in the direction of the stairs. "Make me some felony arrests or something."

The private nodded, little enthusiasm in the gesture, and started to leave.

"And Clementi!" Stryker added. "Tell The Uke to shape up, too, or his ass is grass and I'm the power mower!"

240

A blacked-out Jeep with two sergeants inside rolled up beneath the veranda without Stryker noticing it, but the sudden siren yelp sent both him and Pruett jumping backward as if a cobra had just appeared between their boots. "Stryker!" Carmosino called out. Beside him, Raunchy Raul Schultz was laughing loudly. "You gotta keep your guard up, *troop*! We coulda been a fuckin' old VC *mama-san* intent on liberatin' your loins or something!"

"Schultz!" Stryker ignored Cob Carmosino. "What's that peckerhead doing in one of my MP Jeeps? He can't be out on the street with that cast on!"

"Hey, Mark!" Carmosino ignored him and cut Schultz off just as he was about to explain he was only taking the injured NCO downtown to his hooch. "What did the blind man say as he was passing the fish market down on Tu Do street?"

Stryker's eyes bored into Schultz, but Raunchy Raul could only lift his hands, palms up, in resignation.

"Good morning, ladies!" Carmosino gave Stryker only a second to answer the riddle, and then they were off, two taillights fading in the mist.

"That fucking Carmosino," Stryker muttered, but there was no mistaking the brotherly affection in his voice.

"Quite a card," Pruett remarked, as they started down the steps to the long line of patrol Jeeps.

A unit with two grim-looking eighteen-year-olds aboard slowly cruised by, and he whipped a semiformal salute on them. They nodded without smiling, and Pruett shook his head, remembering his own

241

first years in uniform and the invincibility that came with them. "Self-proclaimed super cops," he whispered.

"Legends on their own mind," Stryker replied just as softly, his words not meant to be insulting but just an observation.

As they passed, Stryker could hear the dispatcher's voice crackling over the radio receiver. "It's now twenty-four-hundred hours, ladies, and martial law curfew arrives in Sin City. So snuggled up to your *manoi*, sit back, relax, and listen, because this is WACO, the hottest station in the nation."

Stryker's frown returned and he pulled out his pocket notebook and scribbled something down in it.

Private Clementi drove by with his partner, an expression midway between don't-look-at-me and I-told-you-so plastered above his smirk, but Stryker didn't look up from his notebook.

"Sergeant Schell must have called in sick tonight." Pruett smiled.

Stryker elbowed him in the side. "Whose side you on, anyway?" It would be a first. Schell hadn't been ill a day in the last twenty years.

"Always an EM at heart." His smile remained intact.

They watched the chaplain's jeep cruise past, PRAYBOY emblazoned across both sides above a gleaming silver crucifix. Both sergeants saluted, received the somber, uniformed priest's blessing in reply, then shook their heads after he was gone.

"Wonder where he's headed at this time of night." Pruett checked his watch.

"Probably down to Tu Do to salvage lost souls."

Stryker climbed into his unit and brought the powerful engine under the hood to life with a twist of the starter toggle. "Jump in," he said, as he unlocked the chain that ran between the steering wheel and brake pedal. He pulled a small, snub-nosed .38-caliber revolver from a pocket in his flak jacket and handed it across the stickshift to Pruett. "Confiscated it from Thomas again this evening," he laughed. "Don't expect no problems out there tonight—it's only Tuesday, you know. But you never *know* for sure."

Pruett gladly accepted the firearm, not bothering to mention the 9mm pistol that hung in a shoulder holster under his fatigue shirt.

Ten seconds hadn't passed since he flipped on the radio in the back seat when a broadcast erupted from its speakers. "Car Twelve, this is WACO. At the sampan docks off Bach Dang and Cuong De, see the QC's. They've got evidence at the scene relating to the Quinn case, over."

Stryker listened to Car Twelve acknowledge the call, as well as two cover units who opted to back him. Stryker reached down and activated the electronic sirens under the hood and sent the roof lights twirling, then headed toward the main gate. An MP wearing sunglasses despite the late hour waved him through with a smile, seemingly not bothered in the least by all the dust. Pruett waved as they screamed past. Prostitutes crowding against the meat-market grill threw kisses back, and one top-heavy whore pressed suddenly bared breasts against the protective screen until rigid nipples popped through the chicken wire.

"Did you see that?" Pruett's head whirled back

around for a second look, but the static post was already far behind them.

"Happens all the time." Stryker grinned proudly.

"I think I'm gonna like this place."

"Yeah." Stryker down-shifted back into second, enjoying the power under his hands as the straining motor protested loudly and the front end dropped slightly before accelerating.

They skidded onto Tran Hung Dao, heading northeast toward the traffic circle at Le Loi, and Pruett watched the tenements that rose up on both sides pass in a dizzying blur. Stryker was one hell of a driver!

"Feel it?" He grinned a death's-head flash of teeth across at Pruett. "Feel the swirl?"

"The 'swirl'?" Pruett's hands clutched to the metal strip around the bottom of his seat, and he hoped the sliver of steel that held it down wouldn't come loose.

"*Saigon!*" Stryker shifted into third as they roared down the middle of the street. He made the siren play music. "Feel her tits pressing down on us from above, John? Feel the intensity of her breath?"

Pruett glanced overhead, and the galaxies seemed to spin about as they turned down a side street on two wheels, taking a detour around a roadblock up ahead.

"I guess maybe it's the way the French built most of these streets so narrow!" he yelled above the noise racing along with them. A National Police Land Rover blocking the alleyway ahead rolled backwards to let them pass and a young, bored *canh-sat* fired a round into the air in salute of their fancy vehicle. Stryker flipped him the thumbs-up, smiling. Pruett glanced back over a shoulder, an unnerving feeling telling him

244

the next shot would be aimed at their backs, but then they were swerving out of the maze of side streets, back onto the main boulevard.

"I guess maybe it's because the streets are so narrow and the buildings so close together!" he repeated his theory. "The emotions generated by this place—*this land*. The emotions generated by these people—and that includes us, buddy—the emotions bounce around instead of escaping like they're supposed to. I guess that accounts for the swirl, know what I mean?"

Pruett gritted his teeth as they sped around the traffic circle on the wrong side. He was sure they were going to flip over this time, and when they didn't there was none of the usual relief flooding into him—just more adrenalin, as Stryker increased speed and slid onto Le Loi sideways before correcting his turn. *I must be getting too old for these fun and games*, Pruett decided sadly.

"Reminds me of the good old days," Stryker continued, mixing the hi-lo siren with the shrill whoops of the yelper. He didn't elaborate, but Pruett almost read his thoughts. "Everytime I make a hot run reminds me of the good old days."

Stryker was thinking about the nights he had ridden patrol with Reilly. They had always worked north together, near Tan Son Nhut, and when someone down south called for help, they would race balls-to-the-wind along Le Van Duyet at seventy klicks, the three a.m. crescent moon ever-watchful over their shoulders. Guns on their hips, a powerful souped-up motor under their hood, the warm breeze in their face and the flares in their eyes, Saigon was *theirs*!

"We used to race down Le Van Duyet," he finally

245

revealed. "There's places out there where it's like a lonely stretch of flat-out highway—and we used to speed down through it, our Jeep's engine sounding like it was ready to blow! You gotta see the lights from that vantage point, John! Zippin' Code-3 downhill, the smiling neon lights of Saigon fast approaching in the distance! It always reminds me of a horny woman, bud, beckoning me, welcoming me home, her thighs spread wide."

They screamed down Le Loi until it dead-ended at Don Dai, then turned east until they came to the slowly moving river. Sampans illuminated by dim lanterns floated far off from shore in the swollen current, and though the water itself was hard to make out in the darkness, the odor of the river was unmistakable.

They rounded another curve, and a dozen VNP units appeared down the road, their park lights blinking but roof beacons off. Stryker doused his own reds and killed the headlights as they coasted up to the scene.

"Don't look good," he muttered as they dismounted. One of the fishermen had found a brightly decorated Easter basket floating in the water. Stryker was confident there were no chocolate eggs or candy inside.

11.

How Many Men Did You Kill Today, Daddy?

CID agent Robert Quinn stood on his third-floor balcony, elbows against the railing, back to the city view. He stared in at Lan, thinking how beautiful she was, how much she reminded him of Xuan in their early days together, before they had married. Before she had born his children.

Quinn's eyes fell to Lan's firm, slender haunches as he watched her squat gracefully in front of the bird cage. Sam jumped eagerly onto her extended forefinger, and she slowly withdrew her hand, until the parakeet was outside its prison for the first time.

Tieng Sam stared about, wide-eyed, at the immensity of his new environment, and promptly alighted in a colorful burst of feathers, flying straight up into the ceiling. He bounced off, fell like a rock toward the floor—Lan rushing out to catch him, gasping—maneuvered into a smooth glide, then flapped his

247

wings again frantically and slammed into the nearest wall.

Quinn shook his head in resignation, and slowly walked in off the balcony, sliding the bug screen closed so the bird could not escape.

Lan rushed up to Tieng Sam, hands outstretched, whispering calm, soothing words to the bird in Vietnamese. He summoned another burst of energy and flew up over her, landing on top of the bamboo drapes covering the front window.

"Tsk, tsk, naughty parakeet!" she reprimanded him, hand outstretched as she rose on her tiptoes, but old Sam was having none of it. He skittered back out of her reach and screeched down at her, angry and confused. "*Robert!*" she called to him for help, unable to reach the bird.

"Leave him be." Quinn walked into the bedroom where Lien and Mang had slept and gently closed the door. "He'll find his way down when he gets hungry."

Frowning, Lan grabbed one of his old nightsticks from the closet and tried coaxing Sam aboard it with light, persuasive jabs to his bright blue belly, but the bird only pecked at the black club defiantly and deposited a small, round dropping onto the teakwood floor at her feet. "*Robert!*" she called out again.

Quinn was not listening. Not to anything from the real world around him anyway. He heard their voices instead. Mang's. Little Lien's. Playing on the floor at his feet with their toys. He looked down, ready to reach for them, and the laughter stopped suddenly, only faint echoes of Lien's innocent giggles lingering in the air.

Limping slightly from the sprained ankle, he moved toward the window and drew the blinds back. He thought he heard Xuan whispering to him in French, but when he turned around he found he was still alone. Painfully, desperately alone.

He glanced down at the open-air restaurant below the window, where he had met her face-to-face for the first time, where he had spoken to her over platters of rice and Vietnamese eggroll and steaming bowls of *pho* soup. Holding his hand up against the dusk of sunset, he thought he saw himself and Xuan sitting at one of the tables, but then a bus honking in the street below brought him out of it and he realized the chairs were empty.

Quinn walked over to a dresser and picked up the small five-by-seven picture of his two children, taken only a month ago. They wore party hats, bright colorful clothes, and a birthday cake with four candles glowing atop it sat on a smooth laquerwood tray in Lien's lap. She sat crosslegged in front of Mang, who was down on one knee, hugging her like only a brother could.

A tear rolled down his cheek, but Quinn didn't seem to notice. He was thinking back to when they first chose names for their children. Xuan had wanted American names. She spent an entire week one time, pouring over old MP rosters he kept in his souvenir chest, examining the different names, finally deciding on Melissa and Justin. But Quinn would have none of that. Even after she opted for Robert Jr., he shook his head adamantly and gave her a list of ten to choose from. And they finally decided on Mang and Lien. Mang, in honor of a much-respected emperor who had played an important role in the history of Xuan's family through the decades. And Lien, after a beautiful flower that was leafy and white, like a lily. It floated only on the most peaceful of ponds.

Once again, Mang and Lien appeared at his feet, playing with their toys. But this time no noise emanated from them, though they seemed to be slapping building blocks together with unusual zeal. No noise until their motions seemed to freeze, and Mang looked up at him, an innocent expression on his face and eyes sad as those of a pet left out in the rain. "How many bad guys did you kill today, Daddy?" his words flew up, striking him like bullets, and then their images shattered, like crumbling frames of mind, and vanished.

Shaken to the depths of his soul, Quinn staggered over to one of the twin beds and sat down on its edge, shaking his head at the pain in his heart. "Why?" The word left him as a sigh. Quinn held out his hands, bewildered, and stared up at the ceiling and heavens beyond. *"Why?"*

"Because you did not love us enough," Xuan's words returned to haunt him. He peered around the room, but she was nowhere to be seen.

They had found Mang's decapitated head the evening before. A fisherman located it floating down the Saigon river, in a brightly decorated Easter basket, complete with bows and ribbons. The child's ears had been cut off with scissors, and his eyes gouged out by a human thumb. Several of his teeth had been jerked out with a pair of pliers, and his nose had been hacked off with a straight razor. The block of meat left over was carefully wrapped in fancy paper and some old police reports — those that had been missing from Quinn's files.

Christiansen was attempting to determine if any of the papers were from old cases that might be even remotely connected with Boardchek, or provide some clues as to his present whereabouts, but they were all soaked through with blood, and his hopes weren't very high. An officer assigned to the morgue was trying to ascertain if the boy had been tortured while still alive, or if the skull had been desecrated after his murder. The head appeared to have been neatly severed from its neck with a single slice from an axe, machete or sword of some type. Stryker suggested they check to see if the madman had left young Mang's brain intact.

Quinn had not exploded into hysterics when Stryker brought him the tragic news. He just returned to his room and sat down on the bed, staring out beyond the balcony railing at something only he could see. Behind him, the eight red lights on his police radio alternately flashed on and off — left to right, left to right — as the memory scanned the different frequencies. Stryker decided he had known all along, had heard the riverfront call when it originally came out. He just didn't want to respond to the scene — no longer had the courage to see for himself.

Instead, he just waited alone in his little fortress of solitude for Stryker or his boys to bring him the bad news.

Quinn stared up at the wall plaque that held some of his medals. He thought about all the others he kept inside the footlocker, not wanting to flaunt the large number of decorations, and he remembered something Xuan once said when she encouraged him to display them all so the children would know how brave he was and what a true hero really looked like.

"Men have three faces, Robert," she told him. "The person they think they are, the person they project to others, and the person they truly are inside. Men have three faces they wear, Robert, but they only have one soul inside, and that's how women like me really judge them. Do not change the way you are, Robert. Let your children see you the way I do, and I assure you, they will not be disappointed."

Quinn thought back to the first time she had accepted his spur-of-the-moment invitation to dine with him at the open-air restaurant. Casting aside her friends' blunt and vocal disapproval as nonsense, she took the seat directly across from him and stared deep into his eyes throughout the five-course meal. "Your eyes are so beautiful," she had told him that evening, "so very serene and *peaceful*. So bright and blue, like the sky at midday when there are no clouds over the Delta. They are the kind of eyes I would like my child to have someday."

"You should see Stryker's," he had said in reply— deeming himself foolish immediately. Would she leave in search of him? But the words had continued to flow forth; he couldn't stop talking in front of her. "You should see Stryker's! They are green, green like the jungle, as green as the rain forest! But your eyes are beautiful too, my dear." He had reached across the table and took her hand in his, but Xuan had pulled free, frowning.

"But mine are brown," he could hear her protesting as clearly now as she had that evening so long ago. "Reilly say they show I full of shit all the time."

"No, no, no, my dear." He had waved her misconceptions aside like wisps of smoke from a joss stick. "Your eyes are beautiful! Beautiful like a . . . *Reilly*?" He had nearly spilled his cup of tea. "Is there no woman in Saigon who hasn't heard of Crazy Jeff?" he had asked incredulously.

"I no think so." Xuan's innocent reply had brought a laugh back to him.

And that was how they had hit it off. Back then, so long ago, during the rainy season.

And now the storm clouds seemed twice as menacing, though the sky outside was as clear and blue as the heavens watching over Mytho, down in the rice-paddy delta.

A vehicle passed by in the street below, and Quinn recognized the motor as that from a U.S. Army Jeep. He returned to the window and looked down, just in time to see an MP patrol cruise by. Bryant and Thomas sat in the front seat, arguing about something good-naturedly. He couldn't make out the words. Probably something about which club to check out next or which string of bargirls to roust for IDs and a flash of thigh.

That goofy Bryant. He smiled without realizing it and thought back to an incident two years earlier, when Quinn had brought some hot dogs home from the PX and told Xuan to fire-up the stove.

"No way!" She had taken a position in the archway to her kitchen, feet braced for business, arms folded over her breasts. "Nebbah happen!"

His jaw dropping, bewildered, Quinn had asked, "What the heck are you jabbering about now, woman?" and Xuan had gone on to tell him Tim's wife, Hue Chean, revealed that, according to Tim, hot dogs were boiled tiger penises. Loins from the lair that made him jungle tough! "Not in my kitchen!" She had waved a dough roller at him. "I no care if they donkey dicks or pony peckers—you *dinky-dau* MPs want to eat them, you order same-same at restaurant in the International! Not my house! Bookoo bad luck, Robert Quinn! Bookoo bad luck, *ching-ching*!"

"How 'bout wombat whangers?" he had asked seriously, and though she had no idea what a wombat was, Xuan promptly threw the roller at him, breaking one of the front windows.

Quinn pulled a photo album from the nightstand drawer and paged through it to his wedding pictures. Xuan's trusting, dedicated eyes looking up at him as they exchanged their vows brought tears to him again, and he couldn't find the strength to turn the page. The album folded between his legs and dropped to the floor.

He lay back on the bed, wanting their voices to return to him, but the room remained quiet. Even the traffic outside, and Lan trying to coax her parakeet back onto a finger, did not interfere with his fantasies.

Robert Quinn had no doubt in his mind that his wife was dead. Twice he had dreamed they found her face-down in some dark back alley off Tu Do, lying under a pile of garbage, naked, maggots wiggling in and out of holes they had burrowed along the edges of her eye sockets.

It was now the waiting stage of the game—torture he was all too aware of after years and years of watching the victims of crime suffer through its aftereffects.

Some of the photos had fallen out of the scrapbook, and his eyes locked onto one showing Xuan and he just before they exchanged the Vietnamese gold wedding bands in front of their witnesses.

The picture brought back a flood of memories, and he thought back to the night when she first accepted his marriage proposal.

Up to then most all of her words to him were childish and playful—sometimes even immature—but when he asked her the question, her smile had faded, and she held her hands out to him, palms up, in the traditional manner. Without even knowing how to properly respond, Quinn had placed his own atop hers. Their eyes met, seeming to scan each other's inner depths, searching their souls for truth, or something just as elusive. And then they withdrew their hands, ready to talk man to woman and woman to man. Lover to lover.

Harsh military police codes and street jargon reached Quinn's ears, and he instantly snapped out of the daze, leaving behind the fantasy world as easily as if he were stepping from a shower.

He crossed through the hallway to his own bedroom—ignoring Lan and her pet (she now had the parakeet back on a forefinger and was whispering soothingly at it, blowing cool, mint-flavored breath against the feathers around its beak).

"Uh, WACO, this is Car 36-Charlie," a young,

nervous voice broke through the static that always swept across the radio net at sunset. "We've got a, well, we've got a pretty gruesome discovery down here. Uh, we've got a —"

"Car 36-Charlie, what is your ten-fourteen, over?" Sergeant Schell's calm, unemotional voice was back in charge, after three lawless night shifts without him.

"In the alley off Duan Thi Diem, between Ho Xuan Huong and Phan Ding Phung, Sarge, over."

"Ten-24, Car 36-Charlie. Ten-13, what you've got at your fourteen there, over?"

"It's a head, WACO," the youth's voice cracked slightly with the announcement, and Quinn felt his face dropping down into rough, callused hands. "A woman's head. It was floatin' in the gutter, wrapped up in a CID evidence bag, Sarge. Some little kids found it clogging up a sewer drain, and they pulled it out by the hair! We saw 'em, sarge — laughin' and carryin' on. They thought they had a big, hairy rat or something for the dinner table. You shoulda' seen 'em beat feet outta here rikky-tik when they saw what they really had, over."

"Ten-24, Car 36-Charlie." For the first time since anyone could remember, Sergeant Schell's voice took on a somber, melancholy tone. "Secure the scene, and we'll get MPI rolling your way, over."

"That's a roger, WACO," the MP private at Ho Xuan Huong and Doan Thi Diem replied softly. "And you better have a unit swing by to pick up Mister Quinn."

Robert Quinn reached over and turned off the radio scanner. He pulled a photo of Xuan from his wallet and kissed it gently, then slid it into a shirt pocket close to his heart. He glanced across the room at a picture of Mang and Lien, and nodded slowly, wiping the tears from his eyes. Then he placed the cold barrel of the .45 pistol in his mouth and pulled back the hammer.

12.

Shout Into The Wind

Sgt. John Pruett wiped sweat from his brow with the edge of his fist, then clamped his free hand back on the steering wheel and resumed swerving in and out of the taxis and bicycles clogging Le Loi boulevard. Sheets of warm, blinding rain swept across his MP Jeep's windshield, and twice he nearly ran down pedestrians who darted out from between parked cars in their frantic attempts to escape the sudden downpour. Up ahead, a clear intersection was jammed without warning by a swarm of sputtering motorscooters when the signal lights changed.

"Damned Vietnamese cowboys!" he muttered as another block passed by without any trace of a street sign. On a whim, he turned left down a narrow back alley and soon caught the flash of red and blue lights up ahead — *such luck*! He had found the crime scene.

Pruett cut his siren, allowing his unit to roll up to the three other Jeeps silently, roof lights throwing strong crimson beams through the floating mist.

A young private came running up, but his confident smile crumbled when he recognized the new NCO from Korea, and he skidded to a halt. "Oh, I thought you were Sergeant Stryker, Sarge!" The youth didn't seem so sure of himself anymore.

"Stryker's with Richards and the Decoy Squad over on Nguyen Van Thoai." Pruett's eyes retained their humorous what-ya-got-for-me gleam. "Checking out another bomb call."

"Well, this ain't the first head I found floatin' in the gutter back down here, Sergeant Pruett—" the MP private forced his chest out slightly—"but it *is* the first one that was ever left in a CID evidence bag like that." He pointed to the decapitated head sitting on the hood of his Jeep, staring back at them, wide-eyed. The plastic bag was half full of blood, and the head was half submerged in it—the crimson line climbing to just above the woman's lips.

"Is she the one?" Pruett asked. "Quinn's woman?"

"You're asking the wrong soldier, Sarge!" The private grew defensive. "I don't mingle much with them CID boys. The only time any of us do is at crime scenes like this, or when we're being investigated for something we didn't do."

"But she does look vaguely familiar." Another MP had appeared in the rain beside the first.

"Vaguely?" Pruett stepped closer to the man. "What do you mean by that?" Then he started over toward the evidence bag.

"Well, she's got the looks of any of a hundred chicks that hang around the meat market, you know? The long hair and the high cheek bones and all that.

But really, Sarge—I've seen her around somewhere."

Pruett pulled a small kit from his web belt and laid it on the hood of the steaming Jeep as another patrol unit arrived behind them. He glanced over his shoulder, recognized Lieutenant Slipka in the haze of flashing lights, then proceeded to remove some forceps from the container. Using them, he gently lifted the evidence bag and turned it round and round in front of a Jeep headlight, checking to see if there was anything floating in the blood besides the woman's head. "Any witnesses?" he asked without looking up at the line cops.

"Just the little kids who found it, I guess," the first MP on-scene reported. "And they all beat feet when we pulled up, Sarge."

When Pruett finally did glance up, a dozen military policemen were crowded around him in a semicircle. Frowning, he peered up at the surrounding rooftops, hoping there were no snipers bearing down at them through cross-hairs just then. "Spread out and check with the residents." He pointed to several leaning tenements. "Somebody must have heard something, seen something." But his main interest was in scattering them. The way they were now, one grenade could take out the whole group.

"Any physical evidence to speak of?" Lieutenant Slipka had appeared behind all the helmets. He stared over at the drainage pipe that led down to the sewers and underground catacombs which crisscrossed beneath the city. There were stories of everything from Army deserters to thirty-foot cobras living in the dark down there.

"I'm pretty sure the decapitation occurred somewhere else," the MP private in charge of the crime scene declared. "Looks like a drive-by dump, sir. And any evidence that might have been abandoned here has surely been washed down into that sewer by the storm."

Slipka seemed to consider what the private said for a moment, slicked his thick blond hair back with wet fingers, then replaced his helmet liner and pocketed his blue-tint glasses after they became smeared with raindrops. "Seems like a pretty sound hypothesis to me," he said, reaching for the evidence bag.

"Does she ring a bell?" Pruett said coldly. He was still new to the 716th and hadn't made many friends yet. He could afford being frank.

Slipka frowned, glanced at his newest NCO, then back at the unblinking eyes inside the bag. "I know Xuan Quinn," he said confidently. "I've met her several times. But I've never met the woman *this* head belongs to in my life." He dropped the bag back onto the Jeep hood and the severed head sloshed about inside not unlike a container of fish being brought home from an aquarium shop.

"Then you don't want me to have CID respond out here?" Pruett pressed Slipka for an answer.

"Christiansen's over at the bombing scene, and the other agents are at a big-time murder-suicide up-town—some Marine major and his house-girl or something. We couldn't get a team down here before morning even if we wanted to. Just take some decent photos, have Clementi over there sketch you a crime scene diagram and get good measurements for it, *savy*?"

"OK, Lou." Pruett offered a semi-formal salute as

Slipka turned to leave.

The officer slid to a halt. "And don't call me *Lou*!" He raised his voice as a bolt of lightning lanced across the skies overhead and thunder clapped a split second later. "I hate it when you guys call me Lou!"

"OK, sir." Pruett offered another salute. "No disrespect intended. That's just what all the cops in New York City call their lieutenants. *Lou* is short for *lieu*tenant, get it?"

"Well, this ain't the fucking Big Apple, Sergeant!" Slipka held his hands up to emphasize the heat and humidity. Thunder applauded the show.

"You hit the nail on the head with that one, sir." Pruett finally dropped his hand when the lieutenant saluted and climbed back into his Jeep.

Slipka got behind the wheel and shifted into reverse, then backed up the alley without taking his eyes off Pruett's. The NCO from Korea nodded slightly as the officer left, conceding the slightest of defeats — neither man seemed offended. And Pruett actually respected the guy. It wasn't often you saw the duty officer touring around town without his own driver. And when the provost marshal insisted a private tag along with him, Slipka always made the trooper ride shotgun — it was his way of "maintaining control of the situation."

"I guess I get the honor of completing all the paper work, right?" The MP who had first greeted Pruett appeared at his side again.

"You the Numba one man on-scene?" He shifted into the local lingo.

"Guilty."

Pruett watched drops of rainwater collect on the

rim of his helmet and the bottom of his chin. "Then I guess the honor is all yours." He smiled. "But *I'll* book the evidence."

He grabbed the evidence bag with the woman's head inside and tossed it into the back seat of his Jeep. "You heard what the lieutenant said." He handed the private his Ft. Gordon Special—a 125 Instamatic. "You don't even have to focus. Do it like they taught you at The School. And make sure you talk to *all* the residents, friend. I want to see five dozen witness statements on my desk by EOW. Sound fair?"

The private seemed suddenly fired-up, eager to accept the challenge. "Got ya covered, honcho!" He pulled the camera from its protective cover and practically fondled it. No one had ever entrusted him with crime scene photos before—that was always left to MI or CID or MPI. Now someone was finally letting him do some *real* policework. And the kid was eating it up.

Pruett glanced about the narrow alleyway. Any investigation from this point onward was nothing but a waste of time, but the book called for it. And you never knew—it just might be connected to the Quinn case somehow.

"WACO to any unit the vicinity Nguyen Cong Tru, the seven hundred block—report of a suicidal subject barricaded at that one-four, third floor. Subject armed with numerous handguns."

Pruett bit his lower lip and started the Jeep, then made rubber burn as he threw the vehicle into reverse. Even though the exact numbers were not given, everyone who heard the broadcast knew exactly where the barricaded subject was at.

Robert Quinn's residence.

When he pulled up into narrow Nguyen Cong Tru street ten minutes later, over twenty other military police Jeeps were already there.

Mark Stryker and Gary Richards were holding back a beautiful young woman in the street in front of Quinn's apartment building. Some "short" MPs had taken up defensive positions behind concrete lampposts and a couple rumbling V-100's, but most just stood around Stryker, feeling no threat of danger from the CID agent holed-up inside the dwelling.

"Thought you had a bombing on your hands." Pruett strode up behind the two other sergeants.

Richards turned, recognized him, and grinned a greeting though he seemed nervous and irritated. "Another dummy device," he revealed. "This time the guy used insulating wire that just melted down when the right connections were made—couldn't carry the charge."

"Saved again by Lady Luck?"

"I doubt it," Richards groaned.

"That's what I thought." Pruett glanced at the jutting breasts of the woman they were trying to restrain. She wore only a loose sarong that was soaked from the rain, and her chest—nipples extended from the cold—bounced about wildly as she tried to break free.

"What about the call down off Doan Thi Diem?" Stryker turned to face him, careful not to release Lan. Raindrops formed on the tip of his nose.

"Well—" Pruett shrugged as the woman also locked eyes with him—"I don't know whose broad's head they found down there, but it wasn't Mr. Quinn's, fellas. What ya got goin' on here?"

"Tell him!" The woman strained against the man holding her, pointing up to the third floor of the apartment building. Tears filled her eyes. "Tell Robert his wife is not dead!" Thunder erupted overhead in a long, rolling crash that hurt the ears and made it seem like the structures around them shook in fear for a moment.

"How 'bout a sitrep?" Pruett's eyes rose from Lan's quivering breasts and turned to face Stryker.

"Quinn's got a third-floor apartment up there," the ex-Green Beret briefed him. "Room thirty-two. He's got himself an MP radio scanner—the whole bit: eight channels. The guy's been taking this thing with his family pretty hard. Who can blame him, really?"

"I think he's been holding onto the possibility Xuan was still alive," Richards added. "That something, some*one* could be salvaged from this tragedy."

"Bob's up there with his service weapon," Stryker continued. "Lan here walked in on him just as— according to her—he was about to blow his brains out. Quinn threw her out."

"He threw me out!" she echoed his words as lightning flashed in the distance.

"Now he won't answer the door in the hallway," Richards added, "And—"

"We've got movement on the balcony," a metallic voice announced over the radio speakers of two dozen patrol Jeeps.

The men around Stryker gazed up, and Robert

Quinn appeared in the archway leading from the master bedroom of his apartment. He was armed with pistols in both hands.

"Any shots fired prior to my arrival?" Pruett asked.

"Negative," Stryker muttered so softly only the NCO from Korea heard him. He moved closer to the building until he was almost directly under the balcony. As he expected, Quinn did not point either of the weapons at him but kept them at his sides, directed limply toward his bare feet.

Stryker sighed in relief. Had the CID agent drawn a bead on him, sharpshooters on separate rooftops across the street would have punched holes through both his eyes with hollow-point slugs.

"We got lots to talk about, Bobby." Stryker raised an open hand in friendship to the dazed investigator, but Quinn didn't seem to immediately see him.

"Go away, Mark," he finally said, waving the stocky MP sergeant back with his automatic.

"No, no, you don't understand, brother. What my men found downtown this evening had nothing to do with Xuan, OK? Nothing whatsoever."

"Don't fuck with me, Stryker!" Quinn's eyes sparkled like fire danced in them as he focused on the MP on the ground for the first time. "Don't go pulling none of your storybook bluffs!"

"Mark wouldn't bullshit ya, Mister Quinn." Tim Bryant had walked up beside Stryker. Anthony Thomas was right behind him. "You should know that by now!"

"And don't you clowns try no group therapy on me!" Quinn dropped one of his pistols and pointed a rigid forefinger down at them. "I'm a *pro* at this game, OK?" The .45 slid through the balcony railing, plummeted to earth, and bounced off the grassy slope without discharging. "I've talked down more hostage-takers and pulled in more attempt-suicides than all three of you have seen porno flicks put together, OK? So don't go tryin' none of your good-guy-bad-guy routine on me! I've been through it all before a hundred times. I'm CID, remember? The Sherlock Holmes of the Green Machine!"

"They're telling the truth, Mr. Quinn!" Pruett swallowed hard and stepped forward from the semicircle of uniformed MPs, into the limelight.

Quinn held a hand over one eye and squinted against the harsh street lights. "What? Who's that?"

"My name's John, Mr. Quinn. John Pruett, fresh over from the Land of the Morning Calm. E5, sir. Regular Army."

"Korea?" Quinn shifted about on the balcony slightly, but did not abandon his other gun.

"Yeah!" Pruett grabbed his cheeks with both hands and pulled. "Now would an ugly mug like this lie to ya?"

Quinn made no reply, but fell into a deep depression when he realized what a scene the stand off was making. Balconies across the street were lined with neighbors he had known for years. He wondered how many of them were hoping he'd blow his brains out. How many had already placed bets on the outcome of the crisis.

"I was there!" Pruett raised his voice slightly as a hot, sticky breeze swirled down through the buildings crowding Nguyen Cong Tru. "I saw the remains you

268

only heard about over the police radio. *I swear to you they did not belong to your wife!"*

Quinn could not see the men below him anymore for the rush of tears clouding his eyes were overpowering, and increasing gusts of wind struck him with stinging sheets of rain. "It's not fair!" he shouted back. "It's just not fair!" He knew things would never be the same. The MPs would never treat him like before after what was happening here tonight. *Life in Saigon* would not be the same without his family. The street would become so cold and impersonal— the risks so useless, such a waste, that he would not be able to justify the pain and the suffering anymore.

"Think it over, Bobby!" Stryker called up to him as, on the ground, Schultz and Farthing scurried past, heading for the stairwell. "There's no hurry! No hurry at all!"

"I love you guys!" Quinn yelled down at them, leaning over his balcony railing slightly. "I know you're sorry to see me go!"

Lightning flashed directly overhead, blinding even those who closed their eyes. And the thunder—in its peculiar Asian habit of embracing the earth with static as it rolled low by overhead—drummed even the thoughts out of many of the weaker men present.

"Of the troops and for the troops!" Stryker heard Quinn scream just before a pistol discharged and there came an explosion of splintering teakwood and bamboo.

When the lightning bolts finally subsided, Stryker glanced up to see Quinn struggling beneath three lanky MPs as Schultz, Farthing and Carmosino attempted to gently subdue him. None of the men appeared wounded.

Pruett had run back to his Jeep and retrieved the clear plastic evidence bag during all the commotion, and as a horrified gasp rose from the onlookers all around, he held the head up for Quinn to see. "You see? I told you, pal! It's not your wife, OK? It's not your wife at all."

"My God!" someone had grabbed his arm for a better look at the contents of the bag. *"My God!"* Tim Bryant fell to his knees, still clutching Pruett's wrist with both hands. Thunder rolled back across the heavens overhead, mocking him.

The severed head floating in the plastic bag of blood belonged to *Tim's* wife, Hue Chean.

13.

Deathstalker

"Watch out, Dong!"

The young shoeshine boy snatched his ten-year-old street partner from the path of the speeding vehicles in the nick of time.

Over a dozen military police Jeeps, lights flashing and sirens screaming, roared past their tiny stall on the curb in front of the Hotel Majestic.

"One two three, motherfuck MP!" The smaller of the two youths jumped down into the gutter after the last patrol unit slid by and directed an obscene gesture at the shiny black helmets. But dusty Nguyen Van Dong, a gleam of old memories in his eyes, merely sat down and brushed himself off.

"Nebbah mind," he said calmly. "No sweat."

The MP Jeeps swerved through a VNP checkpoint and skidded down a back alley that led to narrow Dau street. "Fucking round-eyes," the younger shoeshine boy muttered, taking a seat beside Dong.

"Someday I'm big enough to carry gun I become VC for suuure. Make 'em *di di mau* or die—all go back stateside, you bic?"

"They not *all* bad." Dong smiled, a shiver still in him from the close call. "Why I remember a time when . . ."

The younger boy pulled his knees up to his chin and wrapped his arms around his calves, then made as if listening attentively to his older cousin, while the whole time his ears followed the fading sirens, hoping to hear one of the MPs stack it up.

"Right there! That's the one!" Tim Bryant pointed his bungalow out to Pruett. Behind them, units loaded down with heavily armed night-watch troopers skidded up to the rear of his hooch. The mist drifting in from the canals took on a depressing crimson hue as the roof beams from all the vehicles sliced through it. Eyes appeared between bamboo slats of most of the dwellings on either side. Every American there had his hand on the butt of his firearm, even though this had been declared a friendly housing project years ago. You never knew. Declarations meant nothing in the City of Sorrows. Especially in the back alley slums behind the nightclub district of Tu Do.

"I thought she was out of town!" Stryker was shoulder to shoulder with Bryant as they rushed up the steps, pistols drawn.

"She *was*!" Bryant had a wild, cornered look in his eyes. "But she was due back this morning. And I been on these fucking double shifts now for three days because we're trying to nab this bomber creep!"

"Why Hue Chean?" Thomas was right behind them, an Ithica 12 gauge at port arms.

But then they were at the rear entrance to the bungalow. The door was shattered and hanging from the top hinge. Thomas chambered a round of double-aught-buck into his shotgun.

Left hand held up to silence the other MPs rushing up from over a dozen Jeeps, Stryker motioned Thomas inside with his right.

Bent over, the blond, muscular soldier rushed in, gun barrel fanning from left to right. Stryker was right behind him. Then, after the first two MPs in found cover, Pruett and Bryant entered, and all four men cleared the dwelling as a team.

The bungalow was a shambles. And it was abandoned. There was no sign of Xuan. Or Boardchek.

No blood anywhere, Stryker concluded, after they had searched the house from one end to the other. Bristling with raised M-16's, several MPs crowded both doorways, ready to assist. "Canvass the entire block!" Stryker directed. "I want every resident within a half mile interviewed! Radio for more units. I want a crime scene perimeter set up rikky-tik! And get a CID team over here ASAP! I want this whole place dusted for prints!"

"Maybe it wasn't him at all." Thomas confronted Stryker later, after the bungalow had been sealed off and Bryant was left alone to face his grief. "Maybe she was killed by some madman on the way to market or something. Maybe some crazy fuck had a hard-on for Tim—you know, some past arrest or something. And the asshole went after Hue Chean instead. Isn't that the way it always works, Sarge? Talk tough on the way to jail. But when you finally get out you only got balls enough to go after the cop's defenseless wife or—"

"Or worse," Pruett cut in. "His kids."

Stryker shook his head slowly from side to side. "No," he decided. "It was Boardchek. No one else is as obsessed with revenge as that bastard."

"Bryant and Quinn did hang around together a lot," Thomas recalled now. "Maybe the son of a bitch saw them double dating or something and decided to throw another twist into the investigation."

Stryker picked up a splinter of wood that had once been part of the door, and he examined the knuckle marks inches above the deadbolt. "Yeah." He decided to stay with his gut instincts. "It was Board-chek."

Lan knelt in front of Robert Quinn as he sat on the edge of the bed, contemplating what he had just done. His career was probably over, depending on how Stryker wrote up the report. Outside, the last MP patrol was pulling away.

The rain had stopped but the clouds beyond his balcony seemed even darker and heavier than before. Like they would *dump* on the Saigonese below at any moment.

He could feel their eyes pressing in on him too. His neighbors. The people outside his window who had watched him make a fool of himself. Sure, he was going through hell—but they wouldn't understand. Would they? Christ, this was Vietnam. Families disappeared in the night all the time. Wives lost husbands and fathers lost children every week. Yet when was the last time he had seen a Vietnamese go berserk on his balcony?

Beyond his balcony. He couldn't go out there now—not now. The place where he found his most comfort. His most relaxing hours. They would be watching. Waiting to see what he did next. *Stupid* dinky-dau *round-eye*. He knew they listened for a shot from his apartment. Children laughed down in the street below. Were they laughing about him? Or had another foolish American tried to speak their difficult language and gotten all the singsong vowels wrong again? Were they kids who had played with his son and daughter? Or did they even remember Mang and Lien? Probably not. He had overheard them laughing once about his family. Mang and Lien were just outcasts, ostracized from Saigon society by their peers. Why waste the time befriending them—they were just destined to disappear one day anyway, on their freedom flight back to The World.

Quinn pulled the snub-nosed .38 revolver from the hollowed-out Buffy elephant. *That crazy Thomas*, he laughed to himself. One of the MP sergeants had confiscated his service weapon and backup piece, but Ants had smuggled him a throw-down. Grinning, he had insisted Quinn take it. He couldn't see any cop friend of his being without an off-duty weapon. Especially with what the CID agent was going through right now. "We'll find her, Bob," Thomas had told him. "Keep your chin up. We'll find her. Times are tough right now. But this, too, will pass. Trust me. Time heals all wounds. Things can only get better."

Time heals all wounds, he sighed now, looking up to face Lan. *Except Vietnam.* He opened the revolver's blue steel cylinder and emptied its six hollowpoints. He felt like getting good and drunk, and it just wouldn't do to have a loaded weapon lying around. Booze was a depressant. Every cop worth his salt knew that.

"Let's go out." Lan smiled up at him. "To Maxim's, or the Rex cinema. How does that sound? I'll buy, Robert."

"You have no money," he said matter-of-factly.

"I'll borrow some." She winked up at him.

"I have to monitor the radio." He leaned back and checked the police scanner. "Hey!" he yelled. Only two of the eight channels were lighting up. "Who the fuck took my crystals out?"

Before Lan could admit or deny anything, the phone rang. Quinn tensed visibly.

"I'll answer it," she said softly, swallowing her fear. The telephone had become a symbol of tragedy. She hated the sight of it. "Hello?"

Lan launched into rapid-fire Vietnamese. Her eyes darted back and forth to Quinn's several times. The conversation lasted only a couple minutes, then she hung up the receiver and jumped to her feet.

"We must go!" she announced.

"Go?" Quinn started reloading his pistol frantically. Two of the cartridges slipped from his numb fingers, bounced across the teakwood floor, and rolled under the bed. "Go where?"

"They have come through for you, Robert!" She grabbed a rain jacket and his hand and began drag-

276

ging him toward the door. Quinn slammed the cylinder shut with only four bullets in it.

"Who has come through for me, Lan?"

"The Vietnamese people!" Her smile was genuine. "Someone who saw all the TV coverage of your plight also saw this bastard Boardchek tonight. Word travels fast in Saigon, love. My friends have come through 'in the nick of time'—is that how you say the expression? We now have the location of his safe house!"

Quinn rushed past her for the door. Several frightened tenants darted from their path as he dragged her down the stairwell toward his car.

"WACO, this is Blue Diamond-6!" Quinn all but screamed into his unit microphone as he swerved the scratched and dented o.d. green Pontiac in and out of motorscooters sputtering along Nguyen Cong Tru. "WACO, this is Blue Diamond-6. *Acknowledge!*"

Christ, he thought, slamming the Motorola console several times with his open palm, *have they tampered with this radio too*?

"Blue Diamond-6, this is WACO. *Is that you, Quinn?*"

"Let's dispense with the pleasantries for now, OK?" He pressed down on the transmit lever so hard his knuckles went white from the pressure. "I need some cover cars over at—"

Lightning crackled overhead and a loud pop emitted from the radio speaker, causing Lan to jump over in the seat closer to him. All the modern technology frightened her more than the storms.

Static claimed the net.

Quinn slapped the console several more times. "WACO, this is Blue Diamond-6," he pronounced the base station's call sign slowly so that it sounded like Wake-Ohhhhh, in hopes the extended transmission would break through all the electrical interference.

"Go ahead Blue Diamond-6. Repeat, ten-one-three your last."

"I need backup units to a house north of the intersection of Hai Ba Trung and Hien Vuong!"

There was a slight pause from the dispatcher at the International. Then, "That would put your smack dab in the middle of the Saigon cemetery, Blue Diamond-6. Confirm your last, over."

"*Negative!*" Quinn screamed into the mike as he swerved to the left, narrowly missing two shoeshine boys who had darted out from between some parked cars. "You're thinking of Pham Thanh Gian, WACO. Make it Hien Vuong, got that? Have 'em meet me north of Hien Vuong and Hai Ba Trung. There's a little alleyway that drops down into a housing project. Just have 'em stand by for me there. Two or three district cars oughta be enough."

There came another slight pause, as if the dispatcher was reconsidering, or checking his unit cards and log. "Uh, Blue Diamond-6, this is WACO. We already got several Mike Papa's at that location, uh . . ." The transmission broke unexpectedly. Then, "Suggest you avoid that area for the time being, over."

"Whatta ya mean, 'avoid it'?" Quinn yelled into the microphone. "Whatta ya mean, WACO?"

But no immediate reply was forthcoming. Quinn

hit the battered console several times with his fist out of frustration. "What the hell does he mean 'avoid the area'?" He turned to Lan after swerving through an unmanned roadblock. "What the fuck is going on?"

Lan screamed and brought her hands to her face. Her fingers were illuminated by yellow light, and when Quinn returned his attention to his driving, it was just in time to turn out of the path of an oncoming troop lorry. He lost control, and the sedan fishtailed, then spun around on the wet blacktop as the Vietnamese army truck roared past in the opposite direction, several cursing soldiers waving fists at them then cheering when the Pontiac slid backwards off the shoulder of the road, through a crater of mud, then down an embankment.

The rear fender of the agency car caught onto a protruding tangle of tamarind roots, and the vehicle flipped end over end two more times. Lan's screams mixed with the sound of shattering glass and the fading backfires of the Arvin truck.

"Lan!" He reached for her, grabbed onto her hips as the momentum hurled her body through the jagged shards of windshield glass. *"Lan!"*

The sedan slid down several more dozen yards on its top, Lan's upper torso wedged between the earth and the vehicle's crumpled roof.

"Lan!" He felt her straining thigh muscles go limp as he held onto her and the Pontiac dropped the last couple feet to the bottom of the ditch. Mud poured in through the broken windows on both sides.

The car rocked back and forth, then steadied as more mud filled its undercarriage.

Lan's body had been torn in half at the waist by the impact. Quinn fell back as the car shifted abruptly in its precarious position along the creek bed, and her lower torso flopped back in through the front window, down onto him. Quinn screamed as the blood and tubes and pelvic material gushed from the gaping cavity inside her hips, covering his face and hands.

He threw the slab of meat aside and clawed through the wave of mud filling the inside of the automobile. Yelling for strength, the adrenalin pumping its fight-or-flee juice through his system, Robert Quinn pulled himself from the wreckage moments before the unstable precipice beneath the car collapsed, and it tumbled further down the rocky gorge that overlooked the Saigon river.

Clinging to the same roots that had caused Lan's death, he glanced back down over a shoulder and watched the Pontiac, still on its top, slide down across a sheet of rock — leaving a wide, bloody smear behind.

Quinn froze for several minutes, trying to catch his breath. *What was going on here?* So many years of happiness and prosperity. Now a whole collage of demons and bad luck were coming together to attack him from all sides. *What had he done to deserve this?*

He felt large raindrops striking his face, and when he looked up at the dark, twilight sky, thunderclaps slapped down at him and a powerful downpour struck with all its fury. *Trying to wash me back down the ditch to my death!* he decided, growing defiant. *Trying to have the last laugh!*

"Well, it won't work, Lady Saigon—do you hear me, *cunt*?" He shook his fist at the storm clouds floating in overhead and summoned the last of his strength. "It won't fucking work!"

Quinn looked back one last time at the pool of blood that had been Lan, felt to make sure he still had his revolver, then pulled himself up out of the ditch just as lightning struck the tallest tree on the other side of the gulley.

An icy shiver shot down through him. Smoking and charred, the tamarind was going to crash down on him! End his life before he had a fighting chance. Snuff his soul out the way the crash had claimed poor Lan. *And maybe he deserved it!*

But, no, the tree fell the other way! The earth trembled in protest as it slammed against the rain-soaked ground.

An omen! he decided, gaining his footing and running uphill toward the roadway. *A sign!*

And investigator Robert Quinn sprinted toward the intersection of Hien Vuong and Hai Ba Trung with all his might, quite unaware lightning had destroyed ten other trees in Saigon that evening too.

Military policemen in rain ponchos and steel pots manned roadblocks surrounding the area Quinn was running toward. A private leveled his M-16 at the mud-caked figure rushing down the narrow roadway, but another soldier pushed the barrel up calmly before he could fire. "That's Mr. Quinn," the vet said. "Let the man through."

A huge V-100 Assault tank, steam rising from its

massive tractorlike tires, stood idling in front of a small house in the middle of the block. Two MPs manned swivel-mounted M-60 machine guns on the monster's turrets, and a long .50-caliber barrel hung down from the top and was pointed at a shattered window. Each time the red lights atop nearby patrol Jeeps rotated, the bright beams reflected off tall white letters emblazoned across the side of the track: MILITARY POLICE.

Quinn's eyes began to sting and he rubbed at them before realizing the neighborhood had clouds of floating teargas drifting through it. Their origin: the house sitting silent in front of the rumbling tank.

Quinn shook his head and contemplated rubbing his eyes a second time when he got nearer the perimeter of Reactionary Team troops and saw the menacing-looking battering ram one of the NCOs had rigged to the V-100.

"And mighty damned proud of it, too!" The sergeant they called Smitty folded his arms across his chest and spat at the ground as they prepared the tank for its assault on the house's heavily fortified entrance. Two privates standing in front of him grinned evilly as mechanics hastily tightened bolts and screws that had worked their way loose on the hectic ride over from Fort Hustler.

A long, steel pole — normally used to erect basketball hoops — had been soldered to a metal shield that slid over the tank's front hull. A cement-filled oil drum was bolted to the end of the pole, horizontally. It would do the ramming. On the front of the barrel someone had painted a skull and crossbones, and the words, SORRY CHARLIE!

"What's the situation, Sergeant Smithers?" Quinn slid up to them, panting and out of breath. Smitty gave him a surprised look, then launched into a condensed briefing.

"Got a tip about, oh, zero-nine ago—" He glanced at his black Rolex—"that the scumbucket you been looking for was hidin' in this here dump, Bob." He pointed to the small frame, one-story house with smoke rising from all four windows. "We surrounded it, and tried to sneak in at first, but it was closed up tighter than a Tahitian virgin's snatch—the fucker's got reinforced bars behind all the windows, *on the inside*." He emphasized their exact location. "And the doors are both layered plates of runway tarmac, so we brought the Brute in there." He motioned over to the battering-ram-equipped Assault tank.

"We brought out the bullhorns and all that," Smitty continued, "but got no answer, so we lobbed a couple of CS grenades in through the air holes along the ceiling. Just for laughs, of course."

But Quinn wasn't smiling. "He's gone, Sergeant. He's long gone."

"What?" Smithers rested his meaty hand on the butt of his holstered automatic.

"You can call in Arty, or bring a grunt tank down here and blow the walls down, but you won't find Boardchek. I *know* the son of a bitch, Sergeant! I know him inside-out, and if he was in there, you'd be fightin' one hellacious firefight right now, 'cause he's not the kind of maniac that'll surrender quietly when the heat's applied. Boardchek's in this one for the money, Sergeant. He plans on goin' out like a comet. Not a candle."

Sirens that had been growing louder in the distance were suddenly screaming right up to them, as two blue Air Force SP Jeeps raced down the block, strobes flashing.

"Well, if it ain't the sky cops," muttered Smitty. Specially trained attack dogs strained at their leashes in the back of the souped-up vehicles.

Quinn glanced down at the house some hundred feet away. He could see Stryker, Schultz and Richards's Decoy Squad taking up positions on either side of the front door in preparation for rushing through after the battering ram did its job.

He looked back at the Air Force policemen jumping out of their unit. Moorhouser was one of them. In his mid-twenties, he was of medium height and weight, but carried his chest out in such a proud manner bystanders couldn't help but be impressed. His brown hair was parted down the left and kept close-cropped on the sides — nearly to the extent of being whitewalls — but wavy on top. Always clean-shaven, with never a hair out of place, Quinn thought he looked more at home on a movie set than in a patrol Jeep. Moorhouser had seven medals for bravery in his packet. He was a good man to have on your side. *Good thinking*, Quinn nodded to himself, mentally commending Smithers. Calling in the dogs to track Boardchek was a great idea.

Two growling German shepherds bounded out after the air policemen. Bear and Shogan. Hungry for blood, and the loving pats of reward from their handlers that came afterwards. The dogs were Air Force property, but Moorhouser and his partner *owned* them.

284

Quinn nodded again as he locked eyes with Bear. They were friends—at least as far as he was concerned. When the animals were led past, Shogan snapped at the investigator before being quickly pulled away, but Bear paused to sniff at his knee, then lick his hand, until Moorhouser tugged on the leash, and he was gone.

The night suddenly came alive with the roar of the V-100's engine building up power, and then the lumbering machine was speeding down through the narrow front yard of Boardchek's safe house.

The cement-filled oil drum on the end of the long pole smashed into the steel door, failed to penetrate the barrier, then distintegrated against the ground as the pole buckled under from the pressure and collapsed. Tires spinning, the Assault tank continued forward, and the sharp fenders above the front wheels impacted against brick and wood, forcing in the entire front wall.

Half of the roof collapsed on top of the men sitting behind the machine gun turrets, but protected by their steel pots and flak jackets, they survived the crash unscathed, save for a few minor cuts and bruises.

The line of military policemen surrounding the dwelling moved in like a cautious school of fish, inspecting a morsel of food discarded in their midst, and Quinn dropped down on one knee, pistol extended, expecting Boardchek, crazed and firing two machine guns from the hip, to charge out at any second.

But the house remained silent. Except for the sounds of MPs searching through the debris.

Someone activated the powerful searchlights atop the Assault tank, and as the silver beams sliced through the night, it was the first time Quinn noticed that a fine drizzle had begun falling from the sky again. Vietnamese civilians emerged from their homes to see what all the excitement was about. Many were armed with umbrellas, prepared to weather the next phase of storm that was surely coming. An ancient old *mama-san* set up a soup stand on the edge of the perimeter ropes Stryker's men had set up. Teenagers scribbled graffiti on the CRIME SCENE — DO NOT PASS signs taped to the ropes. Up the block, a *canh-sat* on a Honda-50 clicked picture after picture from his Kodak pocket camera.

Quinn holstered his .38 and started toward the damaged structure up ahead.

Stryker felt the headache coming on long before the first jolts of pain coursed through the lobes where his ears touched his neck. Bryant was wading through the piles of brick, cursing Boardchek and his mother, and some newbie who had come over on the flight with Pruett — Southfield was what his name tag read — was running about with such eagerness he was sure to trip a booby trap or shoot himself in the foot.

When he saw Quinn appear in the doorway, he shook his head in resignation. It was going to be a long night.

There was very little left inside the house to go on, as far as clues went. No furniture. No decorations. Not even a duffelbag. Just piles of brick and cinderblock, and floating clouds of dust, everywhere you looked.

"He must not have been in here, Sarge!" Thomas deduced.

"I'm gonna kill you, Boardchek! You mother-fucker!" Bryant went from corner to corner, pulling up bricks and planks of wood. "I'm gonna crucify your bald-eagle ass!"

Stryker flicked his fingers at Moorhouser, and the air policeman and his partner, their dogs in front of them, rushed in through the doorway.

"He's probably out there right now!" Southfield wiped sweat from his forehead with the back of his hand. Dust had turned it into a grit that gave him a ghostly caste.

"Evening, Sergeant Stryker." Moorhouser nodded slightly but did not extend a hand. Under the circumstances, it was not expected.

"Put Bear to work." Stryker waved his hand to encompass the entire single-room house. "Find something for me, Kimbo. Anything to go on."

"Hey, Mark!" Thomas had located a battered footlocker beneath a landslide of boards. "I think you oughta come take a look at this."

Moorhouser led his dog to the other side of the building.

It didn't take them long to find the trap door. The German shepherds, snouts to the floorboards and tails wagging, went directly to it. Several loose planks were pried up in the center of the floor to reveal a stairwell that led down into a dark basement.

Bear and Shogan both strained against their leashes, attempting to run down the steps, but

Moorhouser and his partner held them back. "Sorry, Sarge. That's as far as my hounds go at this point. Never let 'em down in no tunnels—that's a man's work. Lost too many good animals down underground. Only takes one pissed-off VC, cornered like a rat, to take out the best attack dog. *If* he's armed."

"No sweat." Stryker called Thomas and Bryant over from the footlocker the three of them had torn open a few minutes earlier. "Who wants the honor?" he shone a flashlight down the stairwell, looking for a light switch, but none was visible.

"Let me do it!" The veteran MPs, taken by surprise by the unfamiliar voice, whirled around, expecting to see Quinn volunteering anyway.

"South*field* is it?" Stryker zeroed in on the name tag again.

"Yes, sir!"

Stryker examined his small frame and short, black hair. He looked the typical tunnel-rat part. "Sorry, son. What's your name? Your *first* name?"

"Christopher, Sergeant!" The kid beamed. "Christopher Southfield!" The name rang a bell from somewhere, but Stryker couldn't place it then and there.

"I'm sorry, Chris, but I think this is a job for someone who has been around awhile—"

"The asshole's going to escape if all we do is stand around and argue!" Southfield drew his pistol and charged down the stairwell.

He hadn't gotten past the first few steps when the blast from a double-barrelled shotgun caught him in the chest and lifted the young MP back up out of the black hole. A bright flash of yellow flame following him out, the soldier landed on his back at Stryker's feet, blood spurting from his exposed lungs.

Out of reflex, Stryker, Thomas and Bryant leaned forward into the stairwell and unloaded on the gunman in the basement. Ninety rounds of tracer and copper-jacketed slugs rained down into the dark hole as they cut loose with banana clips on full-auto.

"Masks!" Stryker yelled as he glanced down at Southfield. *How many days?* the thought kept bouncing around in his head. *How many days had the kid been in the Nam? Five? Six?* A single-digit newbie.

Southfield's chest heaved one final time, then his heart stopped and the last spray of blood died, like a fountain being turned off. His eyes were still open, staring up at the ceiling, lifeless, when Stryker dropped the tear gas grenades down into the hole, hooked the kel-light onto the handguard of his rifle, then slipped his gasmask down over his face and started down into what he was sure would be the first stage of hell.

The cellar was small. Perhaps twenty feet by thirty, it covered only half the space of the structure over their heads. Along one wall, as he moved through the thick cloud of gas—flipping his flashlight on and off every few seconds but never letting it burn for long— Stryker discovered an entrance to a tunnel. It's wooden cover was ajar. *Fucking country*, he heard his mind mutter. *All these people know how to do is dig goddamned tunnels everywhere they go! Oughta ship a boatload of 'em to New York so they can build subways.*

Bryant and Thomas were soon up behind him. The rest of the chamber was empty. Through the silver haze, he could see Quinn, gasmask in hand, starting down the staircase.

Stryker flipped his rifle's safety on, slung the weapon over his shoulder upside-down, then drew his .45 and climbed up into the tunnel entrance. The hole was about four feet off the ground and a yard square in construction. All the walls except the one containing the tunnel were reinforced with concrete. Boardchek had obviously torn *this* section of the foundation apart while digging his escape route. Or the VC before him. Or the Viet Minh a decade ago. Or the Frenchmen before even *him*. Planks of wood kept the earthen walls from collapsing. Stryker glanced up over his shoulder. Dust was falling from one corner of the ceiling, where the front tires of the V-100 rested after crashing through the front wall of the house. He hoped the structure would hold another hour.

He motioned for Thomas to follow him in after waiting thirty seconds, then he was gone.

They crawled on their hands and knees—Stryker's pistol poised in front of them, prepared for the worst (yet totally helpless against attack, when he really thought about it)—for several minutes. There were several curves in the trajectory of the tunnel, and they soon lost all sense of direction. When it seemed the floor of the escape route was starting to climb slightly toward the surface, they began hearing strange rumbling sounds overhead.

"This is it," Stryker whispered after they passed an air hole and came to the exit hatch. He pulled his mask off, eyes red and irritated by the tear gas, nostrils burning from the pungent odor. They all felt miserable and exhausted.

The statue of a chipped and discolored gargoyle greeted Stryker as he slowly raised the lid and peered out. Thunder crashed about overhead, and the lightning flashed against the stone creature's face, accenting its half-demon, half-dragon features. Rain pelted down on the two of them. Stryker cautiously turned slightly. Tombstones rose up all around him, some leaning precariously beneath the shifting clouds. In the distance, where there was a small break in the storm front, a sliver of crescent moon hung low in the sky, turning orange, watching over the graveyard.

"Tombstones!" Stryker whispered harshly as he crouched back down in the tunnel again without replacing the lid. He pulled Thomas up closer.

"What?" Bryant moved up on his hands and knees, eyes wide.

"Tombstones!" Thomas repeated what the sergeant had just said.

"We're in the middle of a fucking cemetery!" Stryker was laughing inside, but the death's-head grin would not come.

"Maybe we shouldn't be using cuss words around here, Sarge." Thomas peered out the exit hatch, then quickly ducked back down.

"Nonsense," muttered Stryker, checking his .45 magazine with the palm of his hand before climbing out into the night. "Come on, let's go!"

Thunder boomed about in the ominous skies above, and bolts of lightning seemed to make tombstones move around on their own as Thomas and Bryant and Quinn followed Stryker through the shifting shadows, deeper into the graveyard.

After about five minutes of wandering through the dark, they paused beside an ancient crypt, attempting to get their bearings.

"This is getting us nowhere, Sarge," Thomas complained, dropping to one knee to examine the trampled grass for the tenth time. The cemetery grounds were so poorly maintained, tracking a suspect in this manner was difficult. And the rainfall made things worse.

"The bastard's long gone by now," Bryant muttered, holstering his pistol.

Stryker surveyed the hilltops full of tombstones rising up all around them. He had never been in a graveyard this big, except maybe the one Uhernik had shown him in Hong Kong. "You're right," he conceded bitterly, lowering into a disenchanted squat to catch his breath. "Rest a minute. Then we'll go back and get the dogs."

14.

Contempt Of Cop

Shogan and Bear led them right back to the sunken crypt where they abandoned their first search.

"My mutts don't make mistakes." Moorhouser grinned as he pointed to the marble and concrete doors. "Your crazy man's down in there somewhere." He handed Stryker his XM-203, a combination M-16 automatic rifle and M-79 grenade launcher. *"Enjoy."*

The ex-Green Beret smiled and took the weapon, but he didn't intend to use it. He had been in Vietnam too long to ignore the local customs regarding ancestor worship. And the ghosts would not look kindly on some foreign devil thrashing through their graveyard, tearing down sacred tombs with a brazen display of Western firepower. This was the Orient. Where you ate with chopsticks, slept with temple maidens, and didn't mess with Buddha or the mystery of it all.

"Maybe you better stay here, Tim." Stryker couldn't miss the wildfire in Bryant's eyes. "Like Bobby there, you and Quinn are too emotionally involved with this case to proceed any further."

Quinn stepped forward to protest, but Bryant beat him to it.

"Bullshit, Mark! That's a crock, and you know it! I'm not sure about Quinn, but I'm going with you down there. I'm—"

Stryker rushed up nose to nose with the Spec. 4, grabbed him by the front of the shirt, and lifted him slightly off his feet. "*I'm* giving the orders around here, Tim. *Got that?*" Some of the anger melted from his features as he remembered all the things they had gone through together, but his grip remained firm. "You're too involved in this mess. You're liable to go off half-cocked, or be thinking more about vengeance than your partner's welfare. You might just go down there and get somebody killed, bud." He slowly let the MP back down. "Right now you're only thinking about yourself, and for us to get Boardchek behind bars again, we're going to have to put forth a team effort— you understand what I'm saying?"

He didn't give Bryant time to answer. The suspect already had too much of a head start. There was no telling how big the crypt was, how many exits it had, or how many hiding places. For all he knew, there was some goofy secret stairwell inside that led to the center of the earth, like those pyramids in Egypt.

"Let's go." Stryker motioned Thomas to follow

him. They started down the steps into the dark entryway and vanished in the gloom.

"I don't know about you —" Quinn glided up beside Bryant — "but I'm not just going to stand around and let Boardchek get away again."

"Well, what do you propose we do?" Bryant's eyes seemed dull, empty.

"These mummy caves always got another door." Quinn motioned him away from the MPs gathered near the stairwell. "Let's go for a little walk, *partner*, and see what we come up with."

Stryker felt his gut tighten as they approached the thick stone door at the bottom of the steps. It was slightly ajar. The hinges were rusty, and squeaked — a late-night horror movie squeak — when they pulled it open.

The walls and floor were slick with blood on the inside. "Jesus," Thomas whispered when he almost slipped in the gore.

"*Jesus* got nothing to do with this snafu," Stryker muttered as he flipped the flashlight on, got his bearings, then immediately turned it off again. They were entering a long corridor that ran for nearly a hundred feet beneath the surface of the earth. It was ten yards high, and an equal distance from the floor to the ceiling. It appeared constructed entirely of cement, with brass or chrome plates covering the compartments which housed the coffins. Thomas estimated a hundred bodies waited behind one wall alone. Handles protruded from some of the giant "drawers." He wondered what strength was necessary to pull them open, and what he would find inside. He didn't realize the compartments were permanently sealed, and that the "handles" were for the use of the gods only.

"How ya wanna do this?" Thomas whispered as they both paused at the entrance to the long corridor. It afforded no articles of cover anywhere along the way.

Stryker hesitated a moment, considering, then said, "You wait here, Ants. When I get down to the end, I'll signal you to follow. It looks like there's an opening down there."

"And what if you get your shit blown away?" Thomas whispered back, confident their voices were not carrying more than a few feet.

Their eyes met in the floating dust of ages, and Stryker said, "Well, I guess that's what I get paid for, isn't it?"

Stryker turned away, but Thomas reached out and grabbed his arm. "It don't seem like they pay you *enough* to do something like that, Mark. Your life's worth more than a couple hundred lousy bucks a month. Even *mine* is, for Christsake. What happens if you get halfway down there and that maniac leans around the corner and brings smoke on ya, huh?"

But the ex-Green Beret was gone, rushing down the corridor in a rapid, zigzag pattern, feeling naked as a baby and vulnerable as a virgin. Prepared to die. Aware that this might be the end. And though he might have wished his last battlefield be in a steaming rain forest somewhere outside Pleiku, in the Central Highlands, he knew what he was doing here and now was honorable, for it would bring to justice the killer of his friends. And if he failed, it would be a noble death, and they would toast drinks to him in all the bars of Saigon and tell tales about his exploits for decades and wars to come. The name Mark Stryker would *live*, so long as warriors fought honorably and . . .

All these thoughts passed through the MP sergeant's mind as he reached the end of the corridor without engaging Marlon Boardchek in a gunfight.

He waved Thomas up to his position, then started around the corner.

Slivers of concrete and marble ricocheted in his face as a half dozen bullets aimed at his head shot toward him.

"Get down!" he yelled at Thomas as he dropped to one knee and returned the fire, never really seeing what he was shooting at. After three discharges, he forced his finger off the trigger. His ears were ringing with the harsh noise of cartridges exploding underground.

Thomas was still running. Twice, he slipped in all the blood coating the smooth floor, but he got right back up and kept rushing to his sergeant's aid.

His young eyes glanced up at the brass plaques on either side of him each time he fell. Engraved names and dates-of-death seemed to flash out at him. PHAM. NGUYEN. DIEM. Would they reach out and grab him if his feet didn't keep moving? 1922. 1946. 1954. He felt a terror take hold of him, and he ran faster, fearing, in his horror, he might accidentally shoot Stryker or himself.

But then he was up beside the stocky NCO, and they were both peeking around the sharp corner again. "Motherfucker!" Stryker grimaced as he examined his thumb. "Just like a fucking rook!" In his excitement, he had let his right thumb extend out slightly, and the recoiling pistol slide had cut a deep gouge into the flesh between it and his forefinger.

Another staircase, leading back up to ground level, waited for them around the corner. Boardchek was gone.

They climbed into a sort of greenhouse that kept the weather out, but also the plants. The ceiling and upper walls were made of glass. Vines and low-hanging tree branches covered every inch of their surface on the outside.

The corridor in front of them was slightly larger than the previous one, but it was littered with obstructions. This had been Boardchek's playground. Caskets were strewn about haphazardly, with many hanging precariously from their pried-open compartments. All had been violated. Decaying corpses were everywhere — sitting up against the walls, lying on their stomachs, placed together in grotesque positions of sexual intercourse. The stench in the corridor was nearly unbearable.

Walking slowly, the two MPs abandoned proper procedure for clearing a building, and stayed side by side, years of training and experience suddenly melting away as the power of death pressed in on them, intimidating even Stryker. Their gun hands extended at arm's length, both men clutched their tiger-claw necklaces with their free hands without even realizing it.

The silence in the building was deafening. Anxiety shouted down at them. Thomas glanced up at the glass ceiling. He could see rain pelting against it, but there was no sound. Stryker glanced down at a corpse beside his boot. Chunks of dried-up skin and strands of hair still clung to its skull. A beetle perched on the rim of an eye socket, antennae twitching about at their approach, then retreated back into the dark cavity.

Halfway down the corridor, a compartment door suddenly sprung open and a hand covered with rotting flesh reached out for Thomas! From inside the grave, a man screamed demonically. Thomas yelled in reply, jumping back, and a small explosion erupted from the compartment. A bullet slammed into his thigh, and Anthony went down.

"The devil made me do it!" Boardchek's voice followed the discharge out, and he burst into insane laughter as he pushed the dead body out onto the wounded MP.

Stryker jumped forward and sprayed the doorway with lead, then darted to the side and came back for Thomas. Without holstering his .45, he dragged his partner back several feet.

"Shit!" Thomas gritted his teeth as blood sprayed from his leg wound. "I been dusted by a goddamned ghost, Mark! I been smoked by a fucking *ghoul*!"

Stryker dragged him back behind an upended coffin and laid the coughing MP beside a grinning dead woman. Dust swirled in around them as his boots disturbed the marble floor.

"That was just crazy Merlin, Ants!" Strykers' eyes lit up with the challenge. "And I'm gonna go up there and waste his ass." He had quickly produced a bandage from a pouch on his web belt and wrapped Thomas's leg wound tight until the bleeding subsided from the pressure. "You think you can hold out here for a while on your own?" He quickly reloaded his pistol.

Thomas glanced at the corpses "staring" back at him. *Never abandon your partner! Never abandon your partner! Never abandon your partner!* The words from some long-forgotten drill sergeant back at The School returned to haunt him. "Leave me here, Sarge?" His eyes went wide as the skulls seemed to nod back in anticipation of their new guests' next move. "Leave me here alone with *these* guys?"

"Jesus, Anthony." Stryker reached up and knocked a skull off its neck vertebrae with the back of his hand. "Don't let these guys wreck your karma, OK? I'll be right back." But no sooner had he risen to his feet then Boardchek leaned out from an archway several feet beyond the open crypt and fired a round at them.

The moment Stryker saw the black turtleneck sweatshirt and gleaming bald crown, he returned the fire, sending eight hollowpoints bouncing down after the madman. He quickly ejected the spent magazine and slammed a fresh one into the .45's handle, then sent the slide forward with a comforting crack of steel on steel.

While the MP sergeant was reloading, Board-

chek rushed off down the corridor, but before
Stryker could take aim again, the maniac's broad
back had disappeared out a large double door
constructed of glass. The sound of rain lashing the
walls outside came to them as the doors swung
open, and Thomas yelled, "Go get him, Mark! If
he gets out among them tombstones again, we'll
never find him!"

A string of discharges erupted beyond the doorway just as Stryker reached it, and he ducked out
of habit, but the bullets were not meant for him.
He burst through to the outside, only to find
Quinn and Richards holding Boardchek by the
arms from behind. Two pistols, their slides locked
back on empty, lay on the ground. And Bryant
was rushing forward to strike the murderer of his
wife in the face. It would be the first blow, if he
had his way, in a series that would not end until
the prison escapee was dead.

"Tim!" Stryker yelled, as the first punch
smashed Boardchek's nose to pulp and blood
sprayed across all four men. "This isn't the way to
do it!"

Bryant struck Boardchek twice in the stomach,
then rammed an elbow into the man's mouth as
hard as he could, breaking in several teeth.

"*Bryant!*" Stryker rushed forward and attempted
to restrain the MP. He pulled Bryant off the
prisoner and pushed him away. "This isn't the way!
We'll take him back to the stockade, and they'll
throw him in a hole so deep and so dark it'll be
worse than death! Won't that be better than revenge? When you think about it, won't *that* in

itself be sweet vengeance?"

If Stryker's words were meant to have a calming effect on Bryant, they had just the opposite reaction on Boardchek. The man brought his arms together, lifting Richards and Quinn up like they weren't even there, and hurled both his captors onto Stryker. Richards refused to let go, and the prisoner's sweatshirt ripped down the middle, exposing several sticks of dynamite taped to his belly. "Jesus!" Bryant's hand went to his holster, but his pistol was one of the ones on the ground.

"Stay back!" Boardchek ordered. "Stay back, or we *all* kiss it goodnight right now! Do you hear me? Stay back!"

"You're not leaving here, asshole!" Stryker started moving slowly toward the prison escapee. "You're not getting away from us again."

"Mark," Richards almost hissed his alarm. "Don't set the fucker off on us. *He's nuts!*"

"That's right!" Boardchek's eyes lit up. "Haven't you heard? I'm insane!" He stepped forward and pointed at Quinn. "If you saw what I did to your little girl with my pecker you'd *know* I'm insane!"

Bryant stood beside Quinn now, and he started backing up also, ignoring Boardchek's taunting words as the madman grew nearer.

A panel behind them sprang open just then, slamming into Quinn's elbow, and Bryant whirled around to find Hue Chean's decapitated body lying right in front of them, her pinky finger missing—worms and maggots sliding in and out of the clotting neck wound that was now several days old.

"Jesus Christ!" Bryant grasped the corpse by the shoulders as tears erupted along the edges of his eyes. *She was wearing her wedding dress!*

The huge "drawer" seemed to slide out a bit further, and a woman's deafening scream filled all their ears as the headless body shook and twisted, then appeared to jump up into Bryant's arms.

Stryker used the terrifying distraction to make his move. His mind flashed back to that footlocker they found in the house the Assault tank had rammed. It contained the makings of several bombs. The same components and parts their "mad bomber" had been using during his spree of malfunctioning terrorist acts. Stryker sensed the device now wrapped around Boardchek's waist also was missing one or two vital components that would prevent it from detonating. So Stryker jumped him. Slammed his wrist against the giant's temple over and over until he dropped to his knees and the husky MP sergeant could get him in a disabling chokehold.

"Get it off of me!" Xuan Quinn sat up in the metal coffin after she pushed Hue Chean's bloody corpse off of her. Eyes wide with terror, she screamed at the top of her lungs, hands still straight out as her mind fought to push the horror that had been lying across her for so many hours as far away as possible. Her face caked with blood, she saw none of them, recognized nobody, but sought only to burst free from the casket in which she had been buried alive by the lunatic Stryker was beating into the ground. Xuan's hands trembled as if she were ice cold.

Quinn and Bryant stared at each other for an instant, dumbfounded, then the CID agent rushed over to his wife and took her in his arms. "Xuan! *Honey!* It's OK! I'm here! It's OK! It's over, Xuan! *It's over!*" Quinn sensed Bryant just standing behind him, a dead woman with no head in his arms, her blood leaking down onto the floor from a mutilated throat, but he did not look back. He dared not turn to confront his friend! What words could he find to explain away fate? What could he possibly say?

"Robert, it was terrible!" Xuan cried, shutting her eyes tightly as Quinn carried her from the coffin and guided her to a corner of the crypt away from all the others. "Robert, I'm so sorry! I'm sooo sorry! He took Mang and Lien from me! I couldn't protect them, Robert! Please forgive me! Your children, he took them. I couldn't—"

"Never mind, Xuan." He cuddled her in his arms, hiding her from the cruel world outside, the thunder and lightning overhead, protecting her. "Never mind. It's all over. We'll *start* over, honey."

Xuan wrapped her arms around his neck and kissed him roughly—a long, savage kiss that mirrored what she had gone through the last several weeks. And then she collapsed in his arms, crying, and Quinn held her to his heart. "Never ever leave me, Robert," Xuan pleaded. "Never leave me alone again."

"I won't darling." Quinn felt the tears burning his eyes.

"Promise me, Robert." She forced her eyes to look up at his, and he didn't flinch at all the blood on her face. "Promise me you will never leave me alone at night again."

"I promise." The whisper was pain to his heart.

"Em se yeu anh mac mac," she sighed, legs giving out beneath her. *I will love you forever my husband.*

"Gimme a hand over here." Stryker was trying to lift the dazed prisoner to his feet. Richards rushed to assist him. The dismantled belt of explosives lay at their feet.

Several dozen MPs had responded to the far side of the crypt following the flurry of shots. Black and white helmets were everywhere.

"It doesn't matter," Boardchek muttered, regaining his breath as Richards helped Stryker pull the monster to his feet. "It don't mean nothin'— they're just gonna gimme a plush pad in some funny farm back in The World, ya know." His eyeballs rolled around insanely for Bryant's benefit.

"Shut the fuck up, Boardchek." Richards squeezed the man's wrist so hard the veins crisscrossing his shaved head bulged as he fought to keep a straight face.

Hue Chean's body lay a few feet away, under one of the MPs rain ponchos. The green sheet was short. It was not designed to cover an entire body. Her slender, bare feet protruded from one end, but Tim managed to cover up the bloodstained bridal gown.

"He's right, you know."

Stryker looked up upon hearing the words. Bryant, gun in hand, was blocking their path.

"Don't do it." Stryker produced his most serious expression as he pronounced each word slowly—so there would be no misunderstanding. "Back off, Tim. This is no longer your matter. The fuckhead's *my* prisoner. So holster that weapon, soldier!"

"Shut up, Mark." Bryant was not in the mood for talk. "Save the bullshit for somebody who gives a shit. Boardchek's not walking out of this graveyard tonight alive." He leveled the pistol at the madman's chest, ten feet away.

"He's quite right, don't you know?" Boardchek assumed the accent of a Britishman who was unsure of his sexual preference. His black pupils had rolled up under his lids so that only the whites of his eyes showed. He looked like a seven-foot-tall demon.

"I suggest you put a cork in it!" Stryker whispered to his prisoner, "if you wanna leave here alive."

"But he's right!" Boardchek raised his voice so everyone could hear. "I *shouldn't* leave here. Not tonight anyway. All they'll do back in The World is make me talk to a bunch of fag shrinks and then give me a padded room with a color TV. And I'll be out in no time!" He tried to break free as he lunged at Bryant, leering like a crazed maniac— eyes bulging and saliva drooling from the corners of his mouth. But Stryker and Richards held him back. "A year, two years, and they'll release me! Just look at the stats! It happens all the time!

They'll let me out—you wait and see. *And I'll come back!* You'll have to watch every shadow in every dark alley on your foot beat, 'cause I could be lurking in any one of them! I could just reach out and *grab you!*" He lunged at Bryant again, snapping the handcuffs behind him, and Stryker slammed his elbow into the man's temple twice, sending him to his knees. Several MPs piled on as the two sergeants wrestled with the lunatic, and they soon had a stronger model of cuffs on along with several flexi-cuffs.

"Jesus," muttered Stryker, out of breath.

"Fucking foreign handcuffs," complained Richards. "You were right, Mark. From now on it's nothing but Peerless or Smith & Wesson."

Bryant slowly lowered his .45 automatic. They were all right. The egghead belonged in Bellvue, strapped down to a gurney the rest of his life. Let the shrinks shoot him up with mind-altering drugs and conduct all kinds of experiments to see what made demented creeps like him tick. If there was a god above, maybe Boardchek would overdose, and they could dissect his brain and flush his personality down the toilet.

"You should have seen what I did to his kids!" Boardchek raved madly as they tried to drag him away, but he refused to budge from the spot. His chin pointed over at Quinn. "You should have seen how I violated them! I'm a convicted child molester, you know! It takes a special kind of mentality to come up with the little games *I* devised for those two little brats! You should have been there. Such innocent little babies," he sneered sarcasti-

cally. "The way I —"

Richards slammed his fist into Boardchek's mouth, silencing him.

"Let's get him out of here," Stryker muttered.

Blood dripping from his lower lip, the maniac quickly recovered — he was so pumped up he was feeling no pain. Towering above his captors, he went after Bryant personally. "You should have seen what I did to *that* one!" With his foot he motioned toward the woman lying under the rain poncho. Bryant's knuckles went white as he squeezed the pistol handle, trying to maintain control. "*I fucked her every way imaginable, Bryant-dear!* In the ass, and then her mouth. Over and over, until she came to enjoy it! You hear me, *pig*? She grew to like it! Your old lady gave much better blow jobs than that cunt over there!" Boardchek's chin jutted out at Xuan, who Quinn shielded from view with his protective arms. He started to lead her away from the dark, imposing mausoleum that hung over them like a curse. "Why, she gave such good skull," Boardchek continued, "that the last time I shot my wad, it blew her cock-sucking head *right off*!"

"*Sayonara, slut!*" Bryant's gun hand flew up, and the pistol barked twice.

Thunder crashing overhead failed to drown out the deafening discharges as the hollowpoints burst forth, slamming into Boardchek's chest and catapulting him backwards, out of Stryker's grip.

The huge madman staggered back, refusing to fall, and Bryant calmly moved forward, slowly firing round after crushing round until he was up to his last bullet and Boardchek's chest was soaked in blood.

"This one's for Hue Chean," Bryant muttered, as he extended the .45 to arm's length and fired the final hollow-point into Boardchek's forehead.

Their eyes locked onto each other for an instant, and Bryant saw the fear streak across his face at last. The impact of the bullet punched Boardchek back off his feet as chunks of his demented brain exploded out the bottom of his skull. His wildly twitching frame toppled into an open casket. The dust of death rose up all around him as brittle bones from a long-dead Vietnamese crumbled under his weight.

Bryant's right hand fell to his side, smoke floating from the barrel of the gun it held. He sighed, turned, and slowly walked over to a frowning Sergeant Stryker.

"I had no choice," he said softly, making no excuses as he handed the weapon to Stryker, butt first. "This is Saigon, Mark. It's part of Vietnam." His eyes rose from his boots to meet those of the ex-Green Beret. "And jungle justice called for it."

Then he walked over to Hue Chean's decapitated body, dropped to his knees, and waited for the tears to come—unsure of which gods to pray to.

15.

AWOL From Life

Arlington, Virginia

Stryker decided it must be raining all over the world that week. Fine, misty sheets of drizzle washed across the endless rows of white crosses that extended out on all sides from the funeral ceremony. A large family crypt on a distant hilltop reminded him of everything that had transpired in the Saigon cemetery only a week earlier.

Military policemen wearing full-dress Class-A uniforms fired their carbine salute as the last lines of "Taps" echoed across the green fields. Two buglers had played it, slightly off-time from each other, so that the resulting echoes were as impressive as they were melancholy and sad—something the thousand mourners present would always remember.

Stryker stood at attention with the other members of the honor guard as a high-ranking officer from the Washington, D.C. Provost Marshal's office folded the American flags that had been draped across the two caskets and presented them to the mother of Paul and Christopher Southfield.

Stryker felt a tear growing at the corner of his eye as he watched the woman keep her chin up proudly during the final moments of the double ceremony, refusing to break down like all the other ladies present were doing. *Quite a fighter*, Stryker decided. *Her oldest son is murdered guarding Boardchek at the stockade, and her only remaining child is killed trying to capture the madman twelve thousand miles away.* He decided it must be a terrible twist of fate to cope with. Would her loyalty to her country and its ideals change after all this? After all her family had gone through? The poor woman had lost her husband in Korea.

He would have to speak with her again after the funeral. The Army always granted a dead soldier's friend emergency leave to accompany the body back to The World as an official escort. How many days did he have left in the states? How much time? He wanted to talk to her once more, but he was desperate to return to Saigon. The cold winds of the Atlantic had seemed to age him whole decades as they struck at the very marrow of his bones. He felt like a fish out of water here.

After the ceremony, Stryker returned to his hotel downtown. He wasn't expecting any messages, but after taking a shower (power pressure nozzles attached to the wall and an unlimited supply of steaming hot water was a luxury he had completely forgotten about) for over an hour, he started down into the hotel's bar for a drink when the bellhop stopped him.

"Mr. Stryker?" The young teenager was holding what looked like an overseas cable. The MP sergeant cocked an eyebrow at the youth. He hadn't been called "mister" since he could remember.

"Yes, young man?" He dug into his pocket for a tip.

"From that place." The boy wiggled his nose as if an offensive odor had just assaulted his nostrils.

"Vietnam?" Stryker smiled.

"Yes, sir." The youth exchanged the telegram for the purple currency note and Stryker turned to enter the bar. *"Hey! What's this?"* But the career soldier was gone, and the kid was left to ponder what one hundred *piasters* was worth.

Stryker took a table in the back of the nightclub and ordered a Singapore Sling. He watched the go-go dancer on the front stage as he opened the cable, but she did nothing to arouse him and he ignored her throughout the following succession of drinks.

Stryker smiled when he saw who the cable was from: Pruett. The new NCO from Korea. He decided it was nice for the guy to go out of his way to send a telegram to keep him up-to-date with affairs in Sin City. He made a mental note to bring the man back an eight-by-ten of the president.

Dear Mark,
    Greetings and Salut*asians*!

Life rolls on in the City of Sorrows, but I promised to keep you posted, so here's the low-down. Thomas is doing fine. The bullet missed bone and the vital nerves and they decided to keep him on in Saigon. He'll be on light duty though, for a couple months.

"Another Singapore Sling, sir?"

Stryker looked up from the telegram to find a beautiful Oriental woman in a form-hugging cocktail waitress's outfit bending over his table, a platter of empty glasses in her hand. For a moment he thought he was back in Saigon, but he could tell by her features she was not Vietnamese, and when he glanced over at the floorshow and saw the flaming redhead with the sagging silicone and watermelon thighs he remembered he was in D.C. "You are very beautiful, miss. What's your name?"

"Song-tuk." She smiled warmly and winked. "What can I get you?"

"Ahhh, a Korean princess," he said, thinking of Pruett's wife, Kwang-Im. The team had finally chipped in enough to bring her over from Pusan. He hoped to be back in time to help greet her upon her arrival. "Yes, another Singapore Sling would be bookoo appreciated, my dear." He fought to keep from staring at her ample chest.

"Bookoo?" She focused dark, mysterious eyes on his gold-and-red service ribbon. "You just came from Vietnam?"

"Yes," he sighed. "Funeral detail."

"*Funeral* detail?" She straightened up, looking

slightly shocked.

"Yes, I escorted a fallen comrade back to The World." He glanced out the window at the large snowflakes falling in the street and shivered. He had never wanted to be back in Asia so much in his life.

"Then you are returning after this . . . 'detail'?"

"Yes." He looked her straight in the eyes. "Soon."

Song-tuk set down her tray on the table. "Well," she said, "For now, *welcome home*," and she hugged him tightly. Then, blushing, she vanished, returning to her duties.

A young couple entered the club with a small boy in tow. The child looked Amerasian, but both adults were white. The man looked like soldier material. Stryker wondered if the boy was a war orphan they had adopted. Perhaps he was the guy's own kid, a genuine Saigon souvenir the woman had learned to accept and love. He buried the desire to approach them and ask. And he thought about Robert and Xuan Quinn. He would never forget how, after the shooting in the cemetery, the CID agent escorted his wife to the front gates. A large crowd was gathering there—the security people had quite a job keeping all the curious spectators contained. A small shoeshine boy had stepped forth from the throng and grabbed Quinn's hand. He pulled down on it to get the investigator's attention. "*I* called you," he revealed, refering to the phone call Lan had received. "I'm the one who told you where to find this woman!" And Quinn had wrapped his free

315

arm around the boy and took him home with them. The child would never have to sleep in the streets again.

We solved the bombing case, Mark. Boardchek was behind it all, but then that was your original theory in your first report, wasn't it? The Vietnamese killed in the first bombing were people who testified against him in the child molestation case that originally put him behind bars years ago. Tran Chi Minh was the grandfather of the victim Boardchek sodomized. He testified against him at the trials. Looks like he paid for it with his life.

"Here you go, honey." Song-tuk reappeared with his drink.

"Thanks." Stryker slipped her three five hundred *piaster* bills.

"I get off at two." She placed a cold hand on his wrist. "Perhaps I could show you the city. *The Green Berets* is playing at the cinema down the street."

"That sounds real nice." Stryker's eyes smiled, but he didn't realize his mouth was frowning. He pulled out a pen and scribbled something down on a Miramar Hotel — Saigon matchbook. "Here's my room number."

She bent across the table again, pecked him on the cheek, and glided off through the drifting clouds of cigar and cigarette smoke. Her outfit was one of the mini-skirts then popular in the states and England. He decided he hadn't seen legs like that since Lai, and he leaned back in his chair, envisioning her sitting on his face. He hoped *it* would still pop up after all he had been through the last couple weeks.

He glanced back down at the telegram.

One last thing I thought you should know, Mark. It's about Tim Bryant. The court martial found him guilty, of course. Sentence was thirty years-to-life hard labor at Leavenworth. But the funniest thing happened, and I'll be damned if any of us here can figure it out. None of the guards were injured, but while they were transferring him to Tan Son Nhut for the flight back to the stockade in Kansas, Bryant escaped. Nobody's seen him since. He just dropped out of sight — vanished! My theory is he went underground. Just another nameless face in those back alleys of Saigon the Decoy Squad won't even venture down into. They put his mugshot on the hot sheets for a few days, but I keep finding them wadded up in the trashcan. Something tells me Bryant'll do alright in the Underworld, Mark. Maybe when things cool down a bit, we can track his young ass down and buy a French rocket launcher or stolen tank from him. We could use them to liven up those picnics Carmosino throws down on Plantation road. Bryant knows the street. And he's got the connections. He'll be into big bucks before you know it, Mark. And money changes everything.

Don't bring the clap back with you.

Still in Saigon,

Pruett.

Stryker left the bar without finishing his drink. He walked over to the hotel gift shop, browsed through the magazine rack, and purchased a paperback novel about Green Beret missions in Vietnam. Then he retreated to his tenth-floor room, locked the door, and opened the book to the first chapter. His eyes were continually drawn to the window, however, and he shivered each time he watched the snowflakes swirling down outside. America seemed so cold to him. He had never been so miserable in his life.

Song-tuk never showed up that night.

THE SURVIVALIST SERIES
by Jerry Ahern

#1: TOTAL WAR   (960, $2.50)

The first in the shocking series that follows the unrelenting search for ex-CIA covert operations officer John Thomas Rourke to locate his missing family—after the button is pressed, the missiles launched and the multimegaton bombs unleashed. . . .

#2: THE NIGHTMARE BEGINS   (810, $2.50)

After WW III, the United States is just a memory. But ex-CIA covert operations officer Rourke hasn't forgotten his family. While hiding from the Soviet forces, he adheres to his search!

#3: THE QUEST   (851, $2.50)

Not even a deadly game of intrigue within the Soviet High Command, and a highly placed traitor in the U.S. government can deter Rourke from continuing his desperate search for his family.

#4: THE DOOMSAYER   (893, $2.50)

The most massive earthquake in history is only hours away, and Communist-Cuban troops, Soviet-Cuban rivalry, and a traitor in the inner circle of U.S. II block Rourke's path.

#5: THE WEB   (1145, $2.50)

Blizzards rage around Rourke as he picks up the trail of his family and is forced to take shelter in a strangely quiet Tennessee valley town. But the quiet isn't going to last for long!

#6: THE SAVAGE HORDE   (1243, $2.50)

Rourke's search gets sidetracked when he's forced to help a military unit locate a cache of eighty megaton warhead missiles hidden on the New West Coast—and accessible only by submarine!

#7: THE PROPHET   (1339, $2.50)

As six nuclear missiles are poised to start the ultimate conflagration, Rourke's constant quest becomes a desperate mission to save both his family and all humanity from being blasted into extinction!

#8: THE END IS COMING   (1374, $2.50)

Rourke must smash through Russian patrols and cut to the heart of a KGB plot that could spawn a lasting legacy of evil. And when the sky bursts into flames, consuming every living being on the planet, it will be the ultimate test for THE SURVIVALIST.

Available wherever paperbacks are sold, or order direct from the Publisher. Send cover price plus 50¢ per copy for mailing and handling to Zebra Books, Dept. 1629, 475 Park Avenue South, New York, N.Y. 10016. DO NOT SEND CASH.

THE BEST IN ADVENTURE FROM ZEBRA

WAR DOGS   (1474, $3.50)
by Nik-Uhernik

Lt. Justin Ross molded his men into a fearsome fighting unit, but it was their own instincts that kept them out of body bags. Their secret orders would change the destiny of the Vietnam War, and it didn't matter that an entire army stood between them and their objective!

WAR DOGS #2: M-16 JURY   (1539, $2.75)
by Nik-Uhernik

The War Dogs, the most cutthroat band of Vietnam warriors ever, face their greatest test yet—from an unlikely source. The traitorous actions of a famous American could lead to the death of thousands of GIs—and the shattering end of the . . . WAR DOGS.

GUNSHIPS #1: THE KILLING ZONE   (1130, $2.50)
by Jack Hamilton Teed

Colonel John Hardin of the U.S. Special Forces knew too much about the dirty side of the Vietnam War—he had to be silenced. And a hand-picked squad of mongrels and misfits were destined to die with him in the rotting swamps of . . . THE KILLING ZONE.

GUNSHIPS #2: FIRE FORCE   (1159, $2.50)
by Jack Hamilton Teed

A few G.I.s, driven crazy by the war-torn hell of Vietnam, had banded into brutal killing squads who didn't care whom they shot at. Colonel John Hardin, tapped for the job of wiping out these squads, had to first forge his own command of misfits into a fighting FIRE FORCE!

GUNSHIPS #3: COBRA KILL   (1462, $2.50)
by Jack Hamilton Teed

Having taken something from the wreckage of the downed Cobra gunship, the Cong force melted back into the jungle. Colonel John Hardin was going to find out what the Cong had taken—even if it killed him!

Available wherever paperbacks are sold, or order direct from the Publisher. Send cover price plus 50¢ per copy for mailing and handling to Zebra Books, Dept. 1629, 475 Park Avenue South, New York, N.Y. 10016. DO NOT SEND CASH.